FORBIDDEN

THE BRIDE HUNT BOOK 5

CHARLENE HARTNADY

Copyright © April 2017, Charlene Hartnady
Cover Art by Melody Simmons
Copy Edited by KR
Proofread by Bridgitte Billings
Formatting by Integrity-Formatting
Produced in South Africa

Published by Charlene Hartnady
PO BOX 456, Melrose Arch,
Johannesburg, South Africa, 2176
charlene.hartnady@gmail.com

Forbidden Dragon is a work of fiction and characters, events and dialogue found within are of the author's imagination and are not to be construed as real. Any resemblance to actual events or persons, either living or deceased, is purely coincidental.
With the exception of quotes used in reviews no part of this book may be reproduced or shared in any form or by any means, electronic or mechanical, including but not limited to digital copying, file sharing, audio recording, email and printing without prior consent in writing from the author

First Paperback Edition 2017

DEDICATION

To empathy. The world needs more . . .

CHAPTER 1

"You should have taken the fuckers out." Suddenly his chamber felt too small. The walls were closing in. The air was too thin. His skin too tight.

Blaze rarely showed up unannounced. Granite knew as soon as he laid eyes on the male that something was up. Little did he know just how bad things had become.

Blaze shook his head. "It was clear that they were on a mission scouting the southernmost part of our territory. It was also clear that they had no clue what they were looking for or if they were even in the right place."

Anger churned inside him. "All the more reason to . . ."

"Taking them out would've sent a clear message to those who sent them. Right now, whoever is sending these choppers into our mountain range has no idea if they're onto something or not. They've been on several scout missions into our territory. They zig zag across a grid before returning to . . ."

"It's only a matter of time before they spot something. Before someone fucks up." His heart beat faster at the thought.

Blaze shook his head. "It's doubtful. We're well-trained and camouflaged. Our territory is vast. They're shooting into the dark and hoping to hit."

"Doubtful?" Granite's voice was deep and laced with anger and irritation. It couldn't be helped! "That's not good enough. They could get lucky and then what? Who the hell are these fuckers?"

"Humans. Heavily armed males. We don't know anything more about them."

"It had to be one of those females," Granite shook his head. "There were two who returned home after being on our territory."

Blaze nodded. "Yeah! I suspect that you are right."

"We need to put a stop to these hunts."

Blaze shook his head. "We have had too much success. The whole thing is running better now that we are working with the vampires. The females are carefully screened before being selected to take part. They will eventually grow tired of hunting ghosts and will look somewhere else."

"Except we aren't ghosts, are we?" A low rumble. "If they find any proof, even the tiniest . . ."

"We need to be on our guard. Up the number of scout patrols going out. Our lairs are well hidden."

"What about the mines?"

"They are so deep in the mountains. I doubt that the humans would venture there, and if they did, it would be at their own peril." Granite noticed the tension in Blaze's jaw. The stiffness in his back. The male was just as worried as he was, he was trying to hide the fact.

"And when they bring a whole fleet of aircraft . . . hundreds of males armed to the teeth with silver? We were almost wiped out all those years ago, when humans were still on foot carrying spears and swords. It would be impossible to beat them now. Guns, bombs, bullets infused . . ."

"I know," Blaze snarled. "I have a family . . ." He saw the anger drain from the male and worry take its place. The male dropped his gaze to the floor for a moment. "If anything were to happen . . ." his voice was heavy with emotion. Blaze swallowed thickly, his eyes finding Granite's. "We need to be ready. This Resistance Therapy has to work. If we can beat our silver affliction we can beat the humans. We need time."

"Agreed but it doesn't feel like enough. At this rate we may very well run out of time."

"We need to hide and watch. We need to train harder than we've ever trained before. If it means taking certain calculated risks, then so be it."

"Agreed!"

"The four of us must set our differences aside." The Fire king clasped his shoulder. "If we are not united then we are nothing."

"It was the single biggest mistake our forefathers made." Granite clasped Blaze's shoulder in return and squeezed.

They both nodded and dropped their arms. "There is something you need to know," Blaze sighed. "My son . . ."

he looked away for a beat before looking back at Granite. "His markings are not . . . they are not golden."

"What?" Granite felt his whole body tense. He frowned. "Silver?"

"Not silver," Blaze paused. "Coal's son has the same strange markings. They have no color. The marking is there but it is merely an outline."

"We need to stop these hunts." *What the fuck was wrong with the male?*

"No!" Blaze growled. "It is my belief that these colorless outlines are the new royal markings."

"On what basis?"

"Call it a gut instinct. I am royal," he touched his chest, "my son carries my blood. The most royal of blood. How could he not be a royal?"

Granite could see how strongly the male felt about it. He wanted to argue with him over it because he was being completely biased in his thinking. Blaze was delusional if he thought these colorless markings were the new 'royal.' Granite bit his tongue instead. He finally gave a nod. "We will step up the Resistance Therapy. We will beat this silver affliction and then we will tackle the humans head-on. No more running and hiding. We will stand united and strong against them."

"There is still time. Don't put your males in any danger."

Granite looked Blaze in the eyes. "We are *all* already in danger. Every last one of us."

CHAPTER 2

The big shifter flinched as she pushed the needle into his arm. He made a hissing noise and ground his teeth. She pushed the second and third needle in next to the first. This time he groaned. "Don't be such a big baby." She tried to hold back a smile. Thing was, she'd watched these guys go at each other in full on combat mode. Blood flowed and sometimes bones cracked.

This guy was huge. Even his muscles had muscles. "It hurts," he groaned. Then he grinned at her, despite the pinched look on his face.

"You've been coming for treatments for weeks now, Rock. You would swear this was your first time."

"It still hurts. We dragons are not huge fans of silver." He gripped the top if his bicep, looking down at where the silver needles protruded from his skin. You would swear it was a couple of arrows or a sword stuck in his flesh instead of three tiny needles.

Louise pushed the start button on the timer. "Twelve minutes of suffering, you know the drill."

Rock winked at her. "I would take a silver bullet if it

meant spending time with you, Doc." His gaze dipped to her breasts even though she knew he couldn't see a thing through the white, loose-fitting medical coat she was wearing.

She pulled a pen out of the breast pocket of her coat and opened his file. Rock's eyes moved back to lock with hers.

"So," she clicked the top of the pen. "I need to confirm that you have done no strenuous exercise within the last two hours."

Rock shook his head. "Nope. I have training later this afternoon. Like you said, I know the drill."

She gave him a smile. "How were you after the last therapy session?" Rock currently came in for treatment twice a week. They'd gradually increased his contact time with the silver.

He gave a shrug. "Not too bad. I was at full strength later that same day."

Louise made a note in his file. She felt excitement grow inside her. It was taking longer than she had hoped but they were definitely making progress. "What about redness? Was there any swelling in the area?"

Rock nodded. "Yeah, it was red and slightly swollen but it only lasted for an hour tops."

She made another note. "That's great." When they had first started the treatments the needle mark would be red and raised for at least twenty-four hours. This was fantastic news.

"What about nausea, diarrhea?"

Rock shook his head. "No."

"What about right now, how do you feel?"

"It stings like a bitch but there is none of the nausea or dizziness I felt before." Rock swallowed thickly. "It irritates rather than debilitates. I am weaker. I can feel the silver but it is nowhere near as bad as it used to be. I think we might be able to beat this thing."

She gave a nod. "That's what I'm hoping. We need—"

The door opened, drawing their attention. It felt like the air was sucked from the room as he walked through the door.

Him.

The king.

It was Granite. He had a perpetual frown. His dark eyes narrowed as they landed on her. His mouth was full and sensual. His lips looked so incredibly soft for a moment and then they pulled into a thin line. His muscles seemed to bunch. Especially the ones on the side of his neck. His six-pack became more pronounced, forming a 'V' at the sides of his hips. Not that she was looking or anything.

"Out!" he barked at Rock.

The Earth king wasn't as good-looking as many of the dragon shifters. His nose was too prominent, his lips too full. His eyes were so dark they looked black, yet he was one of the most attractive men she had ever laid eyes on. Which was quite unfortunate since he was also a gigantic asshole. Not that she would ever date him. Firstly, she was there on business and she didn't mix business with pleasure, and secondly, it wasn't permitted. There was a clause within her contract. Strictly no fraternizing with the dragon shifters. It was very clear, while her feet were on this soil—which would be for a while yet—there would be no dragon fun. This suited her down to the ground. *So, no biggie!*

Rock started to stand, his chair scraping on the tile floor.

"Don't move," she addressed the shifter, who looked down at the ground in a submissive manner. He remained half-standing, hovering somewhere in the middle.

She turned her gaze to the brooding king. "I'm right in the middle of a treatment. I'm afraid it's going to have to wait a few minutes."

His frown deepened and he clenched his jaw. She didn't think it was possible but the move made him even more attractive, which pissed her off. She'd only ever been attracted to sweet, kind scholarly types. The total opposite of Granite.

Men who pulled out her chair for her. The type of guy who would walk you to your door after a date without expecting an invitation inside. Somehow, she suspected that Granite would demand. He was the type of guy who would eat you whole if you weren't careful. A not unpleasant shiver raced down her spine. She ignored it.

"Do as I say," he spoke under his breath, flicking his gaze towards Rock for an instant. His voice was a low growl that had her insides turning to mush. *Stupid, stupid insides.*

Rock instantly obeyed, heading for the door.

"Don't go too far!" she shouted at his retreating back. "The timer goes off in six minutes. I need you back then," she quickly added the last just as the door was closing. "That's how long you have." She folded her arms over her chest and tried to give the rude king what she hoped was a death stare.

Louise had a job to do. It was one she didn't take lightly. She would never be able to tell anyone about her time here but it didn't change the fact that the work she was doing was ground-breaking stuff. It was an opportunity of a lifetime. She had been appointed by Blaze, king of all four dragon kingdoms. Yes, she might be on Granite's soil, working with his men, but she wasn't one of his subjects. She certainly didn't take orders from him. They had been told to work together. *Together, damn it.* He clearly didn't know what working as a team meant.

"How long before the test males are immune to silver?"

I'm fine, thank you and you? What an asshole. There was zero small talk. He could at least pretend he had some sort of manners. She sucked in a deep breath. "We're making progress." She recited her findings and the headway they had made. "All three men are withstanding longer contact times and recovering more quickly."

"You call that tiny needle contact?" He made a snorting sound. "How long before we have real progress?" His dark eyes burned into hers.

For a second Louise was tempted to take a step back, or to look away but she held her ground. Only just. "We're years away from—"

Granite made a noise of disgust. "Years . . ." His hands curled into fists. He choked out a laugh, one that held very little humor. "We don't have years. Maybe a year at most. You need to work on months. Six months would be a good timeframe. Get it done." He turned, heading for the door.

It was Louise's turn to laugh and to follow it up with a frown of her own. She shook her head. "It doesn't work like that. There should be limited exposure to the allergen. It needs to slowly—"

Granite turned back. "We don't have time. You are working according to human standards. We are not human. We can withstand—"

"Have you ever had an allergic reaction to silver before?"

Granite shook his head. "I've never come into contact with the metal. I'm careful."

"These treatments bring about a reaction. Patients experience nausea, dizziness. The point of contact becomes red and swollen, extremely painful to the touch. They experience extreme fatigue and weakness, achy joints and fever. It would be nothing short of torture to increase exposure too quickly. Are you saying that's what you want?"

"My males are strong . . . they are in their prime and quite capable of handling it."

"Easy for you to say," she mumbled. "You don't have to go through any of it. Rush immunotherapy has its place, but I wouldn't recommend . . ." She watched as Granite walked towards the stainless steel table in the far corner. "What are you—?" She watched in horror as he picked up a whole bunch of the silver needles. "No . . . wait . . . what?" She gave a strangled cry as he stuck them all into his chest. He didn't so much as flinch as blood began to drip down. By the length of needle that protruded from his skin, she judged that they had sunk about a half an inch into him. She quickly counted twelve silver needles.

The idiot!

"Why the hell did you do that?" She could feel that her eyes were wide. "We never put an allergen into the torso. Only ever in a subject's arm. Are you crazy?"

Granite shook his head. "No, I'm a dragon, not some weak human. I can take it." She noticed that he had beads of sweat on his forehead and that he looked a bit pale.

"Lie down," she pointed to the bed. "I need to remove the needles before you suffer anaphylaxis. You could die."

Granite gave a shake of the head. "I am a dragon and a royal. I won't die from a few pinpricks, I assure you. Add me to your list." His nostrils flared as his breathing rate increased.

"You shouldn't put yourself at risk like that. I'll need to speak with Blaze. Ask permission—"

"Add me to your list. I don't give a fuck what Blaze has to say about it." Sweat trickled from his brow and blood continued to drip from his wounds.

"Please lie down," her voice came out sounding far calmer than what she felt.

Granite shook his head again. He tried to take a step

towards her and stumbled, quickly righting himself. He was sweating profusely, his breath coming in short pants. Louise was sure that if she checked his pulse it would be racing. He kept swallowing deeply.

"Are you feeling nauseous?"

"I told you, I'm fine," his voice was hoarse. His eyes seemed darker. "Add me to your list. Step up the treatments and add me. I will endure with my males."

"Lie down." She pointed to the bed, more insistently this time.

Granite shook his head. "Add me."

"Fine, I'll add you, now lie down so that I can help you." There was an edge of desperation to her voice. He really didn't look good. It was probably just her imagination but even his golden chest marking looked less bright. His coloring wasn't great. His vital signs were deteriorating before her eyes.

"Six months." His breathing was labored. "You need to get this done within six months despite what it takes."

"I can't promise that. I will administer rush immunotherapy as long as your men agree. They will need to understand what it entails though. It won't be easy for them . . . or for you."

"Easy has never been my thing." He closed his eyes and took a deep breath.

"Lie down," she half-whispered. "Please let me help you."

Granite gripped the needles and yanked them from his chest, letting them fall onto the stainless-steel table. A loud clanging sound reverberated around the room. "You can't help me," he growled.

"I'm sure there's something I can—"

"Sex . . ." his voice was low. Those dark eyes locked with hers. It took her a moment to realize what he had said. Her jaw dropped open and she struggled to breathe.

He took a small step towards her. "You can let me rut you."

CHAPTER 3

*S*ex.
Rutting.
Why had he said that?

The alarm went off and Rock sauntered in.

"Fuck off!" he snarled, trying to keep himself from swaying. He already felt marginally better now that the needles had been removed. He still felt weak and sick to his stomach. It was like nothing he had ever experienced before.

"No, stay," the human stammered, her head whipping in the direction of the lesser male.

"Out!" He didn't take his eyes off the little female.

She narrowed her green orbs, giving him another one of her scathing looks. Funny, he'd had females flutter their lashes at him. They usually looked at him with unbridled lust, but the filthy looks she flung at him interested him far more. She gave a small shake of the head. "Those needles need to come out and I need to examine . . ." her voice grew softer as Rock walked back towards the door, obeying his king. *Damn straight!*

The female put a hand up as if to try to stop the male from leaving. "Take the needles out!" she shouted after him. Rock gave a nod and then shut the door behind him.

"On the bed." She pointed to the thin hospital cot in the corner. "Let's get this over with."

Granite felt his lip twitch as he held back a smile. He was not on friendly terms with this human. Or any human for that matter. He didn't trust them. If he smiled, he would give her the wrong impression. She might think he liked her or something. *He did not.* "You want me to lie down so that you can get it over with? It might be easier if you take your clothes off first."

"What?"

"Sex. It's easier when naked. At the very least, naked from the waist down. You could even leave that coat of yours on."

She swallowed thickly and folded her arms across her chest. "That's not funny."

"Do I look like I'm joking?" A wave of nausea rolled through him. Maybe he had gone a little too far. The effects of the silver were worse than he had anticipated.

"I'm not having sex with you." Her eyes were wide.

"You said you wanted to help me." He had to fight to keep his eyes on hers. To stop himself from checking her out. Not that it was possible to achieve with that ridiculous coat covering her from neck to knee.

She rolled her eyes. "Not in that way. I meant clean your wound, maybe dress it for you. You can forget about having sex with me. Besides, it would be in breach of my contact and I'm sure I heard somewhere that dragon shifters are only allowed to have sex with humans on their Stag Runs and if they manage to win someone at The Hunt. There are strict rules. Any type of relationship would be strictly forbidden." She picked up a file on her desk and hugged it to her chest.

"I never once mentioned a relationship. I was referring to fucking. You know when—"

She made a squeaking noise and then quickly pulled herself together within seconds. "Forget it. Even if I wanted to—" her eyes widened and she hugged the file tighter, "and I don't," she put emphasis on the word 'don't,' "it's strictly forbidden."

"So you're one for obeying rules?"

"What and you're not? You're a leader."

"I enforce rules."

"But you don't live by them? Double standards if I ever saw them."

"Sometimes rules are meant to be broken." *Why the fuck was he pushing this?* The human was small. Too small for his taste. It was the silver. He was weak. It was affecting his thinking. A good, hard rut would help.

"Rules are in place for a reason." She licked her lips, looking deep in thought. "Not that I'm in the least bit interested," she cleared her throat, "but I need to know, for scientific purposes if sex really would help or was that just a line?"

He couldn't help the chuckle that escaped him. "Scientific purposes?" Granite nodded. "Yes, sex would really help. A good rutting session would speed up my recovery time."

She put the tip of her pen into her mouth for a moment and sucked on it. He watched as her pink lips closed over the object. *Fuck, but this silver was affecting him.* He could imagine those lips wrapped around something else. Then she tapped the end on her lower lip twice. "That's interesting, I need to look into it." She tucked a strand of hair that had fallen from her tight bun. It was bright orange and wild. There was a smattering of freckles across her nose and upper cheeks. They made her look younger than she really was. Then he realized what she had just said.

"Look into it," he growled. "How do you plan on doing that? Don't think about fucking any of my males." His voice was rough.

Her eyes widened and she sucked in a breath. "I would never—" Her voice had a high-pitched quality and she looked completely shocked. "I'm a professional. I take my job seriously. I'm not having sex with you or anyone else for that matter. Stop being so vulgar."

The little human thought to give him orders. His dick stirred. *What?* His reaction to her insolence irritated the fuck out of him. It couldn't be helped though, the doctor intrigued him whether he liked it or not. She had been here for seven weeks. Had been back to Walton Springs twice in that time and he had yet to scent a male on her. He had yet to scent any form of release on her. Self-inflicted or otherwise. Why he had even noticed was beyond him.

"A professional?" he raised his brows, trying to keep his thoughts out of the gutter. Who was he kidding? This female was prissy, somewhere beyond uptight. There was no way she was going to do something so forbidden. "Good! Keep it that way." Blaze would have a shit-fit if any of his males broke the sacred 'Don't fuck with humans' lore anyway, so best he put it out of his mind. "When should I come back for my next treatment?"

She shook her head, her eyes blazed. "I still don't think this is a good idea."

A wave of dizziness rushed through him and he grit his teeth till it passed.

"Are you okay?"

He ignored the question. "When?" he said, a little more harshly.

She narrowed her eyes. "Day after tomorrow. I will put together a rush program in the meanwhile."

Granite headed for the door. He stopped and glanced back. "Keep in mind that we are shifters. We're much stronger than humans. I want to see this program before it is administered."

She rolled those gorgeous green eyes. *Gorgeous! What the fuck?* They were okay at best. She was very average; small and weak. No curves to speak of. *No!* She was not worth his time or energy.

"Fine," she huffed.

"Six months, female. I won't hesitate to replace you." It was the last thing he wanted. The more humans who set foot on dragon territory the higher the risk.

"Wait just a minute." She put her hands on her hips and he turned back. "Blaze hired me. Not you. I will run this by him before proceeding."

"I told you—"

"No!" she snapped. It sent another bolt straight to his cock. Her composure returned. "I've listened to what you had to say. Thank you for your feedback, I now know your feelings on this."

"Feelings have nothing to do with it."

"I understand your requirements then." She didn't completely lose her cool like he had expected. Instead, she cocked her head. Although she had a calm exterior, he knew she was pissed. Her flushed cheek gave her away. Another tendril of bouncy curls escaped the bun. He had a stupid urge to pull her hair free. To see what she would look like without the coat and all the doctor get-up. She licked her lips – soft, pink flesh – and swallowed hard. He watched her throat work. Granite forced his gaze back to hers. Blazing and hard, there was determination in the depths of those eyes. "I don't take orders from you. I respect you . . . I do, but I wasn't employed by you. We were instructed to work together as a team. Please, can we try and get along? I will report back after speaking with Blaze."

"Make no mistake that this is my territory." He stepped forward and into her personal space. Granite took another step. The female looked up at him, having to cock her neck to maintain eye contact. "I may not have had a say in who Blaze chose to run this originally, but I definitely have a say as to whether or not you stay. Do your reports and feedback to whomever you wish but if I'm not happy with what you come back with, you are gone. Do you understand that, female?"

She grit her teeth but didn't say a word.

"I will replace you in a heartbeat." He clicked his fingers and this time she flinched. "There would be sweet fuck all Blaze could do about it. I hope we have an understanding."

"In other words, we'll get along just fine as long as I do exactly what you say."

He pretended to think about it for half a second. "That sounds about right." He knew he was acting like a dick but she needed to know her place. After today, they all needed her to step it up. They were sitting ducks. This was no time to play nice guy and to sugarcoat his approach. Either the female was tough and would do what she had to or she was gone.

The healer narrowed her eyes. Just when he thought he was going to have to get really tough, she gave a nod.

He exhaled, suddenly realizing that he had been holding his breath while he had waited for her response. The last thing he wanted was to start again with some other doctor. It would add to the time pressures, add to the risk. *No!* He was glad she was staying. Granite spoke as he headed for the door. "Good. I'll see you tomorrow then, you can present your program to me. Make it good!" He turned and headed out, not giving her a chance to respond.

What a complete asshole!
What a jerk!

She felt like throwing something at his retreating back. No, make that his head. If she had a couple dozen eggs, he'd be covered in yolk and the gloopy white stuff . . . *albumen*. That's it, albumen, she couldn't even think of the basic word for egg white. Her brain had stopped working.

Having him that close. Smelling his really manly, really delicious scent drove her insane and she'd pretty much let him walk all over her. Treat her like a doormat. It was not right.

She was crushing the file in her hand, yet she couldn't seem to force herself to let the thing go. This was the most exciting, most interesting assignment she had ever had. It sure as nuts beat her last one. The treatment of rhinitis with the main focus on dust mites. *Yawn!*

This was ground-breaking stuff. If that meant sucking up to the gorgeous, dickhead king then she'd deal. If it meant having to walk the very thin line between both kings, then she'd do it and keep both of them happy if she could. She'd sell the rush immunotherapy to Blaze like it was her idea—he might not bite if he suspected Granite had given the directive. There was no love lost between the dragon tribes. They might get along – only just – but they didn't like one another.

Then she'd get the permission from her patients; but what she wouldn't do – what she would refuse to do – was to put anyone's life at risk. *Forget it!* Granite could go to hell on that one.

There was a soft clang. "Don't mind me, Doc," Rock smiled at her. "Just returning your needles. I took them out ages ago. Thought you might want them back. I don't have any use for them."

"Oh," she managed to get out. Louise forced herself to smile. "Thanks. Are you feeling okay?" She finally forced her hand to ease its crushing hold on the file.

Rock nodded. "Yeah, I'm doing great." He frowned. "I hope you don't mind but I overheard the conversation you had with Granite."

"Mmmhmmm?" She wasn't sure where this was going.

"He's right."

"Well, he can fire me if he wants but I'm not putting any of you at risk." There was a crunching noise as she crumpled the paper in her hand. *Damn!*

"No, not about that, although, he does have the authority to send you packing. I mean about us being able to take more. We're really tough."

"You'd feel very ill. It would hurt."

Rock laughed. "We are built to take pain. We are warriors." He flexed his muscles. He had a fantastic build and was incredibly good-looking, yet she didn't feel a thing. Really weird. Rock was such a nice guy. All five guys who were on the immunotherapy were really nice and super polite. If she had to be attracted to one of them, why couldn't it be someone like Rock? Why did it have to be Granite? King Asshole, as she liked to call him.

"Also, he acts all tough but he's actually a good male. The best kind of male."

"Who?" Like she had to ask.

"My king," Rock paused. "Granite takes his role very seriously. He worries about us. He doesn't sleep at night. He trains harder than any of us. Sacrifices heavily for his people. Deep down inside he is good and kind."

"You could've fooled me," she mumbled, yet somehow, she believed Rock. Granite worked hard. She never saw him having any fun. It was all work. All the time. One small thing they had in common.

The shifter smiled. "You'll have to trust me on this one. He tends to lash out when he is stressed or particularly worried about something. He doesn't trust humans. He has been on several hunts and has won several females but has yet to claim one and bring her home."

"Because he doesn't trust us?"

Rock looked confused for a moment, then he shook his head. "I think that is part of the reason, for sure. He says that he is looking for a female who is sweet."

"Sweet?" Louise made a snorting sound. More like agreeable. Someone who would obey his every command and fall at his feet. "There are plenty of those kinds of women out there." Ladies who would swoon as soon as they caught an eyeball full of him. Not that he needed the ego boost. The guy was just about as arrogant as they came.

"I think all females are sweet," he winked at her. "Especially doctors." Despite his flirty behavior, she got the feeling that Rock was just being nice. She didn't get that yucky, 'wash yourself with soap' feeling she got when guys sometimes flirted with her.

Louise rolled her eyes. "Yeah right."

"I don't understand how he can just walk away from an opportunity with a female."

"Yeah, it must be tough with so few dragon shifter women."

Rock nodded. "We have a couple of shifter females but they prefer to spend time with many of the shifter men. They can have their pick and don't want to settle with just one. There are those of us who would be happy to mate with one of them but they choose not to." He sighed.

"It sounds as if you like someone in particular."

Rock nodded; he had this faraway look. "Her name is Quartz. She is beautiful and kind but she refuses to entertain the idea of us being together. She says that she doesn't want to tie me down. She thinks that I will end up despising her because we would have a childless mating. She feels that no male should be denied offspring. I wish I could change her mind. As much as I would love to have a child, I want her more."

Louise gripped Rock's forearm for a second. "You are a really nice guy. Don't give up, especially if she has similar feelings for you."

"We get along really well. We've been seeing each other for a couple of months. It's not exclusive but neither of us has been with anyone else, which is rare for an unmated dragon female." He grinned. "Who am I kidding? It's unheard of. She still refuses to take things further. She keeps insisting that I go on the hunts. There's a Stag Run in a few weeks . . . she told me I should go, but I don't want to."

"Don't give up."

Rock shook his head. "I won't, Doc."

"One of these days she'll realize that you guys are meant to be together."

"I hope so. That's why I volunteered for this project. I did it for Quartz, in the hope that we can overcome our affliction to silver."

"How will that help Quartz?" she asked when he didn't elaborate.

"You would be able to operate, using a silver blade. Maybe you could fix her." There was a desperation in his eyes. "Not just her, all of our infertile females. You would be able to help all of the non-humans."

Non-humans healed too quickly, making regular stainless steel blades useless. Yet, they died too easily if silver scalpels were used. Making any form of surgical procedure impossible. "You are slowly developing a resistance to the metal. You should also start to heal quickly after coming into contact with silver. You might heal too quickly to perform surgery. I'm not sure that your idea would work."

His head dropped and his shoulders sagged. "I had really hoped it would be possible."

"Look, it is something I will keep in mind. Although, I am not a fertility specialist so I would not be able to test your women or perform any kind of surgery on them."

"It might be possible though?" he raised his brows.

The last thing she wanted was to get his hopes up. "I don't know. Maybe," she added the last when his eyes clouded. "A friend of mine from college specialized in Gynecology, I will contact her."

"That would be great!" Rock grabbed her hand and squeezed.

"Ow!!"

"Sorry, Doc. I sometimes forget how soft and breakable you are."

"Well please don't, it could be detrimental to my health," she had to laugh. "Listen," she pulled in a deep breath. "Don't get your hopes up."

Rock shook his head. "I'll try not to." Then his expression turned more serious. "You'd better run it by Granite before you contact anyone from the outside world."

Louise had to work to keep from rolling her eyes. "I will."

CHAPTER 4

The next day . . .

Louise still couldn't get over it. She had expected to have to argue. At the very least she'd expected to be made to explain a little. She'd put a kick-ass argument together. Had spent half the night on a rush therapy proposal and the other half on coming up with just the right plan to deliver it to Blaze. She'd barely started talking when Blaze had granted her permission to step up the Resistance Therapy. He'd said a couple of things that mirrored what Granite had said yesterday, only in a much politer way, urging her to come up with a cure for their silver allergy as a matter of extreme urgency. He'd seemed stressed and a bit preoccupied, like he couldn't get rid of her soon enough. Then again, the guy was a new father to the cutest little boy. She hadn't been lucky enough to meet his wife and newborn son, but she had seen the numerous framed pictures adorning his desk.

Louise loved babies; there was something about their cute gummy smiles and chubby cheeks that made her heart clench. Then again, that's what they were designed to do. Tug at the heartstrings, make even the most hardened soul broody. Well, it worked on her. She would be thirty-four in a couple of months. That's what happened when a person worked too hard. Their life seemed to pass them by. Louise was married to her job – at least that's what her last serious boyfriend had told her when she'd stood him up at the last minute, one time too many. *Oh well!* She loved her work. She only wished she could find love and keep practicing medicine. Maybe she'd bypass the relationship part and go for artificial insemination. Louise had to bite back a laugh. *Nah!* She wasn't that desperate . . . not yet anyway.

They slowly ascended before hovering over the large patio area in front of the great hall. Home sweet home! It was funny how quickly she had settled in amongst the dragon people.

The ground rose up and the big shifter put her down. She stumbled as his clawed talons released her. Within half a beat she was steady on her feet without a trace of nausea. This whole flying in the claws of winged beasts was getting easier and easier. She'd been transported back and forth from Walton Springs, blindfolded mind you, and had been transported to the Fire castle plenty of times. It was becoming old hat.

Staring at naked men however, was not.

She averted her gaze as her ride shifted into his human form. There were cracking and pulling noises. The guy grunted and then he was all muscle and nakedness. This part of the whole thing was still as embarrassing as hell.

"Would you like me to escort you to your work chamber?" the shifter asked, she could hear that he was smiling. He was a great guy, they all were.

Louise pulled the hood of her thick fur-lined jacket from her head. "No thanks, Stone." She glanced his way, sure to keep her eyes way up, like somewhere above his head. Not that she was even remotely interested in him. She was a human and humans didn't look at each other's privates, they just didn't. Not unless they were into one another, seriously dating, married or all of the above. 'Into one another' needed to at least be a good start.

"Are you . . ." he stopped talking and looked at something over her shoulder.

A few bits of hair had escaped the bun she'd meticulously pinned in place at the back of her head. Her hair was a crazy mess of curls on a good day and a plain crazy mess on a bad day. The curly tendrils that had somehow managed to perform a Houdini feat began to fly wildly about her face and she heard the sound of many wings flapping in unison. She glanced back over her shoulder.

Great!

There were at least twenty of them. They were almost silent, considering how many of them were gradually descending onto the large space behind her.

Crap!

She felt like running away as she caught sight of the golden chest of the majestic dragon at the head of the formation. Its wing span was greater, its coloring brighter. Its eyes so much darker. He was magnificent even in dragon form.

Granite.

King Dickwad.

A shiver surged through her. The familiar sound that marked their shift filled the air. Within seconds, Granite's dark stare landed on her. Her mouth went dry as she took him in. Every last inch of him, in all his glory. *Wow! Just wow.* He bit down on his lower lip as he stalked towards her.

She was so not looking at his magnificent golden chest. Nor was she looking at his ripped abs. She certainly wasn't looking any lower.

She made a croaking noise low down in her throat as her gaze landed on his heavy sacks, his cock. It was so huge it swayed from side to side as he walked. *Oh god! Stop staring. Whatever you do, don't drool. Do not whimper or moan. Eyes up! Eyes up dammit!*

The last thing she wanted was for him to think that she was interested in him . . . because she wasn't. Not even a little bit. Sure, he was really attractive but that's where it ended. The problem was that he'd already caught her staring at his junk. It was a given that he would get the wrong idea. There was only one thing to do about it. She forced herself to look past Granite and at all the other guys. They were all amazing specimens but her stupid eyeballs wanted back on Granite. They weren't interested in the rest. *Tough luck!* She drank them in. Okay, she forced herself to look even though they were naked. She tried hard not to blush and it seemed to work.

"Hey, Doc," Rock gave her a wave.

"Hi!" She waved back, her voice a tad shrill. Her cheeks a tad hot. Okay, so maybe she was blushing a small amount. Who could blame her?

"Doctor Louise, good to see you." Another wave.

"You too, Igneous. Did you have a good training session?" She tried to act normal. Tried to pretend there wasn't a huge lump in her throat. Or that there wasn't a sea of naked men in front of her. One that could adorn any stage, at any strip club, any day of the week. From the corner of her eye, she watched as Granite approached. *Not looking. Not looking.*

Igneous grinned. "Yes, it was—"

"Enough," Granite growled. "Dismissed," he added with a little less venom. *Shit!* He was still approaching. He stopped when he was right in front of her. As in inches away. She could feel his heat, could smell his masculine scent. He was naked. *Naked!*

You're a doctor. You've studied anatomy. You've got this!

"Bye, guys," she gave a tiny wave to the departing warriors.

"Follow me!" Granite strode ahead of her. All she could see in that moment was his ass. His really muscular, bronzed ass. It was a great-looking ass. Beautiful in fact. Could an ass be beautiful? He paused, his eyes still trained up ahead.

Shit!

Granite was waiting for her. *Oops!* She quickly fell into step behind him. Come to think of it, his back was also a thing of beauty. Wide, with broad shoulders. Well-muscled like the rest of him.

"Hi, Doctor!" one of the men shouted as he walked past them in the opposite direction.

Louise smiled and was just about to respond when Granite growled. It was scary. A deep vibration that reverberated through the hallway. The shifter who had just greeted her, tucked his head to his chest and hightailed it out of there. Face ashen.

Granite was a moody SOB, that much was for sure.

He picked up the pace to the point where she was practically jogging to keep up with him. They arrived at a set of large, double doors. Thankfully, he turned towards them or she would have collided with him. The doors were beautiful. A deep, rich wood intricately carved with vines and flowers. It was the doorknob that drew her attention. It looked like it was made from gold. It was encrusted with blue stones – sapphires. They were big and they gleamed. *Had to be fake.*

Granite opened one of the doors, standing to the side while she entered. *Look up! Look up!* Shew, she made it past him without letting her eyes wander.

Wow! The space was huge. Triple volume. It reminded her of a loft apartment in an old building. One that had been completely renovated. It was a mix of modern retro and classic. His office chair was bright red leather, as were the plastic, funky-looking chairs at the boardroom table.

The rest of the furniture was dark, either made of oak or covered with leather. The artwork was the same turbulent dark shade with splashes of red. Ultra-modern stainless steel stairs wound up to a platform above. On the platform was just about the biggest bed she had ever seen. It was unmade. The rumpled sheets had been haphazardly tossed to the side. Black silk. It was his bed.

Granite cleared his throat and Louise jumped.

"You live in your office," she blurted, trying to tear her eyes away from his bed. The place where he slept. Even assholes had to close their eyes from time to time.

"What of it?" He walked to his desk and typed his password into the open laptop on his desk. She noticed how he put his big body between her and the device before doing so. The guy really did have trust issues. It wasn't like she was interested in anything that was on there.

Keep your eyes on his eyes, Lou. You can do it! "It's unhealthy to sleep where you work. Studies have shown that—"

"It's convenient." Granite pushed a few buttons on the device. "I took a look at the proposal you mailed." *Shit!* He didn't look happy. Not even a little bit. Then again, this was nothing new.

She nodded once, clasping her hands in front of her. The doctor looked nervous. This was the first time he'd seen her this way. Her eyes were wide. Her skin so pale that she seemed to have even more freckles on her otherwise flawless skin.

Granite put a hand on the desk next to his computer. He moved to the side so that she would be able to see the screen. Her proposal was open. Granite scrolled down until he reached the part that he was looking for. "I asked you to step it up, Miss Parry. What is this?" He tapped the screen.

"I did step it up." She leaned in next to him and he caught her scent. Honeyed peaches. Fruity and sweet. It was a really good scent. Who was he kidding? It was fucking delicious. He tried to concentrate while she spoke numbers, explaining why they couldn't increase allergen levels higher than she already had on the proposal. Next, she launched into the risks involved with pushing the immunotherapy any harder or faster.

"How old are you?" he asked when she finally finished.

"Excuse me. How is that relevant?"

She seemed so young. Too damned young. "How long have you been practicing? Out of all of the candidates, why were you chosen to assist us?"

The female stood up tall. She pulled a loose strand of hair behind her ear and licked her lips. "I am qualified for this position. Age has nothing to with it. Blaze hired me because I'm the right person for this job . . ." She rattled off her resume, stating awards she'd won and studies she'd conducted. Papers she'd written. The good doctor had even given a year of her life doing humanitarian work in Ethiopia. Working with few supplies and a shoe-string budget. *Blah, blah, blah.*

She used her hands to emphasize her words. "The

studies I conducted on the effect that dust mites have—"

"Dust mites?" he choked out a laugh. He turned to face her, realizing how close they were. Granite could feel the heat radiate off of her. Could hear how her heart raced.

"I don't need to defend myself," her voice was soft as she craned her neck to maintain eye contact. "I already made it through six rounds of interviews and an extensive medical. I had to agree to have my whole life scrutinized. From my birth certificate to any criminal records. I've been under a microscope," she shook her head, "I don't need this from you."

"How old are you?"

"I'm nearly thirty-four, so plenty old enough. Is there anything else you want to know while we're at it?" Not nearly as young as she looked then. He had her file, just hadn't bothered to read it. In this matter, he trusted Blaze. The male would have been thorough. He needed the human to understand who was in charge though. As much as he loved the fact that she had her own mind, he needed her to obey him. Their species was at risk.

"These ratios and contact times, how long before my males and I become resistant to the effects of silver?"

She blinked a few times and then sucked in a breath through her nose. "I'm hopeful the therapy will work, but it's not a guarantee."

"How long?"

She leaned back in, her eyes flashed across the table on to the screen. "Eight months, maybe longer. We can't push any harder than that."

He had to bite back a snarl. "Not good enough, Miss Parry." It came out sounding harsh.

"It will have to be good enough, *Mr.* Granite."

He had to fight a smile. "You can call me *my lord* or Granite."

"My lord?" She gave a snort and then quickly turned serious when she caught his stare.

"It's not good enough, Miss Parry."

"Call me Doctor or Louise."

"It's not good enough, female. Why are you making me repeat myself?"

"We can't make the program fit within a certain timeframe. It doesn't work that way." She sounded exasperated. "It's dangerous. I want no part of it."

"Then pack your bags, you're leaving today."

She folded her arms. "No way. You don't make those kinds of decisions."

"Want to fucking bet?"

"You don't have to swear at me. You're trying to strong-arm me and I don't appreciate it."

Granite put the tips of his fingers to his temples and pushed. "You have no idea of what's at stake here, of the ramifications should this not prove to be a success. This is my kingdom—"

"Yeah, yeah, you're the king and ruler of all. Your chest is golden . . ." She touched his marking with just the tip of a finger. It was just a brush, yet it felt really good. Too damned good. A soft, almost sensual stroke. His dick took notice. It took notice big time. *What the hell?* She did it again, another soft stroke. He knew she didn't mean for it to come across as sensual. By the fire in her eyes and the frown on her forehead, he'd say that the opposite was true. Maybe someone ought to tell his dick, which throbbed. She sucked in a deep breath. "What about when your men are in agony? What if one of them was to die?" Her voice hitched on the last word. She cared. The female cared. *Interesting.*

"I've told you that we are shifters. We don't die easily. In fact, it's almost impossible. It'll hurt," he gave a shrug, "I have spoken with my males and we're ready to do what it takes for our people. They are willing to sacrifice, as am I. We are even willing to take the risk of death."

She held his stare for a long time before finally exhaling through her nose. "It's crazy but let me have another look at the program." She turned back to the computer. After a few beats, she gave a nod. "We can step it up but you need to know that it's against my advice. Also, if I deem the risk too high, I'm slowing things down." She was frowning deeply as she looked up at him from over her shoulder.

"Duly noted." He folded his arms.

Oh fuck! Her gaze drifted to his already hard cock which hardened up a whole lot more under her scrutiny. Her lush pink lips fell open for a moment. Then she did an odd little 'back and forth' thing with her jaw before making a strange noise.

Granite didn't try to cover up. "We need to get this done within six months." He ignored the fact that his dick was trying to get at her on its own accord.

Her eyes widened and snapped back to his. "I'll be going then. I need to run this by Blaze. So—"

"Blaze is fully onboard. Have the proposal back by close of business today."

"No problem!" She began walking towards the door.

"Miss Parry . . . female . . ." he called after her. The doctor stopped walking but didn't turn around.

"There is something I need to talk to you about."

She turned to the side but didn't look at him. "Is it serious?"

What kind of question was that? "Yes," he tried not to growl and failed.

"Okay, sure, but would you mind putting some pants on . . . please?" She waved her hands.

"I'm fine . . . thank you," he added.

"It would be hard to . . . hard . . ." She shook her head and giggled, quickly pulling herself together. Then she chewed on her lower lip, still not looking at him. "I can't concentrate on anything you say right now. I'm sure you need a license for that in certain states. Sheesh!" she exhaled. "You should really put on some clothes." She had yet to look at him.

"No!"

"You have a gigantic erection, please get dressed. It's not appropriate."

"Only if you take some of your clothing off." She was wearing an oversized winter jacket. It looked stupid. Like she was a child playing dress-up in her mother's closet.

"No way." She turned to face him. He could see that she was struggling to maintain eye contact.

"Oh!" she smiled. "I get it. You're one of those guys who gets off on being mean and rude. You probably enjoy whips, chains and spanking."

Just then, an image of this female spread out over his lap, while he spanked her ass, crept into his mind. He could hear her squeals as his hand met her flesh. Could see her glistening pussy nestled between her parted thighs.

"I'm right!" she squealed, pointing at his dick which chose that exact moment to give a twitch.

"Bullshit!" His voice was deep. Too fucking deep. "I'm horny. Seriously fucking horny. That's all. I haven't had sex in a very long fucking time and you were touching me."

Her eyes widened. "I wasn't touching . . . Oh, as in my finger on your chest? That was enough to do that . . . ?" She pointed at his dick . . . again.

His balls felt achy. "Female, just about anything is enough to get me hard after almost six months of celibacy. Jerking off in the shower is not the same as a snug pussy."

She gave a shriek. "You did not just say that." She squeezed her eyes shut for a few seconds. "My ears are bleeding."

"You're a doctor. I'm sure you know how it works. Your ears look perfectly fine to me."

She put her hand up. "Well they're not."

"You act like you've never fucked before."

At this point her eyes were so wide that she looked

comical. Her face was flushed but he suspected that was partly due to the ridiculous coat. She finally squared her shoulders. He found himself leaning forward. He couldn't wait to hear her response. Her eyes flicked away for a moment or two before moving back to his. "No, never."

What?

She licked her lips. "The type of men I've been with in the past, well they wouldn't . . ." She shook her head. "They were the type to make sweet, passionate love." Her lips pulled into a smug, self-satisfied smile. "They definitely didn't do . . . that." She widened her eyes.

Granite couldn't help the laugh that was pulled from him.

"What's wrong? What's so funny?"

"Female. You need to be fucked so badly, you have no idea."

She choked. He'd never seen anyone choke on nothing before but this little human was doing it. Within a few seconds, she was dragging air into her lungs and focusing those green, molten eyes on him. They were narrowed. "That's so incredibly rude. For your information . . ." She put a finger up and wagged it at him. "I may not have had a boyfriend in a while . . . okay a long while, but . . ." She stopped wagging the finger and pointed it at him. "I'm perfectly fine. Better than fine. I don't need a man in my life."

She was so full of shit it was scary. Her answer was perfect though. "I'm glad to hear that. What you do in Walton Springs, on your own time, is entirely up to you.

What you do here, on my territory is my business. My males are taken with you."

She frowned heavily. "Taken, as in . . . ?" She shook her head. "I wouldn't say that just because they're nice to me. You should try it some time."

"You don't need their brand of 'nice,' trust me."

"Just because they're sweet, doesn't mean they have a hidden agenda."

This female was too much. Granite found himself smiling down at her. He quickly schooled his emotions. "Sweet. That's the funniest thing I've heard in a long time. They all want a piece of you. I'm sure you don't need me to spell out which piece, *Doctor*."

She narrowed her eyes. "Nonsense. They're nice guys. But nice isn't exactly a concept you understand."

"Nice my ass. Stay the fuck away from them. If you slip up, you'll be fired and I'll cut the male's balls off myself."

She gasped. "Oh, my god!" She was silent for a few seconds. "You're serious! You would hurt someone like that?"

"Deadly serious. They would grow back but no one wants to lose their balls, even for a couple of days." He palmed his own sacs, noticing how her lips parted and her eyes dilated as she tracked the movement of his hand. *Fuck!* "You should go now. That proposal isn't going to rewrite itself."

He needed to take a long-ass shower. One that hopefully wouldn't clog the drains. Then he needed to speak to his males. If one of them put even a pinky finger on this female, he wouldn't hesitate to remove a certain delicate piece of their anatomy. He didn't need a medical degree to do it.

She gave a nod and turned back for the door.

"And, Doctor . . ."

"I don't think I want to hear this," she gave a groan that tugged on his balls.

Damn, he couldn't wait until the next stag run. *Fuck!* "You should get laid next time you're in Walton Springs."

She sucked in a deep breath and then slowly released it. "Why am I not shocked you just said that?"

"You are giving off this scent. It's driving my males crazy."

"A scent?" She turned back to him, a look of confusion clearly evident.

"Yeah, it's needy and sends out all the wrong signals to my males. It makes risking their balls worth it to them."

"Needy? What the hell is needy? I'm not needy. I've never been needy a day in my life. This whole conversation is grossly inappropriate." The chest area of her jacket rose and fell in quick succession.

"It needs to be said or I wouldn't say it." How innocent was this female? She had no fucking idea. "You are needy. You know that feeling when your breasts feel swollen and overly sensitive? Your nipples tighten, that heavy feeling in the pit of your stomach? That achy feeling a female gets when she needs . . ."

"I get it. My private life is no concern of yours. Now, I'm on a deadline . . . remember?" She spun around and strode from the room.

Maybe he'd been a bit hard on her. Maybe he . . . *No!* He'd never sugarcoated a thing in his life and wasn't about to start now. If she couldn't take it she could go back to her own people. Despite all the gasping and huffing, he knew she was made from sterner stuff. The little human stood up to him. It was one of the things he liked about her. Although 'liked' was probably too strong a word.

CHAPTER 5

The next day . . .

Louise shook her head so hard that a piece of hair fell loose. "No damned way." The guy was crazy. Completely off his rocker.

"Do it," Granite commanded, he was perched on the edge on the gurney. Thank god he was wearing pants this time.

"Your men have been coming for immunotherapy for seven weeks already. You just started. They struggled with today's therapy and they have had far greater exposure than you. You can't possibly start at the same level as them."

"I can and I will."

"Of course you can. Doesn't mean you should though," she muttered under her breath. "How about we get you to their level over the next two to three weeks?"

He ran a hand over the short-cropped hair on his scalp. "How about we start today . . . right now." His eyes were so dark, framed by long, thick lashes. They had no place being on such a masculine specimen of a man, yet they worked somehow. Like his full lips; they helped soften his harsh exterior. Not by much though.

She pulled her thoughts together. "It could kill you. Haven't you heard a single thing I . . ." Louise huffed out a breath, it conveyed her frustration. "It's dangerous. Worst case scenario you could die, at the very least, you'll be in a world of pain. Can't you listen to me and let me do my job?"

She wasn't surprised when he shook his head. "I'm a royal."

Louise wanted to roll her eyes so badly her eyeballs hurt.

"Being a royal means that I heal quicker. I'm stronger. You need to do your job so that I can do mine." He held out his arm and she looked down at it. His bicep was large; his forearm was well-defined. His hand was big and calloused. His skin was bronzed. It was a good arm. A really good arm. The last thing she wanted was to stick it full of needles.

"You'll get sick. Very sick. There will be nausea and possible vomiting. During the treatment, you will experience heart palpitations. Your pulse may become weak and thready. Your body temperature will increase, causing you to sweat profusely. Your respiratory rate will go up. You'll more than likely have an upset stomach for the next twenty-four to forty-eight hours. You'll be weak and dizzy. You will most likely become unconscious. The point of entry will become swollen and painful. In short, you will feel so ill that you'll wish you had listened to my warnings. There won't be a damned thing I'll be able to do for you once you have had prolonged contact with the allergen."

"I can take it." He reached for the needles but she blocked him with her body.

"I will administer the treatment." Thankfully this was her last appointment for the day. Granite was going to need plenty of support once this was over. Medical support of course.

Granite gave a single nod. "Fine, then let's get this over with."

"You won't be able to take care of yourself. Is there someone I can call to help you?"

"I'll be fine." Deadpan. The guy had no clue.

"No, you won't." What an arrogant asshole. Why wouldn't he listen to her? He thought that being a king would somehow grant him special powers. *Wrong!* "A girlfriend? A friend?" She had to try to get through to him. "A family member? You will need help, at least for tonight."

He pushed his arm towards her. "Do it. I can take care of myself."

Fine! She was done arguing. She picked up the first needle and put a hand on his arm to keep it steady. "Stay calm. Turn your hand palm up."

He did as she said. Louise took ahold of his wrist. His skin was warm. "Keep your arm as relaxed as possible and stay as still as possible."

"I think that making me lie on this bed is overkill." He leaned back against the pillow. The upper part of the mattress was tilted to an almost sitting position.

Louise ignored his statement. "You'll feel a pinch as the needle penetrates your skin. I'll place each of the needles quickly and as painlessly as possible. The site will burn during the contact time. Are you sure about this? Fifteen needles for fifteen minutes is pretty hectic."

"I did this the other day, remember?"

"Mmhmmm. You were exposed to a few more needles but the contact time was way less. A couple of minutes, tops." When he didn't respond, she continued. "Okay but don't say I didn't warn you." She pushed the first needle in, then the next and the next, working quickly and carefully until all fifteen were in place.

Granite didn't make a sound and didn't so much as flinch. Once all fifteen were in place, she pressed the button on the timer. Next, she gripped his finger and slid the device on. "This is called a Pulse Oximeter. I'll use it to monitor your heart-rate as well as the oxygen levels in your blood. I won't hesitate to pull the plug if I feel your life is at risk."

She placed a pan in his lap. Granite frowned. "And this?"

"I refuse to clean your puke off of the floor. Use that." She pointed at the pan.

Instead of arguing as she expected, he gripped the edge of the steel container with his free hand and held onto it. His face was flushed and his brow sweaty. It had already begun. The effects of the silver were taking their toll.

"Let me know if you can't take any more. Don't try to be a hero." Granite was a man's man and arrogant as hell. "No one else needs to know what goes on between these four walls. It will stay between you and me."

"I can take it, doctor. Don't you have some paperwork to do or something?" His jaw was set. She noticed that the area surrounding the needles was already looking red.

Louise headed for the other side of the bed, she put a cuff around Granite's bicep. "I don't have anywhere else to be. Monitoring your health is my number one priority. I need to take your blood pressure."

He grunted.

Louise pushed a button on the machine and watched as the cuff filled with air, moments later there was a beeping noise. "Still within normal range." She slipped off the cuff, careful not to disturb the Pulse Oximeter.

Louise made a note in his file, she included the time that had passed. Granite scratched his chest. Moments later, he scratched again.

"Itchy?" She arched a brow.

"Yeah." His breathing was more rapid, as was his pulse. Again, she noted the time and his symptoms. "It's not bad though," he added. His voice sounded a tad hoarse.

Louise checked his chest and neck area, looking for signs of a rash. It was all clear. "You still have eleven minutes to go."

Granite swallowed hard. "It doesn't matter. I can take it."

His heart-rate was slowly climbing. She knew that it would probably end up dropping rapidly. She knew his blood pressure would do the same. "Let me know if you start to have difficulty breathing or if your airway starts feeling tight."

He gave a nod.

His oxygen levels were good but his heart-rate continued to climb. He was breathing deeply, sweat dripped off of him. The needle site was slightly swollen and very inflamed.

"How are you feeling?"

Granite smiled. It wasn't the kind of smile that evoked happiness. Not even close. "I'm doing great. Piece of cake." He scratched his chest.

Louise noticed that he was gripping the pan even tighter. "Are you feeling dizzy? Lightheaded?"

Granite gave a nod. His eyes looked a bit unfocussed and he was swallowing every couple of seconds. "Are you feeling nauseous?"

"I'm fine!" a low growl. "I can handle it."

A couple of the guys had thrown up during their first few sessions. That was with much less allergen over a shorter period. "I need to know what's going on, what your symptoms are. It's important so that I can treat you better."

He gave a nod. That was it. The guy was feeling ill, that much was clear.

"Just so you know, I have water and plenty of paper towels. I worked the emergency room during my residency so I've seen it all. We've just hit the halfway mark."

Louise kept monitoring him. She took his blood pressure, which was through the roof. His heart-rate wasn't fairing much better. The itchiness had become worse, as did the swelling. His body's reaction was normal.

She handed him a wad of paper towels which he used to mop his sweaty brow and running nose.

"We're at the ten-minute mark. I have to say, you're doing great."

"This is great?" He managed to choke out between heavy breaths.

"You're still conscious and haven't shit the bed. You're doing really well."

"If you say so." Seconds later, Granite pulled the pan to his face and emptied the contents of his stomach. Louise held the side of his arm as he retched and gagged. It took a few seconds for him to gain his composure. During this time, she grabbed some more of the paper towels and the water.

She took the pan, replacing it with a clean one and handed him the towel. "You spoke too soon." Granite wiped his mouth. He used the water to rinse his mouth, spitting into the pan on his lap.

"Fuck!" he muttered as his head fell back against the pillow. He closed his eyes.

"Here we go . . ." His pulse began to slow. During the next few minutes, Granite went from a bright red color to a deathly pale.

"What . . . is . . . it?" His eyes were unfocussed.

"Two minutes to go. I don't like your vital signs." She put a hand to his forehead. "Cold and clammy. Your heart-rate is slow and thready. Your breathing is shallow. Are you experiencing tightness in the chest or throat?"

He gave a nod. "My chest . . . tight . . . dizzy," he groaned.

"I don't want to alarm you but you're pretty much dying at this point. Your vitals are deteriorating fast. I don't feel comfortable continuing with—" She reached for the needles.

"Don't," his voice was much stronger.

"But—"

"We're nearly there. I can take it . . ." ten seconds later, Granite's head lolled to the side. His eyes were closed.

"You can take it my ass." She checked his pupils. Louise gave him a shake. "Granite?" She tried again but got no response. He was out cold, his heart-rate was dropping. "This is nonsense," she muttered before quickly removing the needles and hitting the timer.

Using the button on the control on the side of the bed, she lowered Granite some, still leaving his upper body at a slightly inclined angle. Then she put an oxygen mask over his mouth and nose. It clouded as he breathed. His vitals had already improved somewhat. Not nearly enough but at least there was movement in the right direction. The wounds on his arms were bleeding and raw looking. She cleaned and dressed the wounds.

Granite wasn't going to be happy he hadn't completed the whole fifteen minutes but tough luck. He'd almost made it to the fourteen-minute mark. He'd done much better than she thought he would.

At this rate, he might be stable enough to go back to his own room in a couple of hours. She needed to organize a babysitter for the king.

Three hours later . . .

Louise had been told that Granite's brother was coming to check on him, but the guy who strode through the door was the polar opposite of the king. His hair was a sandy blond and a little overgrown. His eyes were the color of a single-malt whiskey. The kind her grandfather used to drink after dinner. Two fingers, neat and in a tumbler. He was also ridiculously good-looking, like a movie star. Not nearly as attractive as Granite though. He smiled broadly. "Did he spew?"

Louise frowned. "Pardon me?"

The guy gave a half-smile, leaning against the door jamb. He folded his arms, reminding her of a surfer. "I can't believe he passed out. He's going to be so pissed," he laughed. "Did he upchuck? I sure as hell hope so . . . he's never going to live this down."

Who was this joker? This could not be Granite's brother. "Are you serious? Granite just went through intense therapy and against my better judgement. It's a wonder he's alive."

Surfer dude gave a one-shouldered shrug. "It's a pity he didn't kick the bucket. One thing less to tease him about.

Oh well! Maybe next time." He strode over to where Granite was resting and began to scrutinize him. There was a smirk on his face. Granite's vitals had improved dramatically since removing the needles.

"Who are you?" She moved to stand between her patient and the shifter.

The guy slapped a hand against his forehead. "My bad! I'm Shale, Granite's brother. I'm the fourth in command and a royal." He touched his chest.

She hadn't even noticed that his markings were golden. Louise gave a nod. "Good to meet you."

Shale gave a laugh, he was peering over her shoulder at Granite. "I wish I had a camera. He looks like shit."

"I wouldn't allow you to take a picture of him. Please step back."

"Please, Doc, you have to tell me, did he spew?"

"I'm not at liberty—"

He chuckled. "He did, didn't he? I can tell by your reaction."

She put up her hands. "No, my reaction did not tell you that and neither did my mouth. Granite is stable and slowly improving. I can't discuss his medical condition with you. I would appreciate it—"

"Come on, Doc. Give me something."

"It was good to meet you, Shale, but I think it's time you left." There was no way she was putting up with this even a moment longer.

He turned serious for a second and then grinned at her. "Don't be like that, Doc. He'd do exactly the same to me.

As would our brothers, Sand and Volcano. Hell, even my sister would give us hell in a situation like this." He gestured to an unconscious Granite. "I'm proud of him, but it's my duty as a brother to give him shit."

"Um . . . okay." If he said so. Then she registered what he had just said. "How many siblings are there?" Her eyes widened for a moment.

"Five."

"Wow! Nice big family. Your folks didn't mess around."

"Yup. That's for sure. They're still very much in love."

"Oh really. That's interesting. Now that I think about it, I haven't seen very many elderly people around."

Shale looked solemn. "Between the humans some years back and the more recent internal battles, we've lost plenty of our elders. Most of them don't live in the lair they're . . ." he seemed to rethink what he was about to say, "somewhere else."

Louise decided not to push it. "Well, it was really nice to meet you but I'm going to have to ask you to leave. Granite needs his rest. It's going to be a while before he's back on his feet." At least another twenty-four hours, maybe more. She wasn't about to give Shale more ammo though so she kept that to herself.

Shale gave her a look that told her she had lost her mind. "You asked for help moving him. You mentioned something about him not being alone for the night. Well," he spread his arms, "here I am, Doc."

"Oh . . . ohhhh. I see. Okay, well, that changes things.

I see no reason why he can't go home. He does need round-the-clock monitoring though." She wasn't convinced Shale was the right guy for the job. He didn't seem all that responsible.

"I've got it covered."

"Granite could experience something called biphasic anaphylaxis. It normally occurs within twelve hours of the initial reaction. Particularly one as bad as Granite's was." She could see that Shale was looking at her quizzically. "It basically means that he could have another reaction just as severe as the one he just had."

"That would be amazing." Shale was grinning from ear-to-ear.

"No, it would not." She was dealing with a bunch of crazy people. "It could kill him."

"I sure hope so." His eyes pulled up in thought. "I really need to try to find a camera . . . or a cellphone . . ."

"No pictures, Shale. This is serious. Granite is your brother and your king for god's sake and you actually want him to die? I think I'll keep him here in the clinic for further observation." The thought of sitting here the whole night was not appealing and completely unnecessary but she couldn't entrust his life to the surfer dude shifter. She'd have to try to get comfortable on the floor or on her office chair. There was no other option. She could not discharge Granite into his care. No way. No how.

Shale shook his head. "He wouldn't stay dead, Doc. He's a strong male . . . the strongest of the Earth people. My brother would not be beaten so easily, I can assure you." He gave a sigh. "I promise not to take any compromising pictures or to give him too much shit when he wakes up."

Louise kept her eyes on him. Not sure what to do.

"Come on, Doc. I mean it. I will make sure that he is well taken care of. I promise, he'll be just fine."

"Okay," she finally agreed. "He needs to keep that device on his finger. It has a built-in alarm which will go off if his heart-rate goes up too quickly. You call me immediately if that happens."

"You will be the first to know . . . I promise."

Louise was sure Granite was on the road to recovery. So far, none of the others had suffered from biphasic anaphylaxis but she couldn't be too careful.

Shale leaned down over the bed. Louise could see that he was about to pick Granite up.

"The hospital bed has wheels. It might be easier than carrying him all the way. I'll stop by first thing tomorrow morning to check in on him.

Shale gave a nod. "I can see that you are worried. Don't be . . ." the shifter winked. "He'll be just fine. I've got this." He pushed the bed towards the door.

She didn't have a good feeling about this. "Are you sure?"

"Couldn't be more sure if I tried." He tossed over his shoulder as he maneuvered the bed through the door. "Goodbye, Doc."

"Bye." Shit, maybe she should go after them. *No!* Granite would be fine. Nothing could go wrong.

CHAPTER 6

The next morning . . .

Louise knocked on the door. There was no answer so she tried again. Nothing. *Dammit.* She couldn't just stand there. Granted it was still really early but surely Shale was not that deep of a sleeper.

Then a thought crept into her mind. What if Shale had left Granite? What if Granite had suffered another attack? Only, worse this time. *What if . . . ?*

She knocked again, harder this time. No answer. Panic welled. She should never have trusted the guy. Should never have left Granite with such an irresponsible person.

Screw it!

Louise pushed the door open and entered the large space. She immediately peered up at the loft area that housed Granite's bed. The sun was still rising, the bedroom was cast in shadows.

"Shale?" she whispered, her voice swallowed in the big space.

"Hello," slightly louder this time.

It looked like there was someone sleeping in that big bed. If Shale had left Granite and if something was wrong . . . Her heart hammered in her chest. She didn't want to barge in but at the same time, it was her duty as Granite's doctor to ensure that he was well.

Louise walked up the a few of the stairs. "Shale," she called, but there was no answer. "Dammit!" she muttered as she hurried the rest of the way up.

There was a pair of those cotton pants on the floor and a . . . a . . . dress crumpled up next to it.

"Good morning," a very feminine voice spoke up. Her voice was a bit husky, like she'd just woken up.

Louise had to hold back a yell. She grabbed her chest.

"Sorry to scare you." The woman was wrapped around a still sleeping Granite. Her dark hair was mussed. Her eyes at half-mast. *Wow!* She was beautiful and naked under the silk sheet.

Louise gave a nod. "Sorry to interrupt like this." She swallowed hard and felt like a complete idiot. She hadn't slept most of the night, worried about him when he'd been just fine. *More than bloody fine.*

She just needed to get the hell out of there before he woke up.

The woman giggled softly and Granite stirred. Louise took a small step back. "I'll come back at a more appropriate time."

The woman smiled. "That might be a good idea." She gave Louise a wink and snuggled closer to Granite.

Louise took another step back, intent on hauling her

ass out of there as quickly as she could, but before she could turn, his eyes flashed open. His dark stare fixed on her. His eyes narrowed as they focused on her. Then he frowned and glanced backwards.

"Good morning, my king." The woman lifted herself onto her elbow, the sheet dropped lower. There were suddenly boobs everywhere.

Louise felt her cheeks heat. It wasn't embarrassment but sudden anger. Why had she wasted even a single moment's worry when here he was ... carrying on like ... like ... this ... ? She realized that the anger was irrational but she couldn't help it. God, there were naked people in a bed right in front of her. Her eyes felt like they were going to bug out of her skull and her mouth felt like it had been filled with cotton wool. She couldn't seem to find her thoughts or pull herself together. *What the hell?!*

Part of her recognized that it was jealously. Pure. Fierce and totally out of place. Why the hell was she jealous? He might be decent-looking ... okay, he was off the charts hot but he was also a gigantic jerk. A total asshole. She didn't even like him so why was she jealous?

Granite rolled onto his back, the black silk only just covered his privates, which were ... she gasped and her eyes widened even more. His erection was back in full force and she couldn't seem to take her eyes off of it.

The woman laughed softly, her voice was husky. "I'll keep an eye on him, healer."

"Great!" She gave a nod and inched a bit closer to the stairs. "I can see that you're fine." She struggled to keep the venom from her voice. "You do that." Softer this time and directed at the woman. There had never been anything between them and there never would be. This was for the best. Louise turned, preparing to get the hell out of there.

"Stop," a growl. "Come back," a commanding tone. Louise turned to face him . . . them.

The lady put her hand on Granite's chest. "But, my lord," husky and filled with promise.

"Get off me and get the fuck out of my bed." His eyes were still locked with hers. Louise couldn't move. She could barely breathe under the weight of his stare.

It was completely irrational but she felt happy for a moment after hearing him kick the other woman out. Then the anger kicked back in. He really was a dick. Here she was feeling all upset that he had slept with another woman and he wasn't even worth it. Not even a tiny bit. It irritated her. She was an intelligent woman. Why was she feeling all wound up in knots over a guy like this?

"No!" she shook her head. "You stay. I'm leaving."

The woman's eyes lit up and she gave Louise a sultry smile. "Are those doctor's orders?"

"Yes," Louise said.

"No!" Granite barked at the same time. "Out!" he added, more fiercely this time.

Louise turned, wanting nothing more than to be gone. She wished she had never come in the first place.

"Not you," Granite growled. "You . . ." he pointed at the shifter, "now!"

The sheets rustled. "My lord, I . . ."

"Now," he growled again and more loudly.

"Yes, my lord."

When Louise turned back, the other woman was curtsying. An actual honest-to-god curtsy and she was completely naked. That, and beautiful. She was curvaceous, yet firm. Her skin was an olive tone. Her dark hair was thick and glossy. Louise shouldn't be staring like this but she couldn't help herself.

"I'm sorry . . ." Louise finally managed to drag her eyes away. She turned her head.

"Don't be silly, healer." The lady walked towards Louise. There was a rustling sound. "I hope you feel better soon, my lord. Please don't hesitate to—"

"Out," he grunted.

What an asshole! Louise turned back. The woman clutched her dress to her chest. "Goodbye, healer," she smiled broadly. It seemed that she was going to allow him to treat her like this after they had just . . .

It had nothing to do with her. Not one little thing. She nodded at the shifter lady, feeling sorry for her, which was crazy since she didn't seem to mind herself. Louise was too angry to talk though. She kept her gaze on the foot of the bed. It seemed like an age before the door finally clicked shut.

"Well . . ." She forced herself to meet his stare. "You are clearly feeling just dandy so I'm going to go—"

"Why did you come?" Granite put a pillow behind his head and pulled himself into a semi-reclined position. He even had the audacity to hook his hands behind his head.

Like he didn't have a care in the world. His erection was still in full force.

"It doesn't matter." All she wanted was to leave. He'd just had sex with another woman and she was noticing how ridiculously huge his package was and how chiseled his chest looked in the morning light. *What the hell was wrong with her?*

She didn't like the guy but apparently, her body had other ideas. Well, her body could forget it. Her brain was in charge here.

"Why are you in my chamber?" he used that same commanding tone.

"I came to check in on you, make sure you were doing okay." *Stupid! Stupid!* "I wanted to check your vitals. Ensure that you weren't still sick, or worse . . . that you weren't . . ." She felt like an idiot.

"Dead?" He raised his brows.

She nodded. "You were unconscious and very ill when I last saw you." Why was she explaining herself to him? He didn't deserve it. She was still holding her medical bag, her arm was getting tired. Her fingers were starting to feel stiff from gripping the handle so tightly.

"You may proceed with your checks."

What? He expected her to still conduct an examination. She couldn't help but frown. "I think you've proven that you're just fine."

"You came here to . . . check my vitals. You're here now so you might as well do it."

He was right. The guy had exerted himself far too soon

after suffering such bad shock. What the hell had he been thinking?

She nodded once and walked towards the bed, dropping the bag at her feet. She opened it up and took out a stethoscope. Then she looked down at the naked, very aroused shifter and realized that she actually had to touch him. *Damn!*

"Maybe you should put some clothes on first." She was acting like she'd never examined anyone half-naked before. Those hospital gowns did sweet bugger all to cover a person. This shouldn't bug her, but it did.

Granite shook his head.

The asshole could see that she was uncomfortable. He didn't give a shit. So she was going to act like it didn't irritate the shit out of her. This was business, plain and simple.

Then again, she really didn't want to touch him. *Yuck!* He and that other woman had been all over one another not so long ago. She knew she was being childish but she didn't want to touch him. She didn't want to be anywhere near him. "No, really . . ." She prayed he listened to her for once. "I don't mind waiting while you shower and dress. I'll conduct the examination after."

Granite shook his head and she felt like hitting him with the stethoscope still clutched in her hand. "I'm ready now," he said.

She had to fight not to look down at his—

"Fine." She pulled out a pair of latex gloves. "Suit yourself," she added as she pulled the first glove on.

"You don't need those." He glanced at her now gloved hand.

She nodded. "Yes, I do." *Asshole!*

"No, you don't. We can't catch anything from one another." He took his hands back from behind his head and folded them across his chest. The move made his pecs pop.

"It's just precautionary," she stammered, trying not to look at his pecs. *His slutty, slutty pecs.*

"Mmmm . . . that's funny." He didn't look like he found it amusing. The opposite was true. "Why didn't you wear gloves yesterday when you were sticking me full of needles?"

"Because you weren't covered in sex juices yesterday," she blurted.

Granite held her gaze for a few moments. Why the hell had she just said that? *Shit!* Then again, she wasn't sorry. It was the truth. Since when did she apologize for telling the truth? Besides, it had just slipped out. He made her so mad she couldn't even think clearly.

"It wouldn't be hygienic and quite frankly I would prefer not to touch you with my bare hands." *Take that, ass-hat!* "You should not have exerted yourself like that so soon after suffering from anaphylactic shock. I'm not touching you until you've showered. That or I'm wearing gloves."

"Sex juices . . ." His lip twitched. "I didn't realize you were going to touch my dick."

Louise made a choking noise. "What did you just say?

No," she shook her head, "you didn't just say that." She looked down at the floor and tried to find her sanity. When she looked up a few moments later he was completely deadpan. Looking the picture of relaxation and calm. Of course he was, he'd just done 'the deed.' "No, I won't be touching you there. Not now and not ever," she added the last unnecessarily.

"Okay, well, then you really need someone to explain to you how things work. How a male and female rut. Better yet, I could show you."

Was he for real? "That is highly inappropriate and . . ." She felt flustered. "It's really rude. My god!" Her voice was raised. "You're some piece of work. From one woman to the next. On that note . . ." She folded her arms across her chest. "How could you treat her like that? You kicked her out like she was nothing to you."

He shrugged. "She is nothing to me."

Louise sucked in a deep breath, she felt her eyes widen. "How can you say that? Oh, my word! You are too much. It's none of my business," she shook her head.

"No, it's not." He moved his arms to his sides. "Examine me. Do it with or without the gloves, just get it done."

Fine! She didn't give a shit anymore. She put the other glove on, put the stethoscope in her ears and listened to his heart.

All good.

Next, she checked his blood pressure. She looked away while the cuff inflated.

"How did I get back to my chamber?" His deep voice almost startled her.

The machine beeped as it gave a reading. "Your brother brought you. He said he was going to take good care of you."

"Shale," Granite growled. "The little prick."

"Yup. He should never have left you alone like that."

"I wasn't alone though, was I?"

Louise had to work not to roll her eyes.

"The fucker!" he added, under his breath.

"Please don't swear like that." His blood pressure had completely normalized. She checked his coloring. "How did you know it was Shale and not one of your other brothers? There are four of you if I'm not mistaken."

"Because, out of all of my brothers, Shale's the dickhead, that's why?"

She wasn't sure why Granite was so pissed off. She didn't ask him. It had nothing to do with her. "How are you feeling? Any nausea?"

"No."

She pulled back each of his eyelids. Everything looked normal. "How are you feeling?"

"I'm fine, just a bit tired."

"I'll bet." It just slipped out.

Granite didn't respond. She hoped he was feeling bad. As in, bad for his actions, not health-wise bad. Even a tiny bit bad would be good, but she didn't count on it. His breathing was normal. "I need to take a look at your wound." She kept her eyes on the area in question.

"Go right ahead."

She ripped the band aid off in one hard swipe. It was a large square. It felt good knowing it would sting him. Therapeutic even. He didn't so much as flinch though. *Pity!* The area was healing well. The wounds were closed and much of the inflammation was gone.

"Why are you so angry at me?" She glanced up at him. His dark eyes were on her while he spoke.

"I'm not." She grabbed some disinfectant and the cotton swabs from her bag.

"Yes, you are. That much is very clear."

"No, I . . ." She glanced back up. He was waiting for her response. Seemed like he couldn't wait to hear it. "I don't like you. You make me angry . . . that's all."

He smiled at her. No, it was more of a smirk than a smile, given that the latter would have been friendly. "That's not it. You like me just fine."

He probably couldn't conceive that a woman didn't like him. That for once someone wasn't falling all over him. "I'm pretty sure that I really don't like you."

He snorted out a noise that told her she was full of BS. "You're either really uptight or you wish it was you waking up in my bed." He paused. "That's why you're so pissed off right now, isn't it?"

Her mouth fell open but she forced it closed. "That's complete rubbish. Neither of those is true. Not even close."

"There's one other explanation – you're angry because you think I got some and you didn't."

"That's the biggest load of—"

"I agree," he nodded. "It's bullshit. You go home regularly yet you never fuck anyone, ever, so it can't be that. That means you're either really stuck up or you're jealous."

Granite had hit the nail on the head. She wished it wasn't true but he was right. He pissed her off even more for picking up on it and calling her out on it. *Asshole.* Who did that? "I'm not jealous of anything," she tried to sound calm and together but failed.

"Stuck up it is then," he nodded. "That's what I thought."

"Oh, my god! I can't believe you." She shook her head. "I'm going to ignore your unwanted, unfounded comments. On second thought, you just called me stuck up so I can give you a piece of my mind in return. You're a male slut and to make things worse, you're seriously rude as well. No, you're more than just rude, you're a rude asshole. I know that you'll probably have me fired for speaking my mind but quite frankly, right now, I don't give a damn. I would appreciate it if you didn't talk to me while I finish cleaning and dressing your wound."

"Some silence would be welcome."

Asshole! Her face burned. She'd allowed herself to stoop to his level. She'd acted unprofessionally. Louise didn't care though. He deserved it. Needed to hear it. Louise continued in silence. Taking her time to clean the wound well.

Once she was finished, she packed her things away.

"Take it easy for the rest of the day. You should be back to normal by tomorrow."

"I'll see you then."

"What?" She was taken aback. She really expected him to contact Blaze and have her fired.

"Tomorrow, Doctor. I will see you then," he spoke slowly. "For our next appointment?"

"Ah, yes. That's right." Louise picked up her bag. She gave a nod and left feeling his eyes on her the whole time.

CHAPTER 7

Later that day...

Louise made her way along the busy corridor that led from the great hall. Many of the men greeted her with a nod or a smile. There were very few shifter women. The one or two she saw on occasion were sweet to her but clearly didn't want to mingle either. She missed girl time. She missed her friends. She'd been thick as thieves with Debbie and Hilary since high school. Both women were happily married with a brood of kids. Louise was godmother to both of their eldest. Not being able to spend time with her two 'besties' was the one major drawback about being there.

She hadn't dated in a long time so although she missed male company, she couldn't blame that on being there.

As she continued on, she spotted a waddling shifter woman up ahead. The woman waved madly at her, blond hair flying. She realized it was Breeze. The woman she had met when she first arrived on dragon soil. She'd seen her once or twice since then.

Breeze was from the Air tribe and married to one of Granite's brothers. The next in command if she wasn't mistaken. They walked towards one another. Breeze was smiling broadly, one hand on her belly.

"Oh, my word!" Louise covered her mouth with her hand. "I can't believe it. Is it really you?" She stopped walking, standing just in front of the female shifter.

Breeze rubbed her distended belly. "Yup! It's really me," she smiled shyly.

"I last saw you three weeks ago." Louise couldn't take her eyes off of the woman's huge and very pregnant belly. "It can't be!" Her stomach had been a small curve back then.

Breeze laughed softly. "Yup, my mate is an Earth male." She said it like Louise was supposed to understand what that meant.

She frowned. "Okay. I'm going to assume that you're not pregnant for nine months like a human woman would be."

"Assuming the human female is mated to a human male you mean? No." She shook her head. "My pregnancy will last four months in total."

Louise sucked in a deep breath. "Wow! So short. No wonder you are so big already."

"Yeah, it's not just that, we—"

"There you are." A really big guy stepped up behind Breeze, he put his hands around her and smiled down at her.

Louise had to keep herself from reacting. Shale had

looked nothing like Granite but this guy on the other hand, looked exactly like him. There were subtle differences but they could be twins. For example, their eyes were carbon copies, only this guy's were lit up, yet filled with tenderness.

"I was worried," he said, brushing a kiss on Breeze's cheek.

She smiled. "I am perfectly fine. We are fine." She rubbed her belly.

The big shifter put his hands on her belly as well. "I am glad." He lifted his gaze to Louise. Gone was any sign of tenderness and affection. In their place was distrust and wariness.

"This is my mate, Volcano," Breeze said, oblivious to the daggers her mate was shooting at her with those dark eyes of his. Now this was a look she recognized.

"I'm Louise, I'm an allergist, I'm working on silver allergy resistance in some of—"

"I know who you are and why you are here." Short and to the point.

"Oh good!" she blurted, sounding like an idiot. Her smile felt frozen in place.

"I was just about to ask Louise to join me for some tea," Breeze said.

Volcano made a noise of acknowledgement. "That's nice."

Yeah right! He hated the idea.

"I have a couple of things to take care of. There was something I needed to discuss with you, if you don't mind." He looked back at Louise, jaw set.

She cleared her throat. "No, of course not."

The shifter led his mate away and spoke with her, looking very serious as he did. Breeze frowned heavily and shook her head. It looked like they were having a disagreement.

Louise felt like she was intruding so she looked away.

A minute or two later, Breeze was back, all smiles. "Would you like to come to my place for tea?"

"If it's okay?"

Breeze wrinkled her nose. "Of course it's okay. Don't mind Volcano." She waved her hand. "He's overprotective of me at the moment. He's overprotective, period. I'm sorry, he doesn't fully trust humans. You'll find that from time to time, especially with Earth dragons."

Louise thought it over for a few moments. "Most of them are really nice."

"Nice." Breeze nodded her head. "Our males are starved for female companionship. They will be very nice." She gave a wink.

"You're saying that they just want to get into my pants and that they're not really just sweet and kind because of my awesome personality?"

"You are very likeable, I wouldn't worry," Breeze grinned.

"If you say so."

Breeze took a step in the direction she had been going. "Are you coming for tea?"

"That sounds great." Louise looked at her watch. "I've got an hour before my next appointment." Some girl time. Just the thing she needed.

It was a short walk. Breeze opened up the door and gestured for her to go inside.

The space was large and airy. It was really homey and open plan like a big warehouse-type apartment. It was similar to the unit she was staying in only much bigger and much . . . nicer, for lack of a better word.

"What can I get you?" Breeze rattled off a list of herbal tea options

"I'll just have water, if that's okay?"

Breeze poured the water and then a glass of what looked like freshly squeezed orange juice for herself. So much for the tea. She gestured to the lounge area. "Please take a seat. I'm afraid I don't have any snacks . . ."

Louise shook her head. "Don't worry about food. I had a huge breakfast, thanks. I always eat lots when I'm feeling a bit down. I guess I'm the opposite to most people. I lose weight when I'm happy and gain a ton when I'm feeling out of sorts. It's called comfort eating."

"You are tiny." Breeze sat down heavily. "You could do with a few pounds." She scooted back in her chair. "Why are you feeling out of sorts? Has something happened to make you feel that way?"

Louise pulled a face. "It's nothing. Don't worry about it." The last thing she wanted to do was to burden Breeze with her problems.

"What's going on? Tell me. Maybe I can help. At the

very least, you'll feel better talking about it."

Flip! She really shouldn't have said anything. Breeze and Granite were family. "Um . . ." She clasped her hands in her lap.

"Tell me." Breeze sat back in her chair and waited.

"Okay . . . I shouldn't though."

"Why not?" She gave a small shake of the head.

"It has to do with your brother-in-law."

Breeze smiled. "Ahhhh, Granite."

"Why do you say it like that?" Louise frowned.

"No reason. What happened?" She folded her arms over her belly.

"It's just that he's so . . . rude and arrogant. He's a jerk and an asshole. He doesn't listen to me . . . not ever." Louise widened her eyes. "You see, we shouldn't be talking about this. I can't talk to you about your family like that. It's not right!"

Breeze gave a laugh. "It's perfectly fine." Then she looked serious for a moment. Then she narrowed her eyes on Louise and scrutinized her. "So, you like Granite."

"What?" Louise shook her head. "No, that's not what I said. We're not in kindergarten here."

"Kindergarten? What is that?" Breeze's brows pulled together.

"We're not young children. You know how youngsters tend to hit a boy because they actually like him? Not that I've hit Granite or anything. Even though I really feel like hitting him sometimes . . . no, all the time. He makes me so mad."

Breeze grinned. "You *do* like him then."

"Arghh!" She let her head fall into her hands. Dragon shifters could be maddening. All of them. Granite just happened to take the cake. "I don't like him, Breeze. Please believe me when I tell you that."

She nodded once but her smile told Louise that she didn't.

"I mean it. I went to go and check on him this morning and he was in bed with one of the dragon shifter women. A really pretty girl . . . she was quite lovely." There was a funny feeling inside her. It was jealousy and not only because the other woman had been with Granite—*What was wrong with her?* It was also because of her curves and beautiful bronzed skin. Louise didn't have the biggest boobs and she was almost translucent she was so pale. She hated her freckles and turned red in an instant if she tried to go into the sun without the highest factor sunblock.

Breeze looked unsure. She was frowning heavily. "Are you sure there was a shifter female in bed with Granite?"

"What do you mean am I sure? Yes, definitely sure. I know what I saw. She was naked with him in bed. They were both naked." Anger boiled up inside her all over again. "To think I went over there to check if he was okay. I was worried about him. Meanwhile there he was . . ." she made a sound of disgust.

Breeze laughed. As in, all-out laughed. She even put a hand in front of her mouth she was laughing so hard. "I'm sure Shale had a hand in this."

"What does Shale have to do with Granite having sex

with another woman?" *Oh shit!* She made it sound like she saw this dragon shifter as *the* other woman, which wasn't true at all. "He isn't healthy enough to be . . . doing the deed. He was a rude, arrogant, asshole about the whole thing just to top it all off. He kicked her out. Not a word of thanks. No goodbye or thanks for the shag. He just kicked her out."

There were tears streaming down Breeze's face.

"What's so darned funny?" Louise asked.

"There is no way that Granite had sex with any dragon shifter female."

"Why not? I know what I saw," she quickly added.

Breeze quirked a brow. "Are you sure about that? Did you actually see them rutting?"

Louise frowned. *What kind of a question was that?*

"You didn't, did you? I know you didn't."

"Well, no of course I didn't actually see them at it." She clutched her chest. *Thank God!* "But that doesn't mean . . ."

"Granite doesn't rut with dragon shifters."

Say what? "Ever?"

She shook her head. "Not ever. Something about sharing with all his males. It's ridiculous of course, not all dragon shifter females are like that." Breeze must have caught her quizzical look because she added. "There are very few females, so a lot of them rut with lots of different males. It's not a bad thing, it's just not something that Granite likes. I think he prefers human females, although he would never admit it. I've heard that he's very picky about who he ruts. Only humans, and then they must be to his taste."

"Really?" Louise felt sick to her stomach. "Are you sure? I saw them . . . saw her . . ." It had been the woman who was wrapped around him and not the other way around. He was still sleeping when she'd arrived. He'd also kicked the shifter out and had mentioned Shale being a— He'd used a choice word to describe his brother. "What does Shale have to do with it?" her voice was soft. Her heart sinking by the second.

Breeze rolled her eyes. "He's always pranking his brothers. He knows that Granite would never rut a dragon shifter female so he sent one to his bed while he was unconscious. That's a classic Shale move. What did she look like? The shifter female."

"Tall and really beautiful. Long black hair, almost down to her bum and . . ." She felt her cheeks heat. "A really great body . . . smoking hot."

"That's Pebble," Breeze snorted out a laugh. "She ruts with many of the males. That female would do anything to get her claws in the king. Not Granite's type by a long shot. He would have been pissed off with her for going along with Shale's silly prank. That's why he kicked her out."

"Why didn't he tell me I had it all wrong?"

Breeze shrugged.

She groaned and covered her eyes. "I called him a male slut and told him that he was a rude asshole for treating that woman so badly. I didn't know. He should have told me." She looked at Breeze who was laughing softly again. "He's an asshole for not setting the record straight."

"Maybe he should have told you, but despite appearances maybe you shouldn't have jumped to conclusions like that."

Louise thought on it for a second or two. "No, I guess I shouldn't have." Another thought struck her. "I'm going to have to apologize." She groaned out loud at the thought.

"It won't be so bad. You'll see." Breeze took a sip of her juice. "Are you ready to admit that you like him?" She smiled slyly.

"No!" Louise said, far too quickly. "I mean, he's really hot, I'll admit that. You'd have to be blind not to, right?"

Breeze nodded.

"Hot, but not my type. Not even close. We have nothing in common. Nope, I'm afraid you have it wrong."

Breeze took another sip of her drink. "I think you like him, I also think he likes you."

"He so doesn't. He's grumpy, bossy and rude."

Breeze nodded, she was grinning broadly.

It was time to change the subject. "Even if I wanted to be with him, and I don't, we can't go down that road. It's forbidden. Against every rule." This line of discussion was making her distinctly uncomfortable. "When is your due date?" She glanced down at Breeze's stomach.

Breeze shut down in an instant. "I'm sorry." She bit down on her bottom lip. "Volcano doesn't want me discussing my pregnancy with you."

"Oh!"

"I'm so sorry," Breeze added. "Like I said, he's really protective at the moment. Besides, Earth dragons are pretty closed off and secretive at the best of times. My mate just doesn't trust humans."

"So it's nothing personal?"

Breeze shook her head. "No, of course not." She sucked in a deep breath and looked Louise in the eyes. "Five weeks, I'm due in the next four or five weeks. We're so excited. I can't believe I became pregnant during the first breeding season." Then her eyes widened like she'd said something wrong. "Forget I said that. It's just that I like you, Louise. I feel like we could be friends."

"Thank you." Louise touched the side of Breeze's arm. "For trusting me enough to tell me. I think we could be friends too and I'm happy for you guys." She didn't want to put the other woman under any more pressure about her pregnancy. "Now, tell me . . . how did you meet Volcano? Was it love at first sight?"

"My brother, the Air king, gave me to the Earth dragons."

"Gave you, as in, like you were a possession?"

Breeze shook her head. "You should see the look on your face. Times are tough. The females of our kind are dying out." Breeze's eyes filled with tears. "Our royal heritage might end up lost. Thunder asked if I would be willing to mate with Earth royalty and I agreed. I was always meant for Volcano but I was allowed to choose which prince I wanted. I was permitted to return home if none of the males was to my liking. To answer your question, yes, it was love at first sight. It was for both of us but Volcano is a stubborn male."

Louise rolled her eyes. "He and Granite are very alike in more than just looks."

"They are and they are not." She smiled. "Volcano wanted Granite to take me as his queen. I thought that it was because he didn't have feelings for me but I was wrong." She shook her head. "I thought I hated him a whole lot back then too. We fought about everything. He was so stubborn and wouldn't listen. He eventually admitted his feelings for me and accepted that Granite and I were not suited for one another. Anyway, both Blaze and Thunder would've declared war if Granite had taken me as a mate. I was destined to be Volcano's mate." She rubbed her belly.

Louise decided not to ask why war would've been declared. She suspected she wasn't supposed to be hearing all of this. "How long have you been together?"

"Almost a year. The best year of my life. I never imagined love could be like this." Breeze sighed, her eyes had a faraway look.

"I'm so happy for you."

"You'll find love too. You just need to be open to the possibility."

"I live here now and will be for the foreseeable future. Relationships with dragon shifters are forbidden so . . ." She shook her head. "Nah! I'm fine on my own."

Breeze gave her a look that told her she was full of shit.

She sniffed the air. "If you say so."

"I do. Although, I might just hook-up with someone when I'm next in Walton Springs. It's been far too long since I had male companionship . . . if you know what I mean."

Breeze nodded, she gave the air a sniff.

Louise had to roll her eyes. "Don't tell me I smell needy and achy."

The other woman pulled a face, then she frowned. "You smell like you're about to go into heat."

"Excuse me?" she choked out the words.

"I can scent that you are about to go into heat. The good news is that the Earth males are not as badly affected as the other three tribes."

"I'm not sure what you mean."

"A female in heat can drive our males a bit mad. They will all want to mate with you."

"Oh, my dear god!"

Breeze laughed. "Don't worry too much about it. It is my understanding that human females come into heat every few weeks so this will be the second time since you arrived here. I can't give you a proper explanation but Earth males are not nearly as affected as the other dragon males. Not for most of the year at any rate. You will be fine." She looked pointedly at Louise. "You should get some human medicine that prevents your heat though."

"You mean a contraceptive?"

Breeze looked thoughtful for a second. "I'm not sure what it's called but it will help our males feel more comfortable around you." She frowned. "Someone should have told you about this."

"Yeah, they really should have." Louise drank some of her water, putting the glass back down on the coffee table.

"We alternate the Stag Runs. Sending different groups in at a time."

Louise wasn't sure what Breeze meant by that. She made a noise of agreement.

"What that means is," she lifted her eyes in thought, "it's going on six months since the last time many of our males have found release with a female. For others, it will be just a month or two, but it's really hard on them."

Why was Breeze telling her this?

"Non-humans are highly sexual. Dragon shifters are no exception. Our males only rut twice a year in total, they suffer greatly."

For whatever reason, Louise's thoughts turned to Granite. He could have dragon shifter women but he chose not to. This meant that he hadn't had sex in a while. No wonder the poor guy sprung an erection at the drop of a hat. No wonder he was so moody.

"It's been a year-and-a-half since my ex and I broke up. I'm doing just fine. Well, mostly." She had been feeling a bit 'needy' and a bit 'achy' as of late and all because of one brooding, rude asshole of a shifter.

"You poor thing," Breeze looked shocked. "That's so unhealthy."

"I'll make a concerted effort to remedy things on my next trip to Walton Springs. The only problem is that I've never really been one for one-night stands. I like to get to know a guy, to have a relationship. I don't have sex for the sake of having sex."

Breeze gave a nod. "I understand, but you said yourself that a relationship would be impossible right now, so you have to do what you have to do. Maybe that means having a . . ." she frowned, "one-night stand." She said the words carefully. "Why do they refer to it as standing in that saying? They should call it a lie-down. It would make more sense."

Louise had to laugh. "Yeah, you're right. It doesn't make much sense." Then she grew serious. "You are right about the other as well. We've only just started the Resistance Therapy so I'm going to be living here for the foreseeable future. At least another year, if not longer." Could she survive a whole year without that kind of physical contact? *No. Not a chance.* Out of nowhere her mind conjured up an image of Granite . . . naked. From his strong wide chest to his six pack. Ridges and valleys that could bring a girl to her knees. Her very dirty mind also pulled up an image of his thick cock. Long and jutting. Her cheeks felt hot, her whole body felt flushed and needy . . . very needy. She hated that Granite had been right about that. Hated her attraction to him. He might not have had sex with that shifter woman this morning, but it didn't mean that she liked him any better. Next time she was in town she was taking care of some very base needs. She was sure that this attraction she felt for the rude king would evaporate once she took care of those basic desires.

CHAPTER 8

The next day...

Every hair on her head had been pulled into a tight bun at the back of her head. Clips held the orange strands in place. He could scent some type of hair product. It was the gloopy, sticky stuff humans used to hold their hair in place, almost like a glue.

At least her skin was radiant and free from the rubbish humans used to hide their faces. There were freckles scattered everywhere, they were more concentrated over her nose and cheekbones though. It wasn't something he had seen on many females but rather something that was uniquely her.

Her lashes were long and fine, they reminded him of strands of light silk. Her eyes were a plain green. Not vivid and sparkling like emeralds. They were much more understated and yet somehow beautiful nonetheless. Probably her greatest attribute, which wasn't saying much. She was wearing that shiny lip covering that humans loved so much. It highlighted her lush pink mouth. It scented of cherry, making his mouth water but only because he enjoyed the fruit. Not because he wanted a taste.

All in all, she was . . . Granite came up blank, he wasn't sure what to think of her. She was not someone he would give a second look. Hell, he wouldn't look a first time. Yet, she was different. She was interesting to him. From the flaming red hair to the smallness of her frame, to her fiery nature. He found himself looking forward to his session today. Looking forward to being stuck with pins . . . *the fuck?*

So here he was, laying down on the bed. A device hooked to his finger. A bedpan in his hand. Getting ready to be stuck with silver until he passed out and he was . . . enjoying himself. He needed his head examined. That was for fucking sure.

The human had said very little to him since he had arrived. Her jaw was set and her body tense. She was trying to avoid eye contact.

Her back was ramrod rod straight and her chin was cocked defiantly. "Turn your wrist palm up," she instructed, using a no-nonsense tone and looking at his hand. Then she fired off a list of questions about his health and general wellbeing while setting out her supplies on the stainless steel table next to them.

She made some notes in a file. "Let's get started." Still avoiding eye contact. Apparently the far wall was much more interesting than he was. "Are you ready?" Eyes on the needles.

He gave a nod. "Yes." It came out as more of a grunt.

He wasn't feeling thrilled about the silver part of this whole process – not surprisingly.

"Same number of needles, only we'll keep the time at thirteen-and-a-half minutes instead of fifteen since you didn't quite make fifteen in your last session."

"Let's try for fifteen. I'm feeling lucky."

She rolled her eyes. He could see her mentally counting to ten. After only five seconds she met his gaze. *Finally.* Her green orbs gave him a scathing look and she shook her head. "Why do you insist on making things difficult? I would prefer it if you didn't pass out this time."

"Let's try for fifteen anyway. I told you I wanted to push it."

She shrugged. "Sure thing, it's your funeral." She pulled a pair of latex gloves on.

"Still afraid I'm going to contaminate you with sex juices?" That was one of the funniest things he had ever heard. *Sex juices.* Never in all his years.

Her eyes widened and she sucked in a breath. "No," she mumbled, eyes on his arm. "Hold still and stay relaxed." She picked up the first needle and jabbed it into him.

Fuck!

"You're still angry at me. Is it because I had a female in my bed or is it something new this time?"

Her cheeks heated, bathing her freckles in a warm glow. She pursed her lips. "I'm not angry." She jabbed another needle into his arm, using more force than what was needed. *Not angry! Yeah, right.* He knew an angry female when he saw one. His arm hurt like a bitch but he didn't so much as flinch. She pushed in another and then another. By the time she reached fifteen, she seemed to have calmed down . . . for the most part.

The little doctor pushed the timer. Then she exhaled. "May as well get this over with." Her gaze met his. "I'm sorry I yelled at you yesterday and that I called you names. I'm sorry I assumed you had sex . . . not that it matters, because it doesn't. Thing is, I was worried about you. I'm a doctor and you're my patient." She groaned. "I'm making a mess of this." She shook her head before looking away.

Granite had to bite back a grin. *Fuck, she was a laugh a minute.* If he wasn't getting ready to puke he would totally laugh at her.

"I know you didn't sleep with her . . . that shifter."

Volcano had told him that the human and Breeze had spent some time together. It looked like he had been one of their topics of discussion. "I wanted to say sorry. For the record, you can have sex with whomever you want." She finally lifted her eyes to meet his. "Whenever you want. Whatever. As your doctor though, I need to advise you to refrain from any strenuous activities for twenty-four hours after a treatment." She gave him a tight smile and pretended to be absorbed by something in his file.

"Why are you still so angry?" He could feel sweat bead on his brow. Could feel his limbs weaken.

"I'm not." Another glance his way.

Granite raised his brows.

She made a small noise at the back of her throat. "Okay . . . maybe I am still angry. You could have told me you didn't have sex with that shifter lady. You allowed me to make a complete fool of myself."

"What difference does it make if I rutted her?"

"It doesn't." She looked calm and collected. "I told you I don't care either way." She looked at the clock on the wall. "Flip, I need to take your blood pressure." She grabbed the armband unit and walked to the other side of the bed. Next, she put the armband around his arm and pressed a button that made it tighten.

He didn't like that she didn't care but he wasn't sure why. "Good, because who I rut and when I rut is no concern of yours."

"Do me a favor and knock yourself out – just don't do it after a therapy session because then it *does* become my business."

"Fair enough." He clutched the pan tighter, trying hard not to throw up. His stomach churned. The area where the needles stuck into him burned. He swallowed thickly.

The device beeped and she made a note of the reading. "It's clear that we don't like each other much, so I think it's best that we keep things strictly business going forward."

"So it wasn't strictly business before?" Fuck, but he felt dizzy. The room spun. "If I had known, maybe we could've done something about you being so stuck up."

"It's that kind of comment you can keep to yourself going forward."

Despite the pain, the dizziness and the nausea, he had to bite back a smile. Oh, how he loved rattling her perfectly coifed cage. It was a small cage at that. A small cage with thick bars and about a hundred locks. The female needed to let loose once in a while.

"It's strictly business from now on." She lifted her lids and peered into his eyes. "Please, let's try and keep it cordial going forward. I've never called anyone a male slut nor have I called someone an asshole. I was tired and not thinking clearly. I'd just sat up half the night worrying while you—"

". . . were passed out." His voice was hoarse and his breathing far too rapid. He couldn't seem to catch his breath.

"I didn't know that," she paused scrunching up her nose. "I felt bad after losing my cool. I don't normally act that way." She clutched her forehead. "I've never called anyone an asshole."

"I'm glad I could be your first." He felt the sweat pour off of him. By now he was panting hard.

"I apologize. I shouldn't have said those things."

"Don't! You can call me whatever the fuck you like . . . just do your job." If nothing else she was a good doctor. He'd come to realize that in that last few days. It wasn't that she knew her stuff, or the awards she had won – he'd finally taken a look at her file – it was that she cared. She didn't like him much but she still cared and that was something.

The female put a hand to his forehead. "You're burning

up. Two more minutes to go."

"You might want to turn around."

She shook her head. A look of concern filled those beautiful green eyes. As much as he tried not to, he gagged. *Way to go Granite, king of the Earth dragons. Weak fuck!* His stomach continued to pitch and roll. *Fucking hell!* He felt like he was five again. Like the time he'd eaten too many chocolate chip cookies. He gagged a second time, tasting bile. He felt weaker than a whelp. "Turn around," he managed to choke out.

Instead of doing as he asked – because that would be too easy – she clutched his shoulder while he emptied the contents of his stomach. Thankfully there wasn't much in there. He'd preempted this little party with the bedpan and had foregone lunch.

She whispered words of encouragement while he gagged some more. The little human rubbed his back until he was done. Then she handed him a warm wet cloth and took the pan from him, replacing it with a clean one.

Granite let his head fall back and closed his eyes.

"Are you feeling a bit better?"

"My stomach . . . yes. Everything else . . ." he shook his head.

"Tell me what I can do." Even though he was fucked right now, his first thought was of those pink, glistening lips around his cock. *Bad idea!*

"Nothing," he groaned.

"Let me know if you change your mind."

Granite gave a nod. He must have passed out because

he was roused when she was removing the needles. There was an instant relief but not nearly as much as he needed. His limbs still felt heavy. His breathing weak.

"Are you still with me?"

"Yes," a groan.

"Do pink elephants eat cheese?"

"Elephants . . ." he barely got the word out. "What the fuck?" a slur.

"Good answer," she gave a soft giggle that warmed him. It was the fever. He wasn't thinking straight.

"I'm going to bandage your wound and then you can sleep it off."

He didn't answer. Was too damned tired. Too sick to his stomach.

Her soft hands clasped his forehead. Her cool touch felt good against his skin. Then her fingers trailed across his scalp. His hair was short. Her touch felt good. So good. It relaxed him.

"Sleep," she whispered and he did.

CHAPTER 9

Two weeks later . . .

The cocktail bar was bustling. It was a Friday night so some of the patrons had come from work. The business suits were a dead giveaway.

Louise took another sip of the sweet, sugary concoction. "What is this called again?"

"It's a . . ." Deb picked up the menu and scanned the contents, "Death by Pink." She snorted out a laugh.

"Mine is a . . ." she lifted the menu back to her face, "Chocoholic's Dream . . . and it sure is." She took another sip and made a sound of sheer bliss, her eyes drifted closed.

Louise laughed. "Anything with that much chocolate is—"

"I can't believe you guys started without me!" Hillary had her hands on her hips and a pretend scowl on her face. She looked at each of them in turn.

Louise jumped up. "Hills!" She grabbed ahold of her friend and hugged her tight.

Hillary hugged her right back. "Okay, okay, I forgive you."

Hillary and Debbie both hugged one another as well.

"We can't help it you're . . ." Deb looked at her watch, "almost an hour late," she said as she took her seat.

"I'm so sorry," Hillary huffed out a breath. "Miles refused to let me leave without reading him a bedtime story and then insisted that I stay until he fell asleep. What can I say? It's really hard to negotiate with a three-year-old." She shook her head. "I couldn't just leave."

"We understand." Louise reached out and squeezed her hand. "So how are John and the rest of the brood?"

Hillary flagged down a waiter. "I'll have what she's having." She pointed at Louise's pink cocktail. It was in a tall, skinny glass with sugar around the rim.

"All good. Busy as anything but good," she smiled. "I'm glad to be out for a while. Let's please talk about something other than school drop-offs, bed-wetting and tantrums."

Hillary had three kids. All two years apart. Her oldest was seven. Needless to say, her life was busy, her schedule crammed. Especially considering she owned a coffee shop.

"I agree whole-heartedly!" Deb nodded her head with such enthusiasm that her ponytail flicked up and down. Her other bestie had two kids. She'd been the first of them to start a family. Her daughter was already nine, her son, five. Deb was a stay-at-home mom and had married her high school sweetheart. She had one of those love-at-first sight relationships that made single people sick. "What's going on with you? Any hot army guys on your radar?" Her eyes were wide and bright. They had to speak up to hear each other over the music.

Louise felt a pang of guilt, but shoved it down. As far as her best friends were concerned, she was working on a top secret government project. Her work was strictly classified, so not something she could discuss with them or anyone else for that matter. Also, as far as they were concerned, she was being housed somewhere remote and lived on an army base-camp. It wasn't a complete lie. Her work was confidential and she did live in a remote place filled with warriors.

"There are plenty of hot guys."

Debbie clapped her hands.

"Don't get too excited. I told you I'm not allowed to date any of them. There's a clause in my contract—"

"That's so boring!" Hillary shook her head, pulling a face that showed how disgusted she was. Just then, her drink arrived. She thanked the waiter while taking it from his hand and swallowing a big sip. She sighed, licking the sugar off of her lips. "So good." She took another sip, smaller this time. "Tell us about all these hot guys. Have you seen any of them without their shirts?" She bobbed her eyebrows up and down.

"Yeah, tell us all about it." Debbie pulled her chair closer.

Louise had to laugh. Both her friends kept their eyes on her. She took a sip of her drink. "Yup," she nodded. "I've seen them shirtless on plenty of occasions." *Like every day. They're sometimes naked.* Her mind wandered to how Granite looked . . . in the buff. Her cheeks felt hot – actually, her whole body felt hot.

"Lucky you!" Hillary cocked her head. "What about your boss? You told us last time that he was being a dick."

Louise shook her head. "My direct supervisor is great. He isn't based in the same place though. My base-camp is run by a bit of a jerk. I have to work with him . . . unfortunately." *A hot jerk. So, so hot.*

"Oh no! That sucks!" Hillary frowned.

"Yup," she nodded her head.

"Is he making life difficult for you? Throwing his weight around?" Debbie asked while taking another sip of her drink.

Louise nodded again. "He was really bad, but he's getting better. I guess awkward would be a good way to describe our working relationship . . . and complicated, really, really complicated."

Hillary raised her brows. "It can't be that complicated. Either he's a jerk or he isn't?"

"Yeah, he is a jerk but at the same time, he feels really strongly about the work we are doing. He's heavily invested in the project. I think that's part of it. We don't get along." She mentioned some of the interactions between them.

"He sounds like a real piece of work." Hillary folded her arms across her chest. "I can't believe he actually told you you're stuck up."

Louise nodded.

"You were right, he's an asshole." Hillary took a big gulp of her drink.

"An asshole on steroids," Debbie chipped in.

"Actually, he might have had a point about a couple of things."

"Like what?" both of her friends asked in unison.

"I'm not saying that it was right of him to have called me that. I do need to say that I called him an asshole first though."

"To his face?" Debbie spluttered.

"No! You . . . did . . . not!" Hillary bounced in her chair.

"I did."

"You? Sweet, kind, get-along-with-everyone Lou? I don't believe it," Hillary shook her head.

Louise played with one of the buttons on her blouse. "This guy knows how to push my buttons. He irritates the hell out of me." Although that wasn't entirely true anymore. Ever since she'd asked to keep things cordial and strictly business, they'd done just that. There had been no more arguments. No more bantering. Granite would arrive for his session. He would become violently ill. There would be a recovery time and then he'd be taken to his chamber. No bickering, no squabbling, no chats. No nothing. Maybe she was nuts but she missed it. "Anyway, to make a long story short, he told me I'm stuck up and that I need to get laid."

"The nerve," Hillary swore. "He irritates me too and I don't even know him."

"I know his type." Debbie put her glass down with a bang. "He probably offered to do the deed himself."

They both stared at her. Louise squirmed in her chair.

"I knew it!" Debbie yelled. "He offered to have sex with you to *help you out*." She did air quotes while she spoke.

"He totally did, didn't he?" Hillary's eyes were wide.

"Look, it's not like that."

"Bullshit. That's sexual harassment. You should speak to your boss about this. File a complaint. The army doesn't take this type of behavior lightly." Hillary frowned.

"He doesn't like me in that way. In fact, I don't think he likes me period. It's not like that."

"How is it then?" Hillary asked. "This is serious," she said, almost to herself. "He can't treat you like that."

"Things have been fine the last couple of weeks. I told you, it's complicated. I know for a fact that he doesn't see me in a sexual way." *Unfortunately.* Where did that come from? Any type of relationship was forbidden. Granite wasn't interested in her in that way anyway, so best she drop it.

Debbie tapped the table with one of her nails. "I still think you should file charges against him, or at the very least have something put on record. You never know what might happen in the future."

Louise shook her head. "Nah! I don't feel comfortable taking that route."

"The guy offered to have sex with you. I'm guessing it happened more than once," Hillary said.

Louise didn't know what to say so she kept quiet.

"I thought so. This isn't right. He's sexually harassing you. He's a bottom feeder, a predator and—"

"No he's not!" There was a firmness to her voice that shocked her. Louise looked from Hillary to Debbie and back again. She realized that she felt protective of Granite. "He's overbearing, annoying and seriously bossy. He can be a huge asshole at times, but he's not a sexual predator. Not even close. I think deep down he's a really good guy with a whole bunch of responsibilities. I also think he is one of the most honest people I've ever met and although he can bug the shit out of me, I guess I like him." *No. She. Did. Not. Did she? Sort of . . . maybe.*

"*Like* like or like?" Hillary narrowed her eyes at her before picking up her glass. It was empty, so she put it back down.

"Oh my god, you *like* like him!" Debbie grabbed her hand. "You *like* like this jerk?" Her voice was laced with shock.

"He's not a jerk." Why did she feel the need to defend him? "He acts like one sometimes," she added. "I'm really attracted him. Like ridiculously attracted to him. If you saw him, you would know why but I don't like him in that way. Even if I did, we can't do anything about it and as I said, he doesn't see me in that way. Can we please drop it?"

"No way," Hillary said, too loudly. A table of suited-up guys turned to look at them. "Wait just a sec—" She flagged down the waiter. Poor guy was run off his feet.

"Another round please." She drew a circle in the air, above the table, with her finger.

The waiter gave a nod and hurried off in the direction of the bar.

"So," Hillary cocked her head, "you like this guy."

"I don't like him. Well, I like him but not in that way. We don't get along. Like I said, it's complicated."

"It's all the sexual tension." Debbie rubbed her hands together. "It makes people nuts." She pointed at her temple.

"I told you, I think he's really hot but he doesn't feel the same about me."

"Why do you think that?"

"I'm not everybody's cup of tea."

"Rubbish!" Debbie gave the side of her arm a slap. "You're as cute as anything."

"I'm barely five foot two with shocking orange hair. My freckles have freckles."

"Just because you're tiny doesn't mean you're not sexy. You have an ass that could crack nuts."

Louise's laugh burst out so quickly she snorted. "My ass can do what?"

"It can crack freaking nuts it's so damn tight." Hillary looked at her pointedly. "Your hair is beautiful too. Especially the color. You should leave it loose some time."

"It's loose enough." Louise had braided her ponytail, which hung down her back. "It's too wild to—"

"Rubbish. You have stunning hair. You used to wear it down once in a while."

Louise leaned forward. "It's wild, crazy hair. A person could go missing in there." They all laughed.

"In all seriousness, I think you should go for him anyway." Hillary's eyes sparkled.

"I can't, it's against the rules. No fraternizing with any of the locals."

"Locals?" Deb raised her brows.

"Army guys. The people who live there," Louise's voice was shrill. "You know what I mean."

"Mmmmm hmmmm." Debbie touched a finger to her lower lip. "That is a bit of a problem."

Granite was completely out. If she wanted to have sex with him – and she didn't – she couldn't. "Granite and I have a strictly business relationship. I'm not going there."

"Granite? What kind of a name is that?" Hillary's eyebrows pulled together in a major frown.

Flip! She hadn't just said that had she? "It's his nickname. He's really built."

"Oh." Hillary's brows went up further. "Okay. You call him by his nickname? I thought it was strictly business."

"Everyone calls him that," she stammered. "It's just how it is. It doesn't mean anything."

"Our drinks are here!" Debbie yelled.

The waiter placed a cocktail in front of each of them. Then he put a shot glass next to each of the cocktails.

"We didn't order those," Debbie said.

"It's from the gentlemen at the next table," he pointed to the guys in the suits who lifted their glasses.

"Thanks, but—" Louise started.

"That's great!" Hillary lifted her shot glass and raised it to the guys who all lifted a drink. "What were you saying earlier about needing to get laid?" she whispered under her breath.

"Yeah, but—"

"Here's your chance. They're cute."

Louise lifted the glass and forced herself to smile in their direction. All clean-cut, nice guys. The one was particularly cute, he had sandy blond hair and a wide smile. He was looking straight at her.

She smiled a bit wider.

"Cheers!" one of the guys shouted across at them. They all drank. The alcohol that burned down her throat was disgusting. It made her want to gag and took her breath away. She reached for her cocktail, taking a big glug.

"Not a tequila girl?"

Oh god! It was the guy. He was there, standing right next to her. Smiling down at her. She shook her head. "No. I'm not much of a drinker. That tasted like battery acid to me."

"You've tasted battery acid before?" he smiled broadly. His dimpled chin and blue eyes sparkled with mischief.

She shook her head. "I'm pretty sure it tastes like that though," she gestured to the empty shot glass in front of her. She noticed that one of the other guys was chatting to Hillary who lifted her hand and pointed at her wedding ring.

"I'm Todd," he held his hand out to her, drawing back her attention.

"Louise." She shook his hand. It was soft and

manicured but his grip was firm. He wore suit pants and a white shirt, top two buttons undone. There were no bulging muscles but he had an athletic build. He also wasn't very tall. Five seven or five eight. He would tower over her.

"Do you want to go to the bar. We can grab something more palatable."

Louise picked up her drink. "I already—"

Debbie gave her a kick under the table.

"Ow!"

Debbie widened her eyes for a second or two. "She would love to . . . wouldn't you Lou?"

"Sure," her voice was a little too high-pitched.

"Great." Todd stepped to the side. He waited for her to go first, following behind her. He stepped in next to her, his eyes on the barman.

"I don't think I can have any more to drink . . . nothing alcoholic at any rate."

He gave her a wide grin. The guy was pretty cute. Definitely her type. "No problem. I can get you a water or a—"

"A water would be great." It had been far too long since she last went on a date. Right now it felt like forever.

The bartender took Todd's order and got to work getting the drinks. A beer for him and a water for her.

He insisted on paying.

"Thanks," she said, as he handed her the drink.

"Sure. So, tell me something about yourself." He leaned up against the bar. Clearly not wanting to head back to the table.

She racked her brain, trying to come up with something other than what she did for a living but came up short. Her work really was her life. It was sad. "I'm a doctor, an allergist to be precise. What about you?" Although she loved her job, most people found it boring.

"I'm an accountant. I 'number crunch' for a living. I'd tell you all about it but I'd have you yawning in no time."

She smiled. They had something in common.

"Let's forget about work. What brings you to Rendezvous?"

Five hours later . . .

They got along and he was cute. She had another Death by Pink and was feeling decidedly light-headed.

"This is it," she pointed to her apartment block. Louise had decided to keep her place rather than sell it. Her current assignment paid really well and included her accommodations, so she saw no reason to let it go. Especially since she wouldn't be staying with the dragons indefinitely. She liked her apartment. It was well appointed, airy . . . *Damn, she was shaking like a leaf.* It might be the ugliest apartment building on the block but it was in a great part of town. She tried to slow her breathing. *Shit, her hands felt damp.*

"Are you sure you don't mind me coming up for coffee?" Todd had his arm resting on the armrest behind her.

Her first instinct was to change her mind and pretend to be tired but she couldn't do it. She needed to grow a pair, she needed to go through with this. Todd was perfect. He was sweet and well-mannered. He was attractive, dammit. The guy was fun to be around and seemed to enjoy her company too. He was really cute . . . just her type.

"I'd like it very much."

Todd's smile widened.

The cab driver told them what the fare was and she reached for her purse.

Todd touched the side of her arm. "I got this."

"You sure? You've paid for everything so far tonight."

"What, a water and a cocktail . . . ?" He swiped his forehead. "Hardly going to break the bank."

He handed the money to the driver and they got out.

Louise felt like her legs were made of jello. Her throat felt dry. She knew that she wasn't in any danger. At least she hoped not. Her best friends knew where she was – or more importantly – who she was with.

They didn't have to have sex. *Oh god!* Why else was he coming up? That's what having coffee meant. It was code for sex. At least, she thought it was. She was so rusty at this whole dating thing.

Todd put a hand to her lower back and she jumped.

"You okay?" he looked concerned. He was so sweet. What was wrong with her?

"Um . . . yeah. I guess I'm a bit nervous."

"No need," he shook his head. "We've had a good time,

haven't we?"

She nodded.

"No reason why we can't keep having a good time. No pressure, okay?"

She nodded, taking a deep breath. "Okay, thanks."

He gave a nod.

Her hands shook as she tried to get the key in the lock. They fell, clanging against the pavement. Oh hell, she was making a mess of this. "Sorry!"

They both went down at the same time and almost bashed their heads.

"I'm so sorry." Louise felt like an idiot. What was she saying? She *was* an idiot.

Todd gave her a kind smile. His eyes had pity written in them.

"I'm making a mess of this." She pinched the bridge of her nose, squeezing her eyes closed for a few moments.

When she looked up he was smiling. "You're not making a mess of anything . . ." he paused, "I like you, Louise. Let's forget about coffee. Meet me tomorrow for lunch instead."

"But the cab already left."

"I took his card remember? I'm sure he didn't get far. Here," he handed her his business card. "Call me in the morning. We can go to lunch or dinner."

Louise shook her head. "I told you, I'm not in town much anymore. My work—"

He shrugged. "I don't care. Call me." He squeezed the hand that was holding the card.

"And Louise . . ."

"Yeah?"

"Can I kiss you?"

"I . . . I guess so." She was so lame. Lamer than lame.

Todd leaned forward and pressed his lips to hers. It felt good. It felt nice. He pulled back and she waited for butterflies to explode in her stomach. It didn't happen. She felt absolutely nothing. *Zip. Nada.*

Todd had his eyes glued to her lips. It looked like he was going to come in for round number two, maybe deepen the kiss this time. Panic welled. "I'll call you in the morning," she practically yelled, quickly pushing the key in the door. "Thanks so much." She leaned forward and kissed him on the cheek. *The cheek!* Oh god, but she was lame.

Her whole face felt hot. Not a good hot. A bad hot.

Todd smiled and nodded. She turned the key. Once inside, she ran until her apartment door closed behind her.

She was going to call Todd in the morning and try again. The guy was perfect. Absolutely perfect. There was something wrong with her. It was all her dammit. Once she figured out what was going on, things would be awesome. She and Todd would be awesome.

CHAPTER 10

Three days later (Monday) . . .

Granite paced from one side of his chamber to the other. After several minutes he put a hand to the glass window and took in the view. Vast, open, beautiful. Normally enough to calm and center him.

It didn't work.

Not today.

He silently growled and paced back towards the door. There was a quick knock and the human entered. Same bun, same coat, same serious demeanor. He was actually happy to see her and it pissed him the fuck off. "It's about time. I called for you two and a half hours ago."

"I was busy with a treatment."

"If I call for you, I expect you to drop everything and to come immediately, am I clear?" He was too afraid to approach her. Too much of a pussy to scent the air. Instead, he took small breaths through his mouth. He'd been desperate to see her and now that she was here he was tempted to send her away without finding out. *Forget that!* He needed to know.

The doctor shook her head. "Drop everything? Impossible. I had already started a therapy session. Once I begin, I need to be there until the end. Furthermore . . ." she continued before he could interject, "I need to monitor my patient for a time afterwards, as well. You should know all of this." She set a file down on a nearby table and put her hands on her hips. "I know you're used to people bowing down to you but I'm not one of your subjects. I thought that we were being cordial to one another. Working as a team and all that."

Granite couldn't help the snort that left him. "Teamwork? The only time I work in a team is when I'm fucking. That's it!"

The human's eyes moved to the ceiling for a moment or two before locking back with his. She mumbled something that sounded very much like 'Give me strength.'

It was time to grow some balls . . . and a dick for that matter. He closed the distance between them and sucked in a deep breath through his nostrils.

Thank fuck!

Granite was so relieved that he almost said the words out loud. *Thank fuck!* He'd spent the entire weekend in a foul-ass mood because he couldn't stop himself from picturing this little female in bed with another male. It irritated him that he cared, but for some reason he did. It wasn't like he was actually attracted to her . . . or was he? *No fucking way.*

Point was, she hadn't listened to him. Then again, why the hell would she take his advice? That would have been way too easy.

"Why are you looking at me like that?" She was frowning. Her full lips pursed together.

How was he looking at her? Shit! He just may have been staring at her plump bottom lip. Okay, so her lips were decent; so were her eyes but that was it. *That was fucking it.* "You don't listen, do you?"

She raised her brows and pointed a finger at him – he loved her sass. "Listen . . ." He could see her thinking it over. Carefully considering what it was he could be talking about. "Oh flip!" she covered her mouth with her hand. She made a groaning noise that hit him straight in the groin. The Stag Run was this weekend, he really needed a female. Any fucking female. He wasn't going to be too picky this time around. "I totally missed my appointment with Dr. Rhodes. With everything that happened – or didn't happen – I forgot all about it."

"What are you talking about?" *What happened? What didn't happen and who was Dr. Rhodes?*

"More like what are *you* talking about? I thought you were referring to my not being on a contraceptive. It would help with the way I scent . . . you know, all 'needy and achy' . . ." She pulled a face like he was full of shit. "Breeze was kind enough to explain to me that it's because I'm not on the pill. I was supposed to see a gynecologist but I missed my appointment."

A pill. Really? Not a chance would a pill help this female.

Not unless it was in the shape of a dick. Granite shook his head. "Yeah, it would help some if you were to take such a pill but not nearly enough. What you need is sex, Doctor. You can try and deny it all you want." *What the fuck was wrong with him?* Why was he pushing this? Pushing . . . all he could think of was pushing up her white coat, tearing off her panties and showing her exactly what she needed. He wanted to make her come and hard and more than once. He squeezed his eyes shut and rubbed them with his thumb and forefinger. "Please just do as I say. You are a distraction to my males." She was a distraction to him and he didn't like it. He didn't want her but couldn't seem to get her off of his mind. It was her scent. It was maddening. She needed to sort that shit out.

"That's the biggest load of nonsense I ever heard. I thought that we were done having these types of conversations. It's inappropriate and—"

"There is a Stag Run this weekend." He'd heard her excuses before.

"Yeah, so what does that have to do with me? Look, why did you even call me here? Was it so that you could lecture me about the way I smell? So that you could make me feel bad about my pathetic sex life? Or lack thereof . . . Not that it's any of your business." Her eyes blazed.

"You're going back to Walton Springs this weekend and you're not coming back here until you've taken care of your problem."

"My problem? You cannot be serious! You're ordering me to have sex or else?"

He folded his arms. He wasn't going to answer her question. He didn't answer stupid questions.

She folded her arms as well and narrowed her eyes at him. "I'm going to email Blaze. This is bullshit."

"Run to Blaze! Do it! See if I give even a small fuck. Why not stand on your own two feet for a change instead of running to that male."

"I cannot believe you. My sex life is my business. Mine. You have no right to tell me what I can and can't do when it comes to my private life." Her cheeks were flushed and a strand of hair had escaped the prison that was her tight bun. He was sure that wasn't the only tight thing on her.

"That's where you're wrong. I *can* tell you what to do if it affects the way things run here. You are an interference. So try me, Doctor. I dare you!"

"You would love to have me fired wouldn't you?" That finger was back up and wagging at him.

"Actually, I happen to think that you're a really good doctor. You take your job seriously. You care about your patients. Firing you is that last thing I want but you are driving my males mad and that cannot be tolerated."

He could see her mulling it over. "You think I'm a good doctor?" She was frowning like she didn't trust him.

He gave a nod. "I do." It was true.

She started to say something and then stopped. "I hadn't noticed . . . my being a distraction." She said it like it was a foreign concept. She also seemed concerned. Agitated even. "The guys all seem fine to me." Then she sniffed her armpits. He had to stifle a laugh. "I don't smell anything . . . Okay, maybe deodorant – the antiperspirant kind but that's it. Are you sure?"

He gave a nod and took a step closer to her. "Your scent is fucking amazing." He gave a sniff and groaned. His dick reacted. How could it not?

Her eyes were on his and she was breathing hard. Her pupils dilated when he nodded. They tracked the movement of his Adam's apple as he swallowed. "It is, really?" her voice was soft and timid.

"Yeah." He took another step, putting him almost flush against her. "Like peaches and cream."

"Peaches and cream . . ." Her voice was dreamy. "And peaches and cream scent of need and achiness?" She frowned.

"You also scent heavily of pussy."

Her eyes widened and her pupils dilated some more. "Oh!" Her pink mouth rounded and his dick hardened.

Granite gave a small nod. "Hot and wet . . . so fucking delicious . . ."

Then the small human did something completely unexpected. She reached up, all the way up. Had to be on her tiptoes and then some. Maybe he met her somewhere in the middle, he wasn't sure. Next thing her pink, cherry-flavored lips were all over his. Soft and clumsy.

So fucking sweet. With a low growl, he gripped her hips and yanked her against him. He tilted his head to the side and took control of her mouth, took control of the kiss. He sucked on her lower lip first, then her tongue, then plundered that mouth of hers. The doctor moaned. It was laced with enough need to have him shooting off there and then. He held onto the tiny bit of control he still had left. Who was he kidding? Control did not factor. Not when she moaned into his mouth for a second time. Not when she rubbed up against him.

One taste.

One touch.

One.

Granite pushed up her coat and the skirt of her dress underneath and cupped her ass. Tight yet lush. Encased in a full set of panties. Cotton, from the feel of it. His dick was so hard it physically hurt.

She gave a loud groan. He pulled back slightly. Her eyes were completely glazed over. Her lips wet and swollen. She leaned back in. She took back his lips. *Who would've thought?* Not stuck-up after all.

Not nearly. She was vocal and so damned receptive.

One touch.

One.

He half-expected her to slap his hand away when he reached between her thighs and cupped her sex. Soaking wet. Dripping. His cock throbbed when she arched into him and moaned long and loud.

Fucking hell!

"I've got you," he whispered as he shoved the cotton aside. Her clit was huge. So swollen and ripe his mouth watered. If he looked down, there would be pre-cum all over his pants. Of that there was no doubt.

"Yes!" she moaned. "Yes!" she cried out, as he rubbed

his thumb over its swollen edge. Another rub. She moaned and he took back her mouth. He gave the swollen flesh a light pinch followed by a slippery rub and she came apart. Just like that. *Done.* Her back bowed and her body went rigid. Her short nails dug into him. Her loud moans and wails were muffled by his kisses. He kept up the slip and slide on her clit.

All he could think of doing was picking her up and putting her against the wall, of filling her. He had yet to put even the tip of his finger in her pussy but he knew she would be tight as fuck. Granite moaned at the mere thought. Her hips rocked against his hand.

He'd fuck her against the wall, then on his desk. Then he'd take her to his bed and take his time. Draw out her pleasure and make her beg. He'd never had a female in his bed before. Or his chamber for that matter. For a few seconds he was so tempted to have her that he shook. He physically shook. The vibrations moved through his body.

No!

There was too much at stake. He should never have let it get this far. Should never have touched her in the first place. He hadn't been unable to help himself. The sooner she found proper release the better. The sooner he could get back to life as he knew it.

Granite pulled away, keeping his hand on her hip. Her eyes were closed. She leaned forward, pursing her lips. *Cute as fuck! No, looking like an idiot,* he tried to convince himself. He pushed her underwear back into place and pulled down her coat.

Her gorgeous – average – eyes flashed open. "What? When . . ." She even swayed a little on her feet but quickly righted herself. The human licked her lips and smoothed her coat.

He made sure that her eyes were on his. "That should not have happened but in a way I'm glad it did. You're going to Walter Springs this weekend."

Her jaw tightened and her hands clenched at her sides. Her scent turned peppery. If she'd been a dragon, smoke would've come out of her nose, but she didn't say a thing.

"You need to take care of your scent problem. This whole . . . thing . . . that just happened proves it. I don't think I've ever made a female come so quickly before." He had loved it. She might be a bit stuck-up but she was sexy as fuck anyway.

Her face turned red before his eyes. From a light pink to all out 'tomato city.' She was about to snap. In fact, he thought she might hit him or kick him. It didn't happen because she pulled in a deep breath instead, and removed some lint from her impeccably white coat. Her composure had returned in full force. *What a pity.* "Thank you for bringing this . . . problem," she paused, "to my attention." She even smiled at him.

The fuck!

"Sure." Granite could feel that he was frowning. He hadn't expected this reaction. "I would say come back anytime but it's against the rules," he chuckled, sounding like an idiot. "I won't say anything if you won't."

She twisted her fingers against her lips and smiled

wider. "No . . . my lips are sealed. Let's put this behind us. It's never happening again so no need to bring it up . . . *ever*," she put emphasis on the word. Even acted like it was the worst thing that could've happened to her.

The fuck!

"Right!" he growled. *Shit!*

"You were right by the way," she nodded a couple of times.

"About?" He felt so off-balance it was scary. He was also sure why he felt like this, which was way scarier.

She blinked a few times. "I think I do need to go home this weekend. I met a guy. We got close, maybe it *is* time to seal the deal. No! It's definitely time to seal the deal. Thanks for showing me that today."

"Sure."

"I'm going to pack a bag. I'm feeling pretty excited about it."

"Good," another growl. Who was this male? Maybe he should have her followed just to be sure she was safe. *No!* She was a mature female, capable of making her own decisions.

"Oh, I almost forgot," she raised her brows. "Why did you call me here?"

"I wanted feedback on the Resistance Therapy." He didn't feel up to discussing it with her right now. He had more important things to do. "But, you can email me a summary."

"No problem!"

"Good!"

"I'll see you tomorrow."

He gave a nod. She didn't seem phased by what had just gone down. *Good!* She was going to take care of her scent problem. *Wonderful! Fantastic news.*

She said her goodbyes and left. Granite turned and hammered his fist against his desk. It splintered into about a million pieces. Thank fuck it was his turn to go on the Stag Run this weekend. He sucked in a deep breath. Saturday couldn't come soon enough as far as he was concerned.

CHAPTER 11

She felt hot all over. Hot and rubbed raw. The shower was great. More than great. She'd made the water scalding and had scrubbed and scrubbed until her skin felt raw. Her hands still shook though. She still felt unclean. Really, really dirty. She couldn't help the clench of her core as she thought about her orgasm.

It had been a doozy. She was sure it had ripped her clean in half. That's how hard Granite had rocked her world. She was willing to give up everything in that moment. Every darned thing. Her job, her career, her life. Everything just to have hardcore sex with him. Sex with Granite would be hardcore and good. Really, really good. He knew exactly what he was doing.

He was also an asshole.

Such an asshole.

As well as an arrogant ass. She wished like mad she hadn't kissed him. She'd made a move on him! Shame coursed through her. She'd never made a move on a guy in her whole entire life. They always chased her. Not that many guys chased her but those few who had been interested, had chased her. Not the other way around.

She had kissed him first. Louise put a hand against the wall and stopped walking for a moment. *Arghhh!* She couldn't believe she had done that. He was arrogant enough to begin with. The last thing Granite had needed was an ego stroke. She'd given him one hell of an ego boost and she felt sick because of it.

Thing was, when he'd said 'pussy,' it had detonated something inside her. It wasn't just that, it was the way he was looking at her as well. Like he wanted to eat her whole. Like he wanted to tear her into pieces, but in a good way. His intense dark eyes had moved from her mouth to her eyes and back. His nostrils kept flaring as he'd taken in her scent. *Fucking delicious. Hot and wet.* The whole thing had turned her brain to mush.

Her cheeks heated when she thought about her orgasm, how little effort it had taken for him to get her there. A few seconds. Ten tops and she had unraveled. It was the best orgasm of her whole entire life and it had taken the guy all of ten seconds. How was that for another ego stroke? One he did not need. That was why she had reacted the way she did. Like she didn't care. Like he had helped her. *Gag!* That pity orgasm he had given her made her feel nothing but pathetic. He'd even commented on how quickly she had come. He looked amused. *The jerk!* He probably thought there was something wrong with her. It had to be a turn off. No wonder he hadn't been able to get away from her quick enough. Shame churned inside of her. All she'd wanted was more. Thankfully it hadn't happened.

One thing was for sure, she was calling Todd this weekend. On second thoughts, she still had his card, she was sending him an email. She was going to have sex with him and she was going to enjoy it, so help her.

Even if she made herself drink ten of those pink cocktails, she didn't care. It was happening, and not just so that she could continue to work here, it was going to happen because she needed to show him . . . Granite. Also, she needed sex and really badly. Her whole body hummed with need.

She sniffed her pits and prayed to god that he was exaggerating about the way she smelled. It was embarrassing.

"I'm so sorry I'm late," she was out of breath and feeling flustered.

"No worries, Doc," Rock smiled broadly. He was already lying on the gurney.

"Give me just a sec to pull your file and then we can start."

"Sure," he gave a nod.

She walked over to the filing cabinet and looked under 'R,' then she went back to the desk. Maybe she'd pulled his file earlier. Yup, there it was. She grabbed the folder and walked over to Rock. "My pen." She felt her top coat pocket and then looked back towards her desk.

"Everything okay, Doc?" Rock was frowning, his features pulled into a look of concern.

"Yeah. No . . . maybe." She bit down on her lower lip

for a second. "Do I smell funny to you?" She walked back over to the big shifter.

He pulled a face. "What do you mean by funny?"

"Funny, as in, do I smell . . . nice?" She wasn't sure how to word this without sounding like a complete idiot.

He gave a nod. "Yeah, sure. You scent of soap and underarm. You scent of you," he said, simply.

Louise shook her head. "That doesn't make sense." She sank down onto the edge of her desk. "Don't take this the wrong way, but do I scent of . . ." *Pussy*. She couldn't say that. "Sexy things . . . ?"

He frowned.

"I mean, god!" She covered her face with her hand for a second or two. This was embarrassing. "Granite said that my scent is driving you guys . . . his males . . . mad. He said I scent of . . . sex," she whispered the word. "Is it true?"

Rock shook his head. "I'm sorry, Doc, but you're asking the wrong male. I am in love with Quartz. I have begun to fixate on her scent. No other female can compare. To me she scents of heaven, of everything pure and sweet and sexy." He made a groaning noise. "It would be better to ask an unattached male. My senses are aligned only to her." It was so sweet to hear him talk. She could actually see the love in his eyes. This Quartz was a very lucky lady.

Before she could say anything, he was on his feet. "Give me a second." He left. Went right out the door. *Gone*.

Half-a-minute later he was back. He had someone else with him. "This is Mountain."

The guy's head was clean-shaven. He gave a nod. "Good to meet you, Doctor."

Rock closed the door and then gave Mountain a nudge. "You need to go and scent the doctor."

He frowned. "I can't do that."

"You can. She needs to know what she scents of. She is worried that her scent is giving the males the wrong idea. She's worried that her scent is too enticing." Rock gave him another small push. "It would not mean anything. She doesn't wish to rut you." Rock glanced her way. "When a male scents a female it is normally an initiation of sex."

"Oh!" She felt her cheeks heat. "This would be purely clinical. No initiation of anything." She remembered how Granite's nostrils had flared earlier, how he'd been breathing heavily through his nose. He'd been sniffing her, openly. Technically, he'd been initiating sex long before she kissed him. It didn't make her feel any better though.

Mountain nodded. He took a few steps towards her and sniffed the air. "Human females smell great to us shifters," he commented.

"Yeah, but that's a generalization. Please can you add to that." She couldn't help that she smelled like a human woman.

Mountain sniffed some more. "I scent soap and toothpaste. I also scent underarm ... it's an antiperspirant. You are wearing body lotion, something that contains almond extract."

"Anything else?" Rock asked.

Mountain gave a nod. "You have a fruity scent, I can't

quite put my finger on the exact fruit."

Peaches. Granite had said peaches. She swallowed hard and gave a nod.

Mountain breathed deeply through his nose and closed his eyes for a beat. "You smell great."

"Are you becoming aroused?" Rock asked.

Oh god! Ground, swallow me whole. Louise didn't know where to look.

Mountain shrugged. "I am a male in his prime. It has been a long—"

"Yeah, yeah . . ." Rock shook his head. "Do you feel like her scent is driving you mad, making you lose control?"

Mountain frowned deeply. "Not a chance! I am a grown-ass male."

"Can you think straight?"

Mountain visibly bristled. "Of course I can think straight. What the hell!" he growled the last.

"Thanks, Mountain. The doctor was worried. It turns out her fears were unwarranted."

Mountain gave a nod and turned his eyes on her. "Take care, Doctor."

"Thank you." She tried to smile but it felt tight and forced.

Once the door closed behind Mountain, Rock turned to her grinning. "I think my king has a bit of a crush on you."

"What? No! No . . ." she added, feeling confusion set in. "No way is that the case."

"You heard Mountain. He is a virile male. He almost always takes two or three females back to the hotel with him."

Louise felt her eyes widen. "You have to be kidding me."

"Dragon shifters prefer one female but he has said that he is worried he will hurt just one female. Dragons have a ton of stamina and six months is a long time," Rock shrugged.

"I see."

"My point being, Mountain is particularly horny . . . excuse my candor. There are more like him, of course. If any male was going to pick up these types of scents on you, it would be him. He thinks you smell good; all human females smell really good to us but it was nothing out of the ordinary. I can call another male and we can conduct the same test but I'm sure it will have the same outcome."

"You're saying that Granite likes me?" *No damned way.*

"Emotion has nothing to do with it. He finds your scent intoxicating and instinct is driving him to rut you." He gave a one-shouldered shrug. "I wouldn't worry about it. He will not be as driven to follow his instincts after the Stag Run. Emotions are running high right now. The scent of testosterone in this lair is nauseating. It always is before a run. The males who are set to go are always the worst affected but we all feel it." Rock pulled a face that would've been comical had she not been so shocked right now.

"I can't believe he finds me attractive."

"No, Doc. Attraction, in the conventional sense, has nothing to do with it. I'm not saying he doesn't find you attractive," he quickly put up a hand. "It's not necessarily the case."

"Okay, so if—"

There was a commotion out in the hall. Rock was the first to get to the door. As big as these shifters were, they sure could move. He turned back. "Get back, Doc."

She could hear meaty thuds. There was even a cracking noise. And loud grunting, followed by a yell.

"A small group of males are fighting." Rock closed the door. "Get to the far side of the room. One of them might shift and burst through the wall."

"What?" she yelled as she did as he said.

"Don't worry!" Rock gave her a tight smile. He followed her, standing in front of her. "I will protect you. Also, the hallways are mostly big enough to accommodate a shift."

"Mostly?" her voice shook. She didn't like the sound of that.

"Get down and stay behind me. You will be just fine." He turned slightly to the side, giving her a reassuring smile.

The commotion went on for a few minutes. There were loud bangs, crashes and more yelling. She flinched at a particularly loud bang. One of her certificates fell off the wall, crashing to the floor below. The frame splintered and there was a distinct sound of breaking glass. Another frame fell and then another.

A loud, terrifying snarl tore through the outside

hallway. It was so loud she felt like closing her ears to ward off the noise. Her blood turned cold. The terrifying sound was followed by complete silence. She realized she wasn't breathing and sucked in a deep breath.

Rock turned to her and leaned down, offering his hand. She took it and he helped her to her feet. Louise smoothed out her coat. Her heart was thudding in her chest.

The door opened and Granite took up the entire frame. The two lines between his eyes were so pronounced it was unreal. His eyes were so dark they looked black. Every muscle was primed. His hands clenched at his sides.

"My lord, I . . ."

He ignored Rock, his intense gaze still locked with hers. The air thinned. The earth may even have stopped mid-rotation. In that moment it felt like they were the only two people in existence. "Are you okay?" His voice was loud, deep. It caused a shiver to run down her spine.

She nodded once. "Yes." It came out soft and breathless.

Granite looked over at Rock for the first time. "Take care of the human," he snarled, then he closed the door.

"Yup . . ." Rock nodded. "He wants to rut you bad," he whispered before giving a chuckle.

"Stop!" She wacked the side of his arm. She wasn't buying it. Not for one second. Even if it was true, Granite still didn't like her and neither did he find her attractive. He just liked the way she smelled – how weird was that? The guy was bad for her. *No!* Risking her career wasn't worth it. Not even close.

"He'll be over it by Monday, Doc. I can see that you are concerned. Don't be." Rock began to pick up her ruined picture frames.

Louise wasn't worried. Not at all. At least she knew what she was dealing with. Granite could go on his Stag Run and she was hooking up with Todd. By next week this would all be behind her. She could forget today ever happened.

CHAPTER 12

Sometime after midnight, same day . . .

Granite knocked. He counted to ten before knocking again. Harder this time. Adrenaline coursed through him. Where was she? Why was she taking so damned long? He could hear movement from behind the door.

He knocked again, holding back so that he didn't break the door down. *Fuck!* He was done waiting. Patience was never one of his strong suits. It never would be.

Granite walked in. The chain on the inside of the door snapped like a string.

The doctor turned to him, her eyes wide. Her hair was pulled into an untidy bun. Tendrils of curls framed her face.

She wore an oversized t-shirt; it was a faded black . . . more grey than black. She wore oversized boxer shorts. Those looked new. They were blue and white. Her legs weren't bad. Short but shapely. Her skin was a milky white.

She had her arms wrapped around her middle. Covering her breasts. He had no idea why. It didn't seem logical that she would do such a thing.

The sense of urgency returned with a vengeance. "Get dressed, you're needed. It's a medical emergency."

"What's wrong?"

"It's Breeze."

"Oh my god! Is the baby okay? Is Breeze okay?" she asked, in quick succession as panic set in. Her eyes widened and her arms fell away from her body, her need to hide from him momentarily forgotten.

He gave a shake of the head. "I'm not sure." He rubbed his eyes and his face. "It looks like she's gone into labor but it's too early. She's worried, afraid and so is Volcano." He huffed out a breath. "I'm pretty fucking freaked out myself."

"Wait a minute." She was frowning heavily. "I saw her yesterday and she said she had a week to go."

"You must remember that our females are only pregnant for four months. They sometimes carry a week overdue, anything less is considered early. Our young are small and helpless. Whelps born too soon often perish," his voice cracked ever so slightly. He cleared his throat.

"It's only a matter of days though."

"At least six days. It might be too soon." He had to look up at the ceiling. His throat was clogging and his eyes were stinging. *Fuck! This wasn't happening.*

When he looked back at her, the human gave a nod. "Okay, fine, I'm not a gynecologist but I worked the emergency room. I've delivered babies before." It looked like she was trying to convince herself. She looked around her chamber and back again. Her eyes were wide, her skin pale. "I delivered quite a number of babies in Ethiopia as well. Shit!" She walked towards him, looking paler by the second. He could hear how her heart-rate had picked up. He could scent fear on her. "I don't have any of the instruments I need. None of the drugs, especially if the baby is a preemie." She pulled in a deep breath. "I've got this though. No problem! We had nothing in Ethiopia either but then again . . . not all of the babies made it." She squeezed her eyes shut. "I know Breeze personally. She's a friend . . . What if I mess up? What if . . . I'm not the right person for the job?" She shook her head.

He gripped her shoulders. "You need to calm down. Volcano and Breeze are panicking enough for all of us. We've had so few births over the years. None of them were early. Our healers are not equipped. You are the most qualified. You won an award for your efforts in Ethiopia."

She gave a humorless laugh. "My efforts were geared at birth control."

"I read the newspaper article."

Her eyes were filled with fear. "I was in the right place at the right time. The birth went like clockwork." She was too modest. A female was too late getting to a hospital. The baby was coming. Her mate had called for a doctor and Louise happened to be close by. She helped birth the child in the back of a car. "Anyone could've delivered that child. All I did was catch. That reporter exaggerated the whole thing. He made me out to be some kind of hero. I'm not."

"Bullshit! You're a good doctor. I believe in you."

She filled her lungs with air and slowly exhaled. "Okay," she gave a nod.

"I will make sure that a healer is close by. You need to understand that dragon females prefer to give birth alone. At the most, they will have a healer with them. Too many people will freak her out even more. Her instincts will be to send you all away."

"Are you sure you shouldn't just send a healer in then?"

He shook his head. "You are the most qualified. You need to trust me on this."

She nodded. "Understood, but I might need to consult with a healer so have someone ready. Also, I need some supplies from my work chamber."

Granite gave a nod. "Make a note of everything you need."

"Okay . . ." She scanned the room, seeing a notebook next to her bed. Within no time she handed a list to Granite.

He held the white paper in his hand. "You have half a minute to get dressed. Put on your white coat and meet me outside."

He didn't wait for her response, instead, he left her chamber and handed the note to Rock. He figured that the human would need supplies and that the male was one of the best equipped to understand what they were.

Rock frowned as he read the list.

Just then, she emerged. The coat buttons were done up wrong and she wore a pair of flip flops. They were a bright red. She carried her black medical bag.

"Hi, Doc," Rock said, he held the paper to his face. "What is a sphygmomanometer?"

"It's that cuff that tightens around your arm to measure a person's blood pressure. Sorry I should have written it in layman's terms."

The male gave a nod, he smiled. "No problem! A stethoscope is that instrument you use to listen to our heart?"

The doctor gave a nod. "I normally take that with me but for some reason I forgot it on my desk today."

"Oxygen tank and mask," Rock read to himself. "Top drawer, right-hand side . . . extra masks," he gave a nod. "A pulse oximeter is that thing that goes on your finger?"

"Yeah. I can't think of anything else that will be of any help. It's not like I can put in an IV or inject either of them." She chewed on her lower lip.

Granite could see her nerves kick in. "You'll do just fine. Rock here will wait outside Volcano and Breezes' chamber so that he can go and fetch something if you suddenly need it." He looked Rock in the eye, giving the command and giving her assurance all at once.

"I am lightning quick." The male winked at the human and Granite felt like punching him. This was a serious situation and he was making light of it.

"Go!" Granite growled, a bit too harshly.

Rock set off like his ass was on fire. Granite took the bag from the human who tried to protest. He shook his head. "Use your energy to walk."

Her eyes were wide but there was determination in their depths. It didn't take long to make it back to the chamber. He rapped twice on the door and entered. The chamber was large.

"Not big on waiting for someone to let you in," the human said.

"No time."

Breeze lay on the bed, her mouth was pulled into a grimace and her eyes were squeezed shut. Her face was red and sweaty.

"Thank god you're back!" Volcano barked as he caught sight of them. The male was pale, he looked like he had just seen a ghost.

He heard the human swallow hard. Heard her heart-rate pick up a notch. Granite put his hand on her back. "You've got this. I'll help where I can." He held back, not wanting to spook Breeze.

She gave a nod and walked to the bed.

Breeze was breathing heavily. Puffing, in and out in quick succession. "It's happening so quickly!" she shrieked. "Oh god! It hurts." A tear slid down her cheek. It took another few beats before Breeze's breathing eased enough for her to talk. The female was so freaked out she didn't react to the fact that there were so many of them in the chamber. Granite didn't think that she had even noticed that he was there.

"How long have you been in labor?" Louise grabbed Breeze's wrist. She held it using two fingers.

"It started with back pain earlier this afternoon. The

pain got worse and worse until it started coming and going. I knew something was up but didn't want to jump to conclusions. I guess I was hoping it would go away. I'm sorry," she turned to Volcano.

The male gripped her hand tighter. "It's not your fault, sweetheart."

"They obviously didn't go away," she whimpered. "It keeps getting worse and worse. I feel like the birth pains are coming one after the other. I keep telling myself that I'm not in labor. I keep trying to pretend . . . but they're so bad I feel like can't breathe or think."

She shook her head. "It got worse and worse until . . . Oh god!" Her grimace was back. "Until, I told Volcano who called Granite." She sucked in air.

"That's it. Breathe deeply." The little doctor also took in deep lungfuls of air. She did so in a rhythmic fashion which Breeze emulated.

There was a knock. Granite went to the door. It was Rock with the supplies. "Stay out here." He noticed that the healer had arrived along with another male. "You must all stay in case you are needed," he spoke under his breath, quickly closing the door. Granite placed the supplies on the table next to the bed.

He could hear Breeze's breathing slowly even out. Granite moved away. His sister-in-law must be in a really bad way; it seemed like she still hadn't even noticed his presence.

"This is all happening so quickly, too quickly." Breeze wiped a hand across her sweaty brow. "I'm so afraid. This shouldn't be happening. This can't be happening."

"It's going to be okay. I'm here for you." Volcano cupped her cheek. "It is normal for an Earth birth to be quick."

"Not this early though." When Volcano didn't reply Breeze continued, sounding way more panicked. "Don't leave me." It hurt to watch the two of them suffering like this. "It's too soon. I couldn't bear it if . . ."

"We need to stay positive," the doctor spoke up. "This baby is coming. There is nothing we can do at this point to stop it. I spent six months in the emergency room and a year in Ethiopia with very few supplies. I've delivered a lot of babies. I've witnessed miracles." She took Breeze's free hand. "You need to try to stay calm. We're going to take this one step at a time. Let's try not to get ahead of ourselves. I'm going to do everything in my power to bring a healthy child into this world. I need to know that you're with me."

"Yes," Volcano's voice cracked. "Thank you," he added, his eyes were misted.

The human's gaze locked with Breeze's who shook her head.

"One step at a time." Louise seemed so incredibly calm. Like she had this. "I'll talk you through it."

Breeze nodded. "Yeah, okay," her voice was small and hoarse. "I'm scared."

"It's okay to be afraid. You need to stay positive though. I'm here for you. Volcano is here. We are going to get you through this. The baby too."

Granite was proud of the human. If she was still feeling fearful, there was no sign of it.

"You need to drink." Volcano handed an open bottle of water to Breeze and she drank deeply from it. His brother grabbed the bottle as another birthing pain hit and she dropped it. His mate made a groaning noise and gripped her belly. Granite inched further back. He shouldn't be here, yet he couldn't leave. He felt like Louise needed him. She kept glancing his way.

The human began her rhythmic breathing and Breeze followed suit. "The contractions are close together, they're strong and go on for close to a minute."

"What does that mean?" Volcano frowned deeply.

"Breeze is already in active labor."

Breeze groaned, she continued to breathe heavily for a time before slumping back onto her pillows, her eyes were closed. Her face was a bright red.

"I need to check your cervix, Breeze. I need to find out how dilated you are." Breeze didn't respond. Volcano was whispering words of encouragement to his mate. "I need to do an internal check." Instead of waiting for a reply, Louise opened her bag and pulled out a pair of latex gloves which she pulled on. Next, she grabbed a tube of clear-looking gel which she squirted liberally onto one of her hands.

The doctor moved to the foot of the bed. From this angle, Granite couldn't see a thing but he averted his eyes anyway. He was tempted to leave the room. He glanced back to the bed and caught her looking at him. Her eyes wide and far too big for her face. Her skin seemed paler than normal. She was putting on a brave face but he could still see the underlying tension. He gave a small nod and kept his eyes on her until she got back to work. Granite looked down at his feet.

"I need you to open your legs for me," Louise said.

He could hear the rustling of the sheets as Breeze complied.

"My hands are a bit cold," the doctor warned. "This will be a bit uncomfortable but it shouldn't hurt."

He could hear a squelching nose as the doctor's fingers entered the other female's body. Breeze made a small sound at the back of her throat. Her heart-rate picked up, as did her breathing.

"Sorry!" Louise said. "All done." He heard her remove her hand and take a step back.

Granite could scent blood. He looked up, his eyes drawn to the gloves the doctor was removing. Her fingers were smeared red.

"Your mucous plug has already come away and you're already seven centimeters dilated."

"What does that mean?" Volcano asked. "Please, healer, we do not understand the way that you speak."

"No, not again," Breeze moaned, doubled over in pain. She grit her teeth for a few beats and began to breathe harder. It felt like an age before she finally sagged back.

"It doesn't sound like you've been in labor for very long, yet you are already far along." Louise sighed, sounding frustrated. "You see," she looked from Volcano to Breeze and back, "human women who give birth for the first time usually take anything from eleven to twenty hours. It can go quicker, of course, no two births are ever the same, but that is the general time-frame."

Volcano shook his head. "A handful of hours at most. Sometimes as little as one or two."

The human gave a deep nod. "That's good. It means that we are right on track. Your contractions . . . birthing pains will be severe." She looked at Volcano. "Hold her hand. Breeze is going to need every ounce of support. The good news is that it'll be over soon. If your labor keeps progressing in this way, this won't take long."

There was a popping noise followed by a gushing sound. Breeze gave a soft cry.

"It's nothing to be alarmed about," Louise leaned forward, looking Breeze in the eyes. "Your water just broke."

The birthing pains continued to come, one after the other. Fifteen minutes later and Breeze began to shake violently. Her teeth clattered. "I don't feel well," she managed to grit out. "I'm sick." Then she leaned over the side of the bed and vomited. Right onto Volcano's feet. If it weren't for the direness of the situation, he would've found it funny. There was not a stitch of humor to be found though.

The human handed Breeze a towel. "You're in the transitional stage. You might feel pressure below. The baby is moving into the birth canal. You will start to feel the urge to push soon."

"Now," Breeze croaked. "It's coming. My baby . . ." she moaned.

Louise frowned, pulled on another pair of gloves and leaned in between Breeze's splayed thighs. "You aren't fully dilated just yet, you—" Her eyes widened.

Breeze groaned.

"What is it?" Volcano yelled.

"Scrap that . . . you *are* fully dilated." The doctor removed the gloves and threw them into the nearby trash. "This baby is coming and it's coming fast."

"Get out!" Breeze screamed. "Out!" Her instincts had begun to kick in. Granite was shocked it had taken this long.

"Breeze honey, take a deep breath," Volcano spoke slowly and gently. "I'll leave if you want, it's—"

"No!" Breeze sniffed, Granite realized that she was crying. "Stay, I'm sorry."

"You have nothing to be sorry about." His brother soothed the damp hair from her brow.

The human walked to him. "I need you to help me set up. I need warm blankets. This room will need to be kept very warm so prepare a fire. A heater would be better . . ."

Granite shook his head. "I'll prepare a fire," he spoke under his breath, not wanting to alarm Breeze.

"I will need towels and warm water." The doctor licked her lips, he could see that her mind was going at a mile a minute.

"No, problem."

Breeze had started to moan. The sound was deeper,

more of a growl. "I need to get up. Help me up."

Louise swallowed hard. Her eyes flashed to Breeze and then back to him. "This baby is coming fast," she whispered, taking a step towards the bed.

Granite caught her hand. "You've got this."

She nodded once. "Stay close in case I need you, please." Her eyes were pleading.

Something in him seized up for a second or two. "I need to stay out of the way but I'm not going anywhere."

"Thank you," she whispered.

Granite realized that he was still holding her hand. He gave a nod and let her go.

He watched as Breeze moved onto her haunches. Volcano had her gown bunched around her hips. Granite sucked in a deep breath. He stuck his head out the door.

"How is she?" the healer asked.

"Doing as well as can be expected," Granite answered. He turned to Rock and rattled off a list of supplies. "Knock once and leave them outside the door."

Next, Granite got to work preparing a fire. Breeze was pushing. Both Volcano and the doctor were saying words of encouragement. Volcano was behind Breeze, holding her up, supporting her every step of the way. He envied the love they had for one another. It had been that way since the day they met. Not that they accepted it initially. Sometimes people didn't see what was right in front of them.

The human had her head between Breeze's thighs. "The baby's head is crowning," her voice was animated.

"He or she has a mop of black hair."

Breeze choked out a sob. "I can't believe this is happening."

"Shhhh. Lean back on me." Volcano held onto his mate.

All too soon, the next birth pains hit. Breeze pushed again.

"You need to stop pushing while the head crowns."

Breeze growled loudly.

"Stop pushing," the human urged.

"Can't," Breeze growled loudly. "Ohhhh. . . . Argghhh . . ." Her voice was so deep. Her skin became scaly for a second and smoke drifted from her mouth and nostrils.

Breeze gave a euphoric yell.

"Oh god!" Louise shouted. When Granite looked again, the doctor was holding a tiny baby. His niece or nephew. Granite felt his eyes sting. Emotion filled him. His throat felt clogged.

"My baby," Breeze said, her voice hoarse. "Give me my whelp."

"What's happening? Our child . . ." Volcano held onto his weeping mate. "Please . . ." his voice cracked.

Louise grabbed one of the towels he had put on the bed. She dipped into her bag and removed some kind of suction device which she used on the little one's mouth and nose. She rubbed the baby with the towel.

The whelp was tiny. So damn small. *Fuck!*

"What's happening?" Volcano yelled.

"Volcano! Please! My baby . . . Give me my baby . . ."

Breeze's voice was so weak, she was trying to tear herself from his arms.

"I just need to—" the doctor muttered as she kept working.

Granite could hear the tiny heart flutter, could hear the small intake of breath. There was a barely audible cry followed by another intake of breath. "You have a little girl. Congratulations." He could hear the emotion in Louise's voice. The baby gave another cry, stronger this time.

Breeze began to laugh through her tears. "She sounds healthy." Volcano moved, allowing his mate to sit down on the bed.

"I need to check her over. Give me a minute." The doctor continued to fuss over the whelp. "She's pink and breathing well. She's active, these are all good signs."

Granite inched closer. He could see his niece's legs kicking. Louise looked his way, she gave him a broad smile before looking back down at the whelp. He couldn't help but smile as well. The whelp looked like she was going to be fine.

"The good news is that she's not caked in vernix; it's that white waxy stuff on her skin. The more premature the baby the more vernix. Also, she isn't covered in much body hair. She's way smaller than I expected but she looks healthy. Here," Louise wrapped the baby in one of the cotton blankets. "Skin to skin would be best." Volcano helped his mate take off her gown and the doctor handed the little one to Breeze. "Lay her on your chest. I'm going to give her some oxygen just as a precaution."

Breeze had tears streaming down her face. His brother did too. Granite swallowed down a lump. If he wasn't careful he'd be next. The human turned on the oxygen. She checked to make sure that the bag was inflating and handed the mask to Volcano. "Put it in front of her face like this." She lay the mask an inch or two in front of the squirming whelp.

Granite was about to go and stoke the fire when Louise stood up and turned to him.

"Congratulations!" She walked over and gripped him in a hug. So small and soft. The scent of peaches and cream surrounded him. He circled her tiny waist and hugged her back. "You're an uncle," she said the words against his chest. His heart gave a squeeze.

"Thank you," his voice was husky with emotion. His eyes still pricked. *Fuck!*

She released him. Granite kept his hands on her hips. A whole lot more of her curls had escaped. Her eyes glinted with excitement, her lips were a darker shade of pink from all the chewing on them. The fire flickered against her bright tendrils. The air seemed to seize in his lungs. Louise's pupils dilated.

Breeze groaned, the sound laced with pain.

"I'm needed," Louise said, under her breath.

Granite released her.

"It's only the afterbirth, the placenta. I'm not sure what it's called in dragon speak," she spoke as she walked back to the bed.

Breeze shook her head. "No!" she groaned again, louder this time.

"My mate is having twins," Volcano announced.

"Twins?" Louise shrieked. "Why didn't I know about this?" Much calmer although he could hear the underlying emotion. "Why didn't anyone bother to tell me?" Her pissed gaze landed on him. Her eyes narrowed.

CHAPTER 13

Twins.
Oh god!

Don't panic! Stay calm. Baby 1 was doing really well. She was pink and active and breathing.

Baby 1! "Granite!" she tried not to yell. "You could have told me," she struggled to sound normal, which was difficult when her teeth were clenched tight.

He moved towards the bed, taking big strides. "We are Earth."

"Get out!" Breeze screamed. "Out!" Her eyes were wide. Scales appeared beneath her skin and her pupils became reptile like for a moment. It was weird.

"I need you to take the baby." She gestured to the infant on Breeze's chest.

"No!" Breeze snapped.

"Let Granite take her," Volcano spoke in a soothing voice.

"No!" Breeze's body folded as her next contraction took her. She grit her teeth. The infant began to slide off of her chest. Volcano picked up the tiny baby and handed her to Granite.

"Go and sit by the fire. Not too close though," Louise instructed.

The infant looked minute in his big hands. He seemed awkward as he cradled her against his chest.

"Take the oxygen with you. Keep the mask—"

"I saw," he grunted.

"Skin to skin. She needs to stay warm. Call me if her breathing changes or if her color changes. Any change . . . you call me."

He gave a deep nod. "I will take care of the whelp. You look after Breeze."

The shifter female was still in the grips of the contraction. Louise could hear as she breathed through it.

Twins. Oh lord! Twin pregnancies were much higher risk. No wonder she'd gone into labor a bit early. It was normal for a multiple gestation. Vaginal births were also not without their risk. Baby 2 was normally the higher risk of the two.

Breeze fell back as her contraction subsided. Volcano was whispering words of encouragement. The guy was phenomenal. It was clear to see that the two of them loved one another.

"Do you know if the babies are fraternal or identical?" She saw their blank stares. "Identical twins don't always have their own sac. Never mind."

Volcano gave Breeze some water. She was shaking again. "I feel that same pushing feeling."

"It looks like we won't have to wait long." It was a good

thing. The longer it took to birth the second baby, the higher the risk. Particularly for a twin birth where the twins were identical. There was a possibility they had shared the same amniotic sac and placenta.

Louise checked for bleeding. Aside from some amniotic fluid, there was nothing. When there was placenta abruption, there was normally a ton of fresh blood. Everything looked normal.

"I need to push," Breeze tried to get up. She was very weak.

"You can do this," Louise looked her in the eyes.

Breeze gave a nod. Volcano was there, supporting his wife with his own body. She pushed her chin into her chest and pushed. The baby crowned immediately.

"The little one has a head of black hair as well," Louise said.

Breeze kept on pushing but the infant's head sucked back. It was normal. She slumped onto Volcano while they waited for the next contraction.

It was on the third one that the baby spilled out in a gush of fluid. Baby 2 was a bit bigger than Baby 1. "Another girl." She grabbed a towel and began to massage. Then she suctioned the infant's airways. The baby gave a solid yell. A carbon copy of her sister.

Like before, Breeze was laughing and crying.

"She looks good," Louise said as she watched the infant punch with her fists and legs. Not in the least bit impressed with what was happening. Her skin was a healthy pink. She gave another yell, louder this time. Then she sucked in a lungful of air. It was one of the best sounds Louise had ever heard.

She realized that her hands were shaking a tad. Her eyes felt moist. *Flip, she was crying.* Not very professional. She realized in that moment how afraid she had been. She'd delivered multiples before. Most had been fine. *Most.* She wiped the tears away.

Louise handed the infant to her mother. Breeze cradled the little one to her chest. Volcano was openly crying. He looked up at her. "Thank you." He gripped her hand and held it for a moment. "Thank you," he repeated.

"My pleasure." And then Granite was there.

He nestled the tiny baby in his strong arms, against his chest. There was a goofy smile on his face. He'd never looked sexier. She had to look away for a moment. "She's fast asleep," he announced, handing the baby to Volcano.

"I'll go and stoke the fire." He sniffed as he walked away. It seemed that the big, bad shifter king had a sensitive side. Maybe there was more to him. He wasn't just a rude, bossy asshole after all.

Louise checked on Baby 1. Her coloring was good. Her breathing was fine. She released a pent-up breath.

"She looks hungry," Volcano announced.

"This is so strange and unnatural," Breeze said, her eyes were bloodshot. There were dark smudges beneath them.

"I will be outside if you need me," Granite announced. He closed the door behind him.

"Are you talking about breast-feeding?" Louise frowned.

Breeze gave a nod. "You Earth dragons are weird."

"Hey," Volcano chuckled, "you just birthed two Earth dragons and you are mated to one."

Breeze smiled back. Volcano brushed a kiss against her lips.

Louise cleared her throat. "I'll be outside as well." She felt like she was intruding on a special family moment.

"No," Breeze sounded panicked. "You have to help me."

"Sure," Louise said.

Volcano was grinning broadly.

"How do I feed them? They need to suck on my mammary glands. Humans have a lot of experience in this." She pulled a face.

"Breastfeeding is very natural," Louise said.

Breeze shook her head. "Earth dragons are the only of our species who feed using these." She squeezed one of her swollen breasts. "I wouldn't know how to even start. They need to suck on my nipples?" She was frowning deeply. She sounded shocked and a bit taken aback.

Louise smiled. "I've helped women before. Don't worry about a thing." She took in a deep breath. "I need to stay close for the next day or two to monitor the three of you. By the time I go, you'll be a pro at it, I promise." She turned to Volcano. "Please, can you fetch us some diapers and some hats for the babies. We need to keep them warm."

"I can't thank you enough." Breeze looked like she was on the verge of tears again. Then she looked down at the bundles of joy in her arms and smiled. Louise could physically feel the love pass between mother and child. In that moment, she'd never felt lonelier or more empty.

CHAPTER 14

Two days later...

A knock sounded at the door.

Granite closed his laptop. "Come in." He frowned, he had no appointments booked.

Sand stuck his head around the jamb. "Can I come in?"

Granite gave a nod. "Take a seat," he gestured to the chair on the opposite side of his desk.

His brother did as he asked. "You said to inform you if the human makes contact with the outside world."

Granite kept his eyes on Sand. He trusted the human. He wasn't sure why but he did. "That's right."

"She continues to look at her Facebook account. She hasn't posted in over a year though."

"Okay." Despite trusting her, he found himself growing impatient. "Who did she contact?"

"A male," Sand frowned. "She has arranged to meet with him this weekend. I wasn't aware that the human healer was going to Walton Springs."

"Well, she is." His heart beat faster. At long last she was

doing what he had instructed. It should feel good, instead, it irritated him. No, it worried him. She was an asset to his people, to all of the dragon shifters, all the non-humans for that matter, particularly if she managed to cure their affliction.

"You look worried," Sand continued to frown. He scrutinized Granite.

"No, it's fine! She mentioned that she was going to contact the male, I must have forgotten about it." He gave a casual shrug even though he felt turmoil inside. "I take it the male responded?" What he really wanted to know was where they were meeting and when.

Sand narrowed his eyes at him. He looked suspicious. The male gave a nod of the head. "Yes, she's going to contact him on Saturday when she gets to town. He's keeping his evening open," his brother smirked.

I'll fucking bet.

"Would you like a copy of the correspondence?"

Fuck, yes! "No," he growled the word. "It won't be necessary. Keep monitoring her internet activity, inform me of anything serious."

"Sure thing."

"Are you sure you're okay? You seem," Sand paused, "out of sorts."

"I'm tired," Granite answered truthfully.

Sand laughed. "And a bit highly strung. I saw your name down for this weekend."

"Yeah." Right now he couldn't muster any type of enthusiasm.

"Don't look so excited about it. I'll take your place," his brother smiled.

"No chance. I can't fucking wait!" Granite grinned. It would be good to get out. Good to unwind. "Are you sure you can handle it here?"

"Absolutely! Besides, Volcano just became a father, he's not an invalid. The male can step in if need be."

The new family was doing really well. His tiny nieces were thriving. Louise had a big hand in it. She spent the first twelve hours at Breeze's side monitoring the three of them. She still called in several times a day. She'd even tried to get out of going this weekend but he'd put a stop to that line of thinking. Things would calm down around here come Monday. He couldn't fucking wait for that to happen.

"You'll be fine," Granite said. "Keep a close eye on the human and forward any further correspondence directly to me . . . to save time," he quickly added the last. He didn't want Sand to get the wrong impression. It was his duty as king to keep close tabs on the human.

CHAPTER 15

Saturday night . . .

"You, my darling and dearest friend, are a chicken." Hillary poked her in the ribs.

"I know. I know." Louise screwed her eyes shut. "I feel awful. Worse than awful. I reached out to him and then I stood him up. Poor Todd!" Louise groaned. "I don't know what's wrong with me. He's such a sweet guy. He's polite and most of all, he seems to be really interested in me."

"Lots of guys are interested, you just don't seem to notice."

"Well, there had better be one who's interested tonight because I'm getting laid, so help me god." *It was going to happen. It was going to happen. It was!*

Hillary raised her brows and just stared at her like she was something the cat dragged in.

"What?" Louise said.

Hillary gave her the once-over, she had a stern look on her face. "Some guys like the school mistress look, but if you're serious about going out there to find sex, then you need an outfit that screams 'available.'"

"There is nothing wrong with what I'm wearing." Louise looked down at her well thought-out clothing.

Hillary blew out a breath and pulled a face. "Are you kidding me? You're wearing a blouse."

"What's wrong with that?"

"A better question would be what's right with the thing?" Her eyes tracked the garment in question. "You have the buttons done up all the way up to your neck." Hillary gave an eye roll. Her friend undid the top four buttons. Hillary paused, she could see that she was thinking it over. "On second thought, take the blouse off."

"What? You're nuts."

"You're wearing a really cute camisole underneath. It even has lace trimming."

"It's an undergarment, Hills. Meant to be worn *under* clothing," Louise annunciated every word like she was speaking to a child.

"It would be perfectly acceptable as a top. Women wear camisoles as tops all the time. I mean, look at you," she lifted her brows. "You have perfect breasts."

"They're small."

"Rubbish! They are most definitely there without being ridiculously huge. You could probably go braless and get away with it."

"Hold on there!" Louise put up a hand. "Let's not get ahead of ourselves here."

"That pencil skirt is really cute, it shows off your narrow waist but it's really long. You need to either cut the skirt shorter or lose the blouse. I vote for the blouse to go." Her eyes widened and she looked excited. "You would look ultra-cute in the skirt with the camisole. Those boots are perfect. John calls them 'fuck me' boots. I'm guaranteed sex if I wear mine. He can't keep his hands off of me, he—"

"Too much info, Hills," Louise laughed. "Far too much."

"You will fit right in where we're going tonight."

"We're not going to that cocktail bar . . . I would hate to run into Todd." Louise shuddered at the thought. She'd feel awful for dropping him after promising she'd call. Make that dropping him a second time.

"Nope, it's a small bar on the edge of town that buzzes on a Saturday night. Apparently it's *the* hook-up hot spot."

Louise gripped Hillary's arm. "Thanks so much for helping me."

"What are friends for?"

"You are the best."

"You do realize that you're not going to be able to sleep with a guy and just walk away, right?"

"Of course I will!" Louise snorted.

"How many one night stands have you had then?"

"Um . . ." Louise pretended to think about it.

Hillary burst out laughing.

"One!" Louise shouted.

"Really?" Hillary folded her arms.

"That new boy in our senior year."

"The two of you kissed at a house party." Hillary

looked disgusted.

Louise nodded like mad. "Exactly."

"You kissed . . . you didn't go the whole hog," Hillary was smiling broadly.

"Yeah . . . and kissing in high school is the equivalent of sex now. Besides, he touched my ass."

Hillary laughed. "Yeah and if I remember correctly you were heartbroken for weeks because he started dating Jenny right after."

"Trevor was a total douche."

"See," Hillary pointed at her. "You even remember his name after all these years. You totally would've dated him if he had asked you out."

Louise shook her head. "No way!"

"Don't talk shit!"

"Okay, alright? Okay. I would've dated him but I'm older and wiser and I can have meaningless, really great sex and leave it at that. I'm going to have meaningless really great sex with no strings attached. Besides, even if I wanted a relationship, I'm leaving tomorrow. It wouldn't work. Long distance relationships never do."

"Okay," Hillary sounded skeptical. "If you say so, Lou."
"

"I do say so."

"And, you're serious about this whole hook-up thing?"

Louise nodded. She'd never been more serious in her whole life.

Hillary reached up past Louise and pulled her hair loose.

"Hey!" Louise gripped her errant curls, trying to tame them. "I can't go anywhere looking like this."

Hillary grabbed her hands. "Do you trust me?"

Louise rolled her eyes. "That's a trick question."

"Do you trust me?" Hillary squeezed her hands and spoke with more conviction.

Louise made a groaning noise. "I'm going to regret this, but yes I trust you."

"Forget the blouse and forget your hair, it needs to be loose. You'll look amazing! Those guys aren't going to know what's hit them. They'll be falling all over themselves to get at you."

Granite gestured to the bartender for another beer. The drink was placed in front of him a few moments later with a clunk.

He leaned back against the dark wood and scanned the room. It was a small establishment. There was an upper level sitting area, a dance floor and the bar. The place was jam-packed. It was like this every Saturday without fail.

Females visited just in case the 'special ops' guys were in town. Namely, them, the shifters. The various tribes all took turns and then not every eligible male would go at once. Smaller groups frequented the bar almost every Saturday night.

As per usual, there were far more females than males in attendance. All hoping to snag themselves one of the Special Forces males. There was also a large number of human males, hoping to pick up the leftovers. Of which there were plenty. There were half-dressed females everywhere. At least half a dozen tried to catch his eye as he continued to give the place the once-over.

Thing was, Granite wasn't feeling it. Not even one bit. It pissed him off.

"Hey! Are you listening?" The human female beside him gave his arm a tug.

"Ah . . . yeah." He locked eyes with her.

She gave him a wide smile. The female was very pretty. She was tall and curvy. Her hair was blond and fell down her back to just below her shoulder blades. She had an easy smile and a relaxed disposition. "I asked if you were enjoying yourself."

"I'm enjoying myself just fine." He was bored to death and couldn't understand why.

The side of her mouth tipped up. "What is my name?"

"Why is that relevant?"

"You should at least know a girl's name if you're going to take her home."

He couldn't help but smile. Granite liked her candor. He still wasn't feeling it though. "Is that right?"

"Yeah, it most certainly is." She licked her lips. They were a bright and fiery red.

Why was he delaying? He'd sworn to himself that he would grab the first single, willing female and be done with it. Here she was.

"It's Jessica, Jess for short."

Granite gave a nod.

"You're supposed to tell me your name. That's how this

works."

He picked up his beer and took a swig. The female pulled her lower lip into her mouth as she watched his throat work. He set the beer down and gave another slow nod.

After a long paused she continued. "Then you buy me a drink and we talk."

Talk? Nope. She could forget that.

"We'll laugh and then you'll whisper something really dirty into my ear." Her pupils dilated. He could scent her arousal. It did sweet fuck all to his own libido.

The fuck?

He took another sip and folded his arms, his eyes on her big blue orbs. "Then we'll high-tail it out of here. You won't be able to keep your hands off of me in the back of the cab. We'll kiss. We'll—"

A flash of red at the door caught his attention. Bright red. *No way!* Curly red. *No fucking way.*

It was the little doctor. She laughed at something her friend was saying. Her hair. By Claw, it hung down her back, thick and heavily curled in tight spirals. It seemed brighter somehow. It was the kind of hair a male might fist during rutting. It was definitely that kind of hair. The wild kind.

She was wearing more than most of the females in this place, yet she was half-naked in comparison with her normal attire. Her breasts. Fucking perfection. Like two ripe peaches. Soft and small but big enough to suck and squeeze on. His dick woke up.

The fuck?

"Hey . . ." Someone leaned in against him. "Are you listening? It's rude not to listen when a girl is telling you exactly what she plans on doing to you."

He glanced down at the pretty blonde and then back at the doctor.

Louise's eyes widened and she took a step back. She'd recognized one or two of his males. She'd realized where she was.

Smack bang in the middle of the Stag Run.

It was funny how her eyes zoned in on him. It happened immediately, like she could feel him staring. Recognition flared in their depths.

Then she turned back towards the door. *Fuck!* She was going to leave. Her friend grabbed her by the arm and spun her back around.

"What's up? What's wrong?" Concern etched her voice.

"Um . . . I can't be here." Louise's eyes tracked back to him and then quickly back to her friend when she caught him still watching. "We're going," she ground out. "Now." There was a pleading edge to her voice.

"Why?"

"Please, just trust me on this. Please don't argue," quickly delivered.

The other female gave a nod and they made their way to the door.

Not a fuck!

"Hey, big guy . . ." the blonde cooed, putting a hand on

his chest. "What's going on inside that head of yours? A girl might get worried."

"I prefer women." Granite extricated himself from the female's grip. "Have a good evening."

Her mouth fell open but he didn't give a shit.

Without overthinking it, he moved towards the exit. He needed to speak with the little doctor. She shouldn't leave on their account, on his account. That was bullshit. She had just as much right to be here as anyone else. Besides, at least if she stayed he could keep an eye on her. He realized that he'd been worried about her out with some asshole male. Nope, she was staying right here, right under his nose

CHAPTER 16

Fifteen minutes earlier . . .

"The Cockpit. The place is seriously called The Cockpit?" Louise had to laugh.

An engine revved as the cab pulled away from the curb, leaving them stranded. She could hear the sound of music and laughter coming from inside the bar.

It seemed to be really busy even though it was only nine o'clock.

"Apparently, and if the gossip is to be believed, some Special Forces guys are here almost every weekend. They're big and buff and raring to go."

Her mind immediately wandered to Granite but she pushed thoughts of him away. The guy was probably already doing the horizontal mumbo jumbo with some or other bimbo. She smoothed down her skirt and took a deep breath.

"Ready?" Hillary bobbed her eyebrows.

"Yeah."

"Well you look gorgeous."

Louise grabbed Hillary's hand and gave it a squeeze. "Thanks again. I know you have better places to be on a Saturday night."

"Are you kidding, I never get to go out anymore. Not to places like this. You know how much I love people watching." She gave Louise a wide smile.

"Now let's get in there before we freeze."

Louise nodded and they headed into the bar. The place was bursting at the seams. There were so many scantily clad women it was obscene. There were also truckloads of guys.

Hillary turned to her. "Wow!" Her eyes were wide. "You can't possibly leave here alone. I think we just arrived at Candy Land." She clutched her chest dramatically. "Oh my god but there are some gorgeous guys in here."

Louise laughed, looking in the same direction Hillary was looking. A couple of buff guys stood at the bar.

Wow! Not bad. Maybe there was a football convention in town or something because . . . Wait a minute . . . wait just a—

No!

No way!

Louise took a step back as she realized that one of the guys was Igneous. Suddenly the guy next to him looked familiar as well.

Special ops guys?

The Stag Run!

OMG! That meant that Granite was here as well. She

felt her skin prickle, her whole body felt hot. She turned her head and there he was. His dark eyes were on her, his face impassive.

He wore a plain, white t-shirt and faded jeans. It was nuts but he was actually more attractive somehow with his torso covered. Maybe because she knew what was underneath those clothes.

There was a woman talking into his ear. With those long legs and narrow waist, she had to be a model. Her hair was blonde and so straight it was sickening. She turned to her side, showing a curvy silhouette. Make that a swimsuit model.

She had to get the hell out of there and right now. Louise turned to make an escape.

Someone grabbed her arm and twisted her back around. It was Hillary. She'd forgotten all about her friend in her haste to beat a retreat. "What's up? What's wrong?"

"Um . . . I can't be here." It was like her eyes were drawn to him. The blonde was pressed against him, still talking. His gaze was still firmly on her. The temperature went up another few degrees. "We're going." Louise looked Hillary in the eye. "Now!" she all but begged.

"Why?"

"Please, just trust me on this. Please don't argue." *Please listen to me. Please.*

Thankfully Hillary nodded. Louise huffed out a breath and made for the exit like her ass was on fire.

Once outside, she leaned up against the wall next to the door and gulped in some air.

"What's wrong?"

"I'm suddenly not feeling well. Please, can we go?" Louise pushed off from the wall, already pulling her cellphone out of her purse to call a cab.

Her friend narrowed her eyes and scrutinized her face. "I'm not buying it. What's going on?"

"Those special forces guys in there." Louise pointed her thumb to the door behind them.

"Yeah?" By the spark that had appeared in Hillary's eye, she could tell that her friend knew where this was going.

"Well, they're the same group of guys I share a barracks with. I'm working with them. There might even be one or two of my patients in there." *Granite is here!* Adrenaline rushed through her. "I can't talk about that though. It's..."

"Confidential... Yeah, yeah." Her eyes lit up like the fourth of July. "He's here isn't he?"

"I don't know who you're talking about," Louise tried to feign ignorance.

"The guy you have a thing for."

"I do not—"

The door to the bar opened and noise flooded outside along with a man. A really big man. A man who stole the air from her lungs and made the ground feel shaky just from one look.

His dark, intense eyes narrowed on her as the door closed behind him. "Doctor," his voice was deep.

Hillary grabbed her chest and... swooned. It looked like she might fall over.

Louise ignored her friend. "Granite," she tried to keep her voice even. Thank god it worked.

Hillary made a soft squeaking noise in the back of her throat when she realized who he was. When she realized that she had been right in her assumptions.

Granite narrowed his eyes. "Where are you going? You only just got here."

"Um . . ." *Flip, why did he even care?* He should be happy she was leaving. "I just thought I would . . . get out of everyone's hair. I didn't realize . . ." she let the sentence die.

Granite frowned. *Wow!* He was so hot. The jeans hugged his thighs like a second skin and the white t-shirt pulled tight around his chest and biceps. His chest markings were just visible above the V of his collar.

"Bullshit!" a low growl. Louise was sure that Hillary swooned again. She even put the back of her hand to her forehead. Granite took a step towards her. "You are more than welcome to stay. You have every right to be here. Don't leave on account of . . . us."

"Yeah, but . . ." All the guys were all here to hook up. Then again, so was she. It felt weird though. "I don't want to get in the way of anything or . . ." She didn't want to see him with that other woman. Any woman for that matter. She *was* jealous. How had this happened? "You didn't have to run out here and leave your date. Go back, go do your thing." She shooed him with her hands, feeling like a complete idiot.

"That female is not my date. I've never dated

anyone . . . ever." He opened and closed his hands a few times. It made his biceps pop. "I don't date," he added.

"Oh! Well, date or no date, you left her all alone in there."

"She is an adult and can take care of herself. It's freezing out here." His gaze drifted down. Her already hard nipples hardened up a whole lot more. Goosebumps popped up all over her body and it wasn't just because of the temperature.

His dark eyes flashed back to hers. "You should go back inside before you catch a cold or something."

"I . . . I don't know about staying," she stammered, feeling off kilter. She had a thing for Granite. *Shit!* She had a thing for him. This was not good.

Granite gave a shrug. "It's up to you. I think you should come back in but if you wish to leave then, go ahead," he gestured towards the road.

"Maybe we should just stay. I'm Hillary by the way." She held her hand out to Granite.

Granite turned to Hillary, he looked down at her outstretched hand and back up to her face before finally taking it. "Granite."

She grinned like a fool. Louise rolled her eyes. Hillary kept on shaking his hand with no letup in sight. She looked star-struck "You can let go now, Hills."

"Oh yeah!" She dropped his hand. "Sorry!" Hillary was blushing wildly.

"See you later." He looked at her, his expression was unreadable. Then he was gone, swallowed by the noise and laughter.

"Oh my god!" Hillary covered her mouth with both her hands. Then she jumped up and down like a nine-year-old girl. "He's so hot! Oh, my god . . . you were right about that. I think my panties might be wet."

"Hillary!" her voice was laced with shock.

"You're going back in there."

Louise shook her head. "Nah, that wouldn't be a good idea. I just . . ."

"He really likes you."

"More like the other way around," she mumbled. Granite liked the way she smelled, she almost laughed out loud at the absurdity of it.

Hillary gasped. "I knew it! You *like* like the guy."

"Maybe . . . I think it's more of a lust thing. He still irritates the shit out of me on most days. We would fight like mad if we ever got together – not that it would ever happen."

"Just think of the make-up sex."

"Even if I wanted to start something with him, he doesn't date and I would lose my job. It ain't going to happen. Let's just go." She implored Hillary with her eyes and wrapped her arms around herself. It was darned cold.

Hillary made a noise of frustration. "No! Let's just stay. Forget about Granite. There are so many yummy guys here."

Hillary was right. Granite had gone back inside, back to his blonde bombshell. He was going to get lucky tonight. The thought angered her. She hated feeling so jealous. The best thing she could do was meet someone and take the plunge herself. She needed this. More than anything, she needed to forget him. Louise gave a nod. "Okay, but we stay away from . . ." she almost said *the shifters,* "the special forces guys."

Hillary clapped her hands. "Oh goody! Let's go and get a drink."

They made their way through the throngs of people. Louise kept her gaze front and center. She was going to try to forget that Granite was there. She wasn't going to look over at that side of the bar. She didn't want to see that swimsuit model draped all over him, or, even worse, see him leave with her. They might even already be gone. For a second or two, she was tempted to look but she managed to stop herself at the last second.

Hillary found a space at the bar and raised her hand to the bartender. She ordered them some ciders.

"Hey, Doc!" It was Igneous. He put up a hand and grinned broadly. There was another shifter standing next to him who nodded at her.

"Hi!" She didn't want to get into a conversation. They were staying away from the shifters.

"Good to see you." There were a couple of ladies hanging around the guys. Two of them gave her the stink eye. A third acted like she couldn't care. Like she was too cool for entire world.

Hurry up, Hills!

"Good to see you too. Are you having a good time?" Lame question.

Igneous nodded. "Most definitely." The shifter let his eyes slide down her body. *Oh no!* "You look different, Doc. Really different." He lifted his brows as his eyes locked back with hers.

"Yeah, well . . ." she didn't expand, gave a small shrug instead.

"I like it." He looked at her lips. The ones she had recently applied some Super Stay Caramel kisses lipstick to. It was overkill. Total overkill. The lipstick together with the eyeliner and mascara. Sure, her eyes looked huge and her lips as well, but heck, it was overkill. She should have left it at lip gloss and some blush for her cheeks.

"Thanks," she smiled. The bartender finally brought the drinks and Hillary paid. *Thank god!*

"No really." Igneous took a step towards her. "It's good to see you out of that coat. I didn't know you had such a banging body."

He did not just say that!

She gave a small, tense, smile.

"And your hair." His eyes widened and he made a groaning sound. "It's striking," he nodded, suddenly more serious. "You should wear it like this more often." He reached out to touch one of her curls.

A low growl sounded.

Igneous instantly pulled his hand back like he had been burned.

One of the ladies giggled, they all blushed. She had heard that growl before. Her back prickled. Louise slowly turned.

"I think you males have something better to do," he spoke so low that she could hardly hear him. She may have lip read what he was saying.

Granite turned his gaze to her for a moment. "Glad you changed your mind." Before she could answer, he headed to the bar.

A lady bartender pretty much dropped what she was doing in favor of serving him. Of course she did. Look at him. *Just freaking look* . . .

No!

She tore her eyes away. He was buying drinks for his non-date. His booty-call.

"Hey." Hillary handed her one of the drinks and then linked arms with her. "Let's go find us some single guys."

"You're married, Hills," Louise smiled.

"Of course I am. The guys are for you."

"Guys . . . Really? I don't think so. One is enough for me." All she wanted to do was turn back towards Granite. Was the bartender flirting with him? Was he flirting with her? She couldn't picture Granite flirting. Not in the conventional way anyhow.

"Let's go then," Hillary said, dragging her away.

Louise stopped dead. "No way! Isn't that . . ."

"It's Todd," Hillary whispered. "What the hell is he doing here?"

"Oh my word! He had better not see me." They were rooted to the spot. Todd was with the same group of guys he had been with the previous week. There were one or two ladies in the group as well.

"Let's back up," Hillary whispered. "Slowly," she added as Todd turned his head. Towards them. His eyes lit with recognition.

Damn!

Then he smiled. Smiled. Something eased in her. He wasn't mad that she had dropped him for a second time. "Hi Todd!" She could hear that Hillary was smiling.

"Hi!" He walked over to them. "Good to see you." He gave Hillary a hug and then hugged her too, adding a kiss on the cheek. "This is a surprise. So good to see you." He let his eyes linger on her before turning to Hillary.

"You too," she mumbled. It *was* good to see him. It reminded her of how cute he was and how sweet. What was wrong with her? Why wasn't she feeling anything? "Um . . . Todd, about not calling . . ."

"Forget about it," he said. "We're here now aren't we?"

She smiled. "Yeah, we are." Todd really was cute in his button-up shirt and dark blue jeans. His hair had that just styled look.

"What can I get you ladies to drink?" he turned his head to Hillary as he asked. How attentive to include her friend. He was such a nice guy. Louise was going to make more of an effort this time.

CHAPTER 17

Granite couldn't keep his eyes off of her. He tried to force himself to look around the room, to choose someone else, but he couldn't. His gaze kept moving back to her. An hour and a half passed and adrenaline still coursed through him. First Igneous and now the human. He felt his blood heat in his veins. If he wasn't careful smoke would come out of his nose.

Igneous was one thing. At least he could warn the male off. *Fucker!* If he allowed him to continue on that particular path, half his males would be sniffing around her in no time.

Look at her. Just damn well look. She threw her head back and laughed at something the human was saying. The sound was so fresh, so free. Her wild, beautiful hair tumbled about her shoulders and down her back. The color made her stand out head and shoulders above the rest even though she was a tiny thing.

The male whispered something in her ear and she laughed again. What a little pussy he was. Not much of a warrior. Not much of anything, yet she hung onto his every word.

Who knew that hiding beneath that coat was a body a male could kill for. His hands curled into fists and he had to force himself to unclench them.

"Wow!" a female whispered in his ear. She gave his bicep a squeeze – or tried to at any rate. "Do you want to get out of here?"

He shook his head without even looking at her. "Not with you, I don't," he rasped.

The female stomped off. Her heels clacking on the tiled floor. He couldn't bring it in himself to care.

"Why don't you go over and talk to her?"

"What?" It was Rock. The male looked amused. "What the fuck are you talking about?"

"The human. You are clearly taken with her."

"I'm not taken with her," he snapped. "Okay," he shrugged, "maybe I'd like to fuck her, it doesn't mean I'm taken with her though."

Rock grinned. "Whatever. You should go over there."

Granite shook his head. "She looks perfectly happy with that human."

"Bull!" Rock gave a chuckle. "I've seen the way she looks at you." The male put up a hand. "Before you get all weird, she looks at you with lust-filled eyes, not starry ones. She wants you to fuck her just as much as you want to give it to her."

"Yeah right!" He put his warm beer down on the bar. "She hasn't looked at me once since coming back inside."

Rock nodded. "Exactly."

Granite waited for a few beats but Rock decided not to explain the statement. "What the fuck do you mean by that?" His temper was already flared.

Rock laughed and he had to fight the urge to punch the prick. Pop him one right in the nose. He clenched his teeth instead. "She hasn't looked at you once. Not once. Isn't that a bit strange?" He widened his eyes. "She's purposefully not looking because she's into you . . . She wants you . . . sexually . . . that much I can tell you."

"Aren't you hooking up tonight?" Granite asked as the male put his arm around Louise's waist. *Fuck!* His blood was almost at boiling point. He could feel it simmering.

"Nah!" Rock drew his attention back. "My heart is taken. The only reason I am here is because Quartz insisted that I go."

A laugh was torn from Granite. "Unbe-fucking-lievable! You and Quartz?"

"Yeah."

"I take it she hasn't agreed to mating you yet though."

"It's just a matter of time."

Granite nodded.

"Um . . . my lord." Rock was looking in the direction of the doctor.

"Yeah?" He tried to sound bored even though he was anything but. He refused to follow the male's gaze. He'd stared enough for one day.

"They're leaving," Rock sounded a touch panicked. "That human and your female."

"She's not mine," he rasped, his eyes moving to the

three of them. Sure enough, they were walking towards the door. He noticed how Louise kept her eyes on the door ahead. No looking left or right.

By Claw, Rock was right. At least, he hoped the male was right. He was about to find out.

"Take care," he rumbled as he made his way to the little doctor. There was no way he was letting her go without a fight. They both had one night, might as well put the time to good use.

****

They were going to Todd's place for coffee. They'd drop Hillary off first and then it was happening.

There was a tiny voice inside her that told her she couldn't go through with it but she forced it down. The closer they got to the door, the louder that voice became. She eventually stopped walking. "I just need to . . ." She was about to head to the ladies room to tell Hillary that she couldn't leave with Todd when a deep voice sounded behind them.

"Leaving so soon?" The rough yet smoky notes gave her shivers all over her body. Both she and Hillary turned. Todd walked on for a stride or two before turning around as well.

Flip! Why was he harassing her? Where was the blonde? "Yeah," she gave a nod, trying to sound nonchalant and failing. There was a definite edge to her voice. "We're heading out. Thanks for suggesting I come back in, turns out you were right." A bit more upbeat. She tried to force a smile but it quickly faded when Todd hooked an arm around her. She didn't like possessive bullshit on the best of days, let alone when a guy hardly knew her.

Louise forced herself to stay put when what she really wanted was to shrug out of his grasp. Granite looked down at where Todd's hand curled around her waist. His frown deepened and he seemed to bristle. His muscles bulged. Especially the thick ropes on either side of his neck. "I need a word," his eyes lifted back to hers.

He tried to run her life at work, which was pretty much all the time. She might find him ridiculously attractive but she sure as nuts wasn't going to let him walk all over her here too. Louise squared her shoulders. "Can't it wait until Monday?"

Granite shook his head. "No!"

It was a simple word. She waited for him to elaborate and was just about to tell him to go to hell when Hillary stepped forward. "You go. This looks serious. I'll keep Todd company for a minute or two."

Todd shook his head and Granite's jaw tightened.

"Actually . . ." Todd cleared his throat. His eyes had a frightened look but who could blame him. "We were just . . ."

Granite's hands clenched at his side. His muscles popped some more. His jaw tightened.

Oops! This was going downhill fast. Best she have a quick word with Granite. He obviously didn't like Todd. Maybe he did like more than just her scent. This seemed a lot like jealousy to her. Not that anyone had ever been jealous over her before. "Okay," she interrupted what

Todd was about to say. "I'll be right back." She glanced his way.

Todd's eyes widened and he sucked in a breath.

"Two minutes," she added. Louise walked to the other side of the room, Granite fell in next to her. She didn't owe Todd an explanation yet she still felt bad for leaving him standing there like that. "We need to make this quick," she turned to Granite as soon as they reached the wall. The place was still busy, only not as much as before. She noticed that many of the shifters had left already.

"Don't leave with that male," Granite said as his dark gaze locked with hers.

She gave an exasperated sigh. "Why not?" She didn't tell him she hadn't planned on it, that she'd changed her mind. "He's a really nice guy. We're going for coffee."

His mouth twitched but he quickly turned serious. "Coffee. Right."

"Look, you were the one who told me I needed . . ." She swallowed hard. "Not that I'm doing this because you told me to. Make that, you ordered me to. I'm not! You don't get to tell me what to do when it comes to my private life."

He clenched a hand around the back of his neck. His nostrils flared as he released a breath and dropped his arm back to his side. "I shouldn't have given you that directive and I shouldn't have called you stuck-up."

"No, you shouldn't have," she still used an argumentative tone because—*What? This was an about turn.* She hadn't expected him to say that. Louise looked around the room. "Where's your hot blonde?"

"I don't know and I don't care." He moved closer, only inches away. He smelled so darned good. Like the forest with a bit of musk and a lot of man. He also smelled like soap and freshly ironed laundry. "There is only one female who has my attention right now. That female is you."

Oh! Oooohhhh! Flip! Really? He was jealous! She schooled her emotions . . . or tried to. This shouldn't come as a surprise to her, but it did.

"Don't leave with that male. I want you to leave with me."

She laughed. It was short and a little bit hysterical. "I can't leave with you, Granite. Even if I wanted to I—"

"You can." He grabbed a handful of her hip and squeezed, pulling her closer as he did. There were only inches separating them.

Shit! His hand was on her. She felt its heat seep through her camisole. His hand. She could barely breathe. Definitely couldn't think straight. "But the contract. The clause . . ."

"That clause only applies on Dragon territory. You are not permitted to rut a male on Dragon land. I'm only permitted to rut a human on the Stag Run. There is nothing stopping us from—"

She shook her head. "We have to work together. We . . ." This wasn't happening.

"We're adults." He made a growling noise. It was laced with frustration. "We're attracted to one another. It's getting in the way of our working relationship. Don't even try to deny it."

She opened her mouth to do just that but shut it again. She couldn't, in all honestly, go against what he had just said. The air buzzed with sexual tension. She gripped her bottom lip between her teeth instead. Could she do this? Could they do this and have a good working relationship afterwards?

"Fuck, Louise." He leaned in, burying his face in her hair and sniffed. *Oh god!* He was sniffing her in deep breaths that had her heart-rate sky-rocketing. She felt each inhalation right between her thighs. It was also the way he said her name. His voice thick with need. It stripped away some more of her resolve. Made her brain turn mushy.

"I don't know if . . ."

"One night. Just one." His mouth was right by her ear. "I want to feel your body tighten around my cock when you come."

Holy mother of . . . She swallowed hard, finding it difficult to breathe.

She shuffled from one foot to the other. "Just like that, you went straight for the kill. No small talk, no dinner, no—"

"No!" a growl. "None of that shit. I'm giving it to you straight. We're both here tonight looking for a fuck."

As much as she wanted to deny it, she couldn't.

"I don't do flowery bullshit. I want to taste every inch of you. Touch you until you shake with need. I want to make you come more times than you ever knew possible."

Oh god! She actually felt something drip out of her at

that last admission. Her clit throbbed. That heavy sensation was back and she had a feeling it wasn't going to go away soon. She put a hand on his chest. She should push him away, she really should.

"I know you feel the same way. Don't fight this. I tried but it won't work. We're fucked if we don't do this now."

Yeah, working with him would be hell. Her hand gripped the material of his shirt. She couldn't take her eyes off of his. He had her tied up in knots.

"Louise," a low groan. The way he said her name almost had her coming right then and there.

She whimpered and he crushed his lips against hers. His other hand cupped her jaw as he deepened the kiss. Her toes curled. Her body pressed against his, almost of its own accord. Every nerve-ending buzzed. He released her moments later. She felt half-drunk and had to suck in a deep breath to bring herself back to her senses.

"So damned receptive. Let's get out of here."

She gave a nod. Was she really going to go through with this? *Yes.* Excitement coursed through her.

Oh hell! Todd. Her gaze shot back to the exit. There was no sign of him, only Hillary who was grinning like a maniac. She gave Louise a double thumbs up and Granite chuckled.

He took her hand. "Let's go."

"Todd left," Hillary said, as they walked up to her. "Um . . ." she glanced at Granite and then back at Louise. "I called a cab. It should be here any minute." Her grin grew wider.

"We can give you a lift." Granite pulled a set of keys out of his pocket.

Hillary gave a shake of the head. "I'm good."

"We'll walk you to your cab." It felt weird saying 'we,' like they were an item or something. They were not an item. Not even close. This was just one night.

Hillary gave a nod. "Sure."

They walked outside. *Damn, it was cold.* Granite put an arm around her and pulled her close. It is just sex. Just sex, she reminded herself. He was being nice because he was about to get some. The two of them didn't get along. They couldn't have a conversation without arguing. There was nothing more there than an attraction that just wouldn't quit. It was a good thing. There was no future for them. *One night.*

She chewed on her lower lip, feeling his heat, his hard body. His name suited him.

"I'll see you tomorrow," Hillary said. Louise realized that a cab had pulled up to the curb.

"No you won't," Granite said.

Hillary grinned some more. You would swear that she was the one going home with Granite. "No problem! I'll see you next time you're in town," she winked at Louise. *Winked!* Hillary didn't wink . . . ever. She was acting like a teenager. Then again, they both were.

Louise stepped forward and hugged her friend. "Thanks for everything."

"Enjoy yourself."

Despite the cold, Louise felt her cheeks heat. She didn't

answer. Instead, she watched while Hillary climbed into the cab and watched as the vehicle drove away.

"My car is this way." Granite slid his arm around her and led her to the parking lot. He headed for a black SUV and opened the door, helping her in.

Then he climbed in himself and started the car, cranking the heat. "It isn't far."

"Wow! This is nice for a rental."

"It isn't a rental and neither is the apartment."

"Oh!"

Heat began to flood the car and she almost groaned in pleasure as it warmed her. She should've worn that blouse.

"There's almost always a group of shifters in town." He glanced her way for a second before looking back at the road ahead. "We own a couple of apartments around town. We also own these vehicles." He gave his steering wheel a tap. "It would be crazy to rent vehicles and to pay for hotel rooms."

"Mmmhmmm, that makes sense." Her hands shook a bit so she clasped them in her lap. She couldn't believe she was doing this. Louise squeezed her eyes shut for a few seconds trying to calm herself down.

"You don't have to be nervous." Granite glanced in her direction. He smiled and her breath caught in her lungs. Granite actually smiled . . . at her. Wonders would never cease. The smile was gone almost as quickly as it arrived. "We can have coffee," he flashed her another smile.

She rolled her eyes and laughed. "Yeah, sure."

Within a half a minute they'd driven to a gated entrance

that led into an underground parking area. Granite used a card and the gate opened.

He drove down and parked. They got out of the vehicle and headed to an elevator. Granite put his arm back around her. "You should've worn a coat."

"Yup, I should have." This felt awkward. So stilted.

The elevator door closed and Granite pushed a button. Then he turned towards her and her knees almost crumpled. His eyes were dark and lust-filled. He gripped her hips and pulled her against him. He nuzzled into her neck and sucked on her skin. Then he kissed and nipped his way to her ear. When his tongue laved at her shell, she whimpered. When he sucked on her lobe, she moaned. "I can't wait to be inside you," his voice was hoarse. It did things to her she didn't think possible.

There was a ding and the elevator door opened. He gripped her hand and led her into the hallway. The floors were wooden and gleamed under the lights. There was artwork on the walls. It was pretty fancy. Then he was unlocking a door and pushing her inside. He flicked the switch. The place was really nice.

All modern lines and finishes. It reminded her of a hotel room and in a way it was used as one so it made sense. He walked into the open-plan, well-appointed kitchen and flicked on the kettle. "I'll be back in a sec."

Granite returned a moment later holding a sweater. He put it over her shoulders. Then he went into the kitchen and pulled out a mug and set it by the coffee-maker.

"What are you doing?"

"I promised you coffee."

"You did, but I was expecting you to rip my clothes off and have me on my back in seconds."

Something in the depths of his eyes flared. "That's not how I operate. I promised you coffee." He scooped a generous amount into the coffee-maker.

"Coffee at this time of night? I'm not sure . . ."

"You're going to need it."

"Oh!" Now that was exactly what she expected from him.

He poured the water into the machine and turned it on. "Would you like something to eat? I can fix you a sandwich."

The thought of eating made her stomach clench. "No thanks. I'm good."

"Sure?" He raised his brows. "You're going to need your energy." His eyes narrowed on hers.

She tried to look away and couldn't. "I'm sure. The coffee will be perfect."

He finally broke eye contact and pulled the coffee from the machine, pouring her a cup. "Cream, sugar?"

She didn't take cream but somehow she knew this coffee needed to be cool enough to drink down quickly. Granite was not the patient type. "One sugar and a good splash of cream."

He nodded once and spooned in the sugar, adding the cream. A couple of stirs later and the coffee was placed in front of her on the counter. "Take a seat," he gestured to one of the bar-type chairs. They were stainless steel with white leather.

"I'm going to hit the shower."

"Okay." He was perfect just the way he was.

"You're welcome to join me." His gaze lowered to her lips.

The thought of getting naked straight off the bat was terrifying even though she'd shaved and waxed and plucked and pulled. Louise shook her head. "No, I'll drink this." She raised the steaming cup. "Unless . . ." she had a terrible thought. "I actually need a shower." She sniffed her pits. "Do I, need one?" Her eyes felt wide but she couldn't help it.

Granite's mouth turned up at the corners. He was almost smiling. His eyes shone as he stalked towards her. Granite leaned in, putting them nose to nose. "You smell delicious. I've told you this before. Peaches and cream." He brushed a kiss on her lips. "And wet, hot pussy."

Her girl parts got a whole lot wetter as he said it. Louise put down the cup.

Granite's nostrils flared and he kissed her again. Soft and sweet. So unexpected. "I'll see you in bit."

She gave a nod, watching as he left the room.

God!

Oh god!

Flip!

Louise covered her face with both her hands. She was smiling wider than she had ever smiled. It felt like her face was going to split in half.

Oh, sweet Jesus!

This was really happening. She heard the shower go on in the next room. Granite was probably naked round about now. He was gorgeous naked. So hot it was crazy.

She picked up her coffee and took a big sip and then another and another.

Then there was silence as the water was switched off. She took a big gulp as nerves hit. There was no way she was backing out of this. No way in hell.

She heard him approach, watched as he put his arms up to grab the door jamb. *Oh lord help her!* He was dripping wet, a white towel rode low on his hips.

Screw what was left of the coffee. The mug hit the counter with a clunk.

Louise slid off the chair and like a moth to a flame, she walked right up to him stopping just shy of his big body. Then she leaned up onto her tippy toes and kissed him. He tasted so darned good. Like every guilty pleasure she'd ever had. She groaned as he lifted her off her feet.

Granite turned and walked into what had to be the bedroom. Her eyes were closed as he devoured her mouth. She wound her arms around his neck. Pushed herself up against him. He was warm and damp. His muscles rippled underneath his skin.

With a soft grunt against her lip, he lay her down on a . . . single bed. *What?* Granite pulled back a bit further. "I don't like using the main bedroom. It gets its fair share of traffic."

Yup, she could only imagine what when down when the shifters came to town. Although, she wouldn't have to imagine it for much longer. She was about to experience it first-hand. His chest was broad, well-muscled, as was the rest of him.

Granite kept those dark eyes of his on hers as he picked up one of her legs, putting it over his shoulder. He unzipped the boot and took it off, then removed her sock as well. He did the same with the other leg and then hooked both legs over his shoulders.

He kissed the inside of her leg. His eyes still on her.

Her heart felt like it might beat right out of her chest. The side-lamp was on and the room was well lit. He nipped her inner thigh and a pent-up breath rushed out. He gripped the edge of her skirt and eased it up as he kept up his attention on her inner thigh, using his mouth and teeth, slowly working his way down.

"Lift your ass," he instructed.

She did as he said and he pushed her skirt up over her hips. She felt embarrassment flood her for a second. Her panties would be soaked, she was that turned on.

Granite tore his gaze off of her and looked down between her legs. His nostrils flared as he breathed deeply.

She knew what he would see, Louise was wearing a black lacy set. Darker colors worked better against her white complexion. *Oh god!* The way he was looking at her between her thighs made her want to squirm. She tried to control her breathing. He wasn't even touching her, yet everything felt like it was tightening, clenching and throbbing under his scrutiny.

Granite leaned down and sucked on her sex right

through her lacy panties. The lace rubbed against her swollen clit. Louise's hips bucked and she grit her teeth wanting more. Oh how she wanted more . . . needed to have his mouth on her.

"So fucking delicious!" he groaned against her, causing goosebumps to breakout all over her body. She felt him shove the material aside, felt cool air against her most intimate place before his hot tongue laved her.

She made a whimpering noise and threw her head back. She groaned when he sucked on her clit. None of her exes had ever sucked on the tiny bundle of nerves before. It caused her breath to catch and her back to bow just a little. Another hard suck followed by more of that laving. Her back bowed a whole lot more. She felt his finger at her opening, pressing against it. It felt thick, like his thumb maybe. Her hips were rocking against his face but there was nothing she could do about it. The finger pressed a tad harder, threatening to breach her. He sucked on her, just as the very tip pushed in.

Her mouth fell open, her eyes widened. She gripped his head with both her hands, her body jerked as an orgasm ripped through her. It was huge, it was earth-shattering. It was everything she dreamed it would be with his mouth on her, working her. She made a weird noise from the back of her throat, sounding more like a primal creature than a human being. It couldn't be helped. She was no longer in control of her own body, he was. Right here and right now, he owned her.

CHAPTER 18

"So damned sweet," he rumbled, his mouth still against her swollen flesh. He had to be inside her within the next minute or his dick might just self-combust of its own accord. He glanced up, her head was tossed back, her mouth slack. She licked her lips and blinked a few times. Then he looked back down at her pink-flushed pussy. It was glistening with her release. There was a thin strip of fur, it was the same orange as her hair. *So damned pretty.* "I'm going to fuck you now, Louise."

She gave a nod and turned her hazed-over eyes to him.

Granite crawled up her sexy body. He gave a tug on the edge of her top. "This needs to come off."

She nodded again and lifted her arms. Granite pulled the garment off of her. Her hair was wild about her face and shoulders, so vivid against the white pillow. He loved it.

Her breasts were encased in black lace. He could see her pink nipples through the fabric. Her soft curves were like ripe, little peaches. He nipped at one of the nubs through the lace and she moaned. There was a pearl clasp in between her breasts. He gave it a flick and her soft curves popped out. Small and sweet. *Oh so fucking sweet.*

Granite had to groan as he took one of the ripe raspberry tips into his mouth and sucked. So did the little doctor. She rocked her hips forward. Or tried to, but he was in the way. He could feel the heat from her pussy. Could scent her need. He had meant what he said, this female needed to be fucked almost as much as she needed her next breath and by the way she was gulping down air, it was a whole hell of a lot.

Granite moved his attention to her neck. He licked and sucked her flesh there as well. He gripped her knee and pulled it up. He pulled his towel free, feeling the wet lace against his straining dick.

He needed inside and he needed it now. Granite reached between her legs and yanked at the fabric; it tore like thin paper in his hand. Then he stuck a finger inside her, deep inside. Louise cried out something he couldn't make out, her hips jerked forward.

So fucking receptive. Very wet but so fucking tight he needed to be careful. Careful was the last thing he wanted right now. Every instinct he possessed told him to take her and to do it now. Her scent was maddening.

Granite took back her mouth as he lined up his tip with her opening. Her legs closed around his hips and she rubbed her wet heat against him.

"Oh god!" she groaned into his mouth. "Oh!" Another moan as he pressed his tip against her welcoming flesh. Despite being so tight, it felt like her pussy pulled him in.

Her flesh sucked him down. Tight, yet so welcoming he couldn't suppress a groan as more of him slid inside her. Using gentle thrusts and a circling motion, he slowly entered her slick pussy. He grit his teeth and breathed through his nose. All he wanted to do was ram himself inside her, he had a feeling he would come in seconds if he did. This was about her first. All her.

The little female writhed and moaned. Her fingers dug into his shoulders. "Oh, Granite," her voice was filled with awe. Her hips kept rocking, moving faster than his were. Clumsy and sexy in equal measure. Her moans were thick with lust. His balls pulled tight.

"So good!" he moaned.

"Mmmmhmmm . . ." she arched against him.

His hips finally hit hers, he was balls-deep. Although Granite stopped moving, she continued to pant. He had her pinned down so she couldn't move. Not an inch. He kissed her hard and deep.

Granite pulled out slowly before plunging back into her . . . hard. She bit his tongue, not so hard to draw blood but hard enough that it stung . . . a bit. It sent a bolt of pleasure right to his balls. He almost came there and then. Thank fuck he managed to hold back. He grit his teeth for a few seconds, feeling sweat bead on his brow.

Then he pulled back and thrust again and again. Her legs tightened around him and her finger dug deeper. Her pussy fluttered on the next thrust and then she was coming on a long drawn out moan. More receptive than he'd ever experienced before. He had to fight to keep from tumbling with her as her sex spasmed hard around him.

He groaned as she began to come down. Granite kept moving, kept his thrusts controlled and rhythmic.

"Oh my . . ." she moaned; her breathing was loud, it filled the small space. Granite slowed even more until he stopped moving entirely. He'd give her a minute to catch her breath and then all bets were off.

Louise buried her face in his chest and groaned. It wasn't a good groan. It was an *oh-fuck-what- have-I-done* groan. Granite lifted his head so that he could make eye contact. It was the weirdest thing, she had this 'just come' grin on her face and yet she looked . . . embarrassed. "Are you okay?"

She bit down on her lower lip for a second. "I'm sorry!"

"What could you possibly have to be sorry about?"

"I couldn't help it."

She wasn't looking at him, she was staring at his chest instead. "Couldn't help what?" He cupped her chin and forced him to look at her.

Her eyes were wide. "Um . . ." she gave a tight smile. "I come so easily with you . . . it's so embarrassing."

"It's amazing. I love how your body reacts to mine. How easy it is to get you wet, how just a simple touch can get you off."

She frowned. "It's not a bad thing? You see, I'm not normally like this. Not that . . ."

He kissed her softly. "I love it. Fucking love it. Let's see how many times we can make you lose it before sunrise."

She gave a nod, looking unsure. It was up to him to show her that he meant every word he had uttered. Every last one.

She felt like an idiot. What was it about this man? It was as if Granite had a detailed map of her body outlining every single nook and cranny. He was tuned in to her like no one else before. It was embarrassing. He had yet to come himself. It wasn't like she hadn't noticed. She couldn't help it though. There was nowhere to hide, no way to play it down. Each of her orgasms had blasted through her. Her body was helpless but to react. She had tried so hard to hold it together but feeling him inside her, so deep, so full, had been her undoing. His movements were powerful, each movement precise.

His cock throbbed, their bodies still joined. "I want to take you from behind." His eyes had a feral look.

It sent a thrill through her and she nodded. Her belly felt coiled tight. That heavy feeling was back. She'd come twice already and she wanted more. It was unbelievable but she wanted it all, everything he had to give. She only prayed it would be enough. That she would be able to walk away without a backwards glance. Even worse, that she would be able to work with him, see him often. He was a patient. *No!* She wasn't going to think about how she'd crossed the line. Rules aside, it was her own line.

Granite pulled out of her and she felt empty and achy. "Let's get you out of this." He tugged at her skirt. She shrugged her bra off her shoulders and unzipped the skirt.

All the while, her eyes were drawn to his cock. It was a thing of beauty. So long and thick, slick with her juices. His sacs weren't as big as she remembered them. They were pulled up tight against his body. She licked her lips, wanting to suck on his long length, wanting to fondle his balls. She'd love to make him come with her mouth.

"Don't . . ." Granite gave a low growl.

Her eyes flashed to his. They were crinkled at the sides. Amusement etched in their depths. "Don't look at my dick like that, it won't take much to make me come and I'd really like to find release buried deep inside your tight body."

He had a way of speaking that turned her on and in a bad way. His words made her feel hot all over. Granite gripped the edge of her skirt and pulled it off, taking what was left of her ruined underwear with it.

"On your hands and knees," he used his bossy tone. She didn't mind so much right now. Not when her core was begging to be filled. Begging for more.

Louise did as he said, arching her back so that her ass would be in the air. Her butt was one of her best features. Hillary had been right about that.

"So pretty." He squeezed her ass and ran a finger down her slit. It was so slippery down there she almost felt embarrassed. How could she think about anything though when his thumb circled her clit? Just once but it was enough to make her moan. She had to bite her lower lip to stop herself from begging him.

"Go down onto your elbows and brace yourself," he

gripped her hips as he spoke.

She whimpered as his tip breached her opening. Just the very tip. *God but he was big.*

She lowered herself and braced against the mattress. Her face plowed into the soft duvet as he thrust into her, right to the hilt. It took her breath away. Full and stretched to capacity in an instant.

Granite didn't give her a chance to catch her breath, he kept driving into her using hard, powerful thrusts. The coiling sensation increased. She made moaning noises with each hard shove. The moans sounded choked. Her breasts were mashed up against the bedding. Her knees barely touching. Her eyes were wide. Her body tensing. More coiling. More heaviness. A louder, higher-pitched moan was torn from her. The sounds of his body slapping against hers filled the room. Her body made a wet suction noise each time he withdrew. This was sex at its most raw and primal form. It was better than all the sex she'd had to date all rolled into one.

Granite was grunting. His hard breaths were almost as loud as her own. His fingers dug into her. He gripped a handful of her hair and pulled lightly as his body began to jerk into her. His movements turned frantic, his noises animalistic.

It was enough to send her spiraling. She yelled into the bedcover as her body let go. All that pent-up ecstasy coursed through her in a rush of endorphins and pleasure so blinding it made her eyes water.

Granite roared. She felt hot spurts inside her. He jerked

a few times before slowing. Then he caged her with his body, his head was against her back. He was breathing heavily, they both were.

What now? Did she gather her things and leave? Did he want her to stay? Hillary was right, this was her first time at doing anything like this. Sex for the sake of sex. It was the best sex she had ever had but she hadn't thought of what would happen after.

Granite pulled out of her. "Don't move," a soft rumble.

Within a half a minute he was back, warm towel in hand. He wiped her clean. It seemed that the king of the Earth dragons could be a good guy if he wanted to be.

Then he pulled her into his arms. Like they were lovers or something. "Why are you so tense?" he asked as he began to tickle her back using the tips of his fingers.

"I don't really know what to do." Louise lifted her head so that she could look at his side profile. Granite lay on his back. "Should I leave?"

"I told your friend not to make plans with you tomorrow. I spoke of fucking you until the sun came up. I meant it." He glanced her way. "I meant all of it. You are mine right up until we leave tomorrow."

Mine.

It sent a shiver coursing through her. She knew he didn't mean it like that, but still. Louise gave a nod.

"I take it you don't need a long rest to recoup?" she smiled.

Granite shook his head. He took ahold of her hand and pulled it beneath the sheet. His dick was hard and thick.

"This is what you do to me. I want you again. Once was nowhere near enough."

Louise curled her fingers around the length of him and all of his features turned pinched and tense. She felt his muscles tighten.

"You are the one who needs a break," his voice was deep and husky.

Instead of answering him, she curled her hand around his thick girth and gave his dick a long, hard tug. Granite's eyes rolled back and he groaned. "Careful female."

Louise smiled as she tugged on him again, this time rubbing one of her fingers over his tip.

"That's it," Granite smiled as he rolled on top of her. They almost fell off of the narrow bed. Louise laughed, it quickly turned into a moan as he pushed into her. Granite kissed her as he sank deeper.

CHAPTER 19

Granite turned another pancake. It was golden brown perfection. His stomach grumbled. The scent of bacon filled the small kitchen. A dish of the crisped pork was in the warming drawer.

There was orange juice and some maple syrup on the table. His stomach grumbled again. It was turning in on itself at this point.

He hadn't been able to get enough of the little doctor. It was one rut session after another. Thankfully, she had seemed just as eager. They'd finally fallen asleep as the sun was rising. He hadn't meant it literally when he'd talked about rutting her all night and yet it had happened. Granite was worried that she might be a bit sensitive this morning.

They didn't have huge amounts of time left. Enough for a shower and some leisurely breakfast.

Using the spatula, he eased the pancake out of the pan onto the growing stack and poured in some more batter. Then he angled the pan so that the batter spread out evenly, placing the pan back on the stove.

"Wow!" her voice was croaky. "I didn't know you could

cook."

He had to smile at the sight of her. Hair a wild mess. Eyes heavy with sleep, or lack thereof. Her cheeks were flushed, her lips swollen. In short, she still had that just fucked look and he loved it on her. "Good morning," he smiled.

She returned the smile. It went from lazy to a wide grin in a few seconds. She was clearly remembering all the things they had done last night. Each position, every orgasm. There had been a number of those. The female remained as receptive as she had been at the start. It was a rare gift and he'd taken full advantage of it.

"Morning." She looked down at her bare feet, the smile had turned a tad shy. *Shy!* After everything that had gone down. It was really sweet.

"I like your shirt."

She blushed. *A blush!* It was refreshing. "Sorry!" a whisper. "I hope you don't mind?" She fingered the cotton. It was his shirt. The white one he'd worn last night. It looked amazing on her.

No! She looked amazing in it.

"Take a seat," he gestured to the small dining-room table. More of a breakfast nook really. "I'll get you some food. Pour yourself a glass of orange juice. There is fresh brewed coffee if you would prefer."

Her eyes widened and she made a moaning noise that went straight to his dick despite their marathon fuckfest.

"I'd kill for some." Her eyes moved around the small kitchen until they landed on the pot. "No fair by the way."

She glanced back at him. "You showered."

He looked down at the towel wrapped around his waist.

She gave a soft snort, drawing his attention back to him. "I still smell like . . . well . . ."

"You scent of sex and of me," his voice took on a feral edge.

She turned, leaning back against the counter like she needed the support. "Oh! Well, that's okay then."

It was more than okay. She'd scent of him for a couple of days. Two or three tops. He found he liked his smell on her. Not in a possessive way. Not to stake a claim or anything. It wasn't just his scent. It was the smell of endorphins. The ultimate scent of satisfaction and relaxation. Her scent together with that just fucked look had his dick hardening up. He was a sick bastard. That was for fucking sure. Then again, he was looking at six more months before he would be able find release inside a female again. Unless he was successful in finding the right female on the next hunt. Granite wasn't holding his breath. That had been a dead-end so far. It didn't help that he couldn't trust any of them. It something to worry about another day.

Louise turned back towards the cupboard that housed the mugs. She reached up on her toes. It was a view he could get used to. Lean thighs, her ass so close to being on display that his dick took notice . . . even more notice.

The scent of burning caught his attention. "Shit!" he muttered as he flipped the pancake. It was streaked with black and beyond salvaging.

He pulled one of the drawers open and scraped the burned pancake into the bin.

Louise pretended not to notice. She fixed a coffee for herself and then turned back to him. "Can I make you a cup?"

Granite shook his head. "I'll have some juice."

She gave a nod and poured him a glass, placing it in front of one of the plates. Louise took a seat, sipping her coffee. He liked that she didn't feel the need to fill the silence. Most females had that urge.

"I'm nearly done here." He poured the last of the batter into the pan, going through the pancake-making motions.

She gave a nod. "No problem."

"How are you feeling?"

Louise cradled the mug in both her hands. "Tired," she smiled, hiding behind the mug. "Good though." Another shy smile as she took another sip of her coffee. The scent of her arousal wafted towards him. Still peaches and cream but mingled with a good dose of his own scent.

He tried hard not to take it in too deep into his snout and failed. Despite coming half a dozen times in her tight body, his balls pulled tight. Granite ignored his body's reaction to her. This wasn't the time. He needed to get her fed, so he flipped the pancake instead.

He willed his semi to go down. Thinking of anything and everything to make that happen.

Maybe they could have breakfast and a quickie, if she was up for it. He didn't normally rut females once the sun came up but he'd make an exception for her. She could use one more fuck. He'd take it slow and careful. He'd make sure it was good for her.

Twenty minutes! Just twenty! He made the promise to his dick. *Go down! Not right now.* Granite slid the pancake onto the stack. He said a prayer of thanks as he felt his erection subside.

He placed the pancakes and bacon in front of her, sliding in on the seat next to hers. "I'm sorry! We don't eat straight eggs." Straight eggs. *What the fuck were straight eggs? Who said that?*

She gave a nod. "I know. I've been living with the dragon shifters for a couple of months now," she said it in a mocking tone.

Of course she knew, what was wrong with him?

"I completely understand," she added.

"Help yourself." He pointed at the pancakes.

Louise took one.

"You're supposed to add a slice or two of bacon and lather the whole thing in maple syrup. It's delicious." All he could think about was her pussy as he said the word. His mouth watered. *Delicious.* It was an understatement.

She nodded, taking a pancake.

He took two, suddenly needing to fill his mouth with something sweet. He had a feeling the maple syrup wouldn't cut it. She still scented of arousal and need. His reaction was perfectly normal.

They ate in silence for a few minutes. He polished off the first pancake and started on the second.

She took another small bite, chewed and swallowed

before putting down her knife and fork. Louise grabbed a napkin and wiped her mouth.

"I hope you're not done?" He raised his brows.

Louise shook her head. "Nope, still eating. There was something I wanted to say though." She wrinkled her nose.

Shit! She didn't strike him as the type to give a declaration of love. To go all gaga on him. It happened on occasion though, despite ensuring that females understood that it was only sex. Despite making it clear that there would be no tomorrow or future of any kind. Fuck, he rarely ate breakfast with them. Of course, he'd feed them, he wasn't a complete bastard but he'd be sure to stay on the other side of the kitchen. Once that last mouthful was down the hatch, he'd get them on their way. Every now and then, there were tears. He had not expected this from her and quite frankly he was disappointed.

"I crossed the line. This thing between us . . . not that there's an us . . ." she sucked in a deep breath. "This can't happen again," she shook her head. "I'm going to finish eating and be on my way. I need to go past my apartment anyway." She looked down at herself. "I could do with a long shower."

"You can shower here." What a pathetic thing to say. If the female wanted to leave she should go already. He gave a shrug to show that he didn't give a shit either way.

Louise shook her head. "I really need to change. I can't be seen in last night's clothes."

"My scent is all over you," he blurted. "Some of the males saw us leave together. They will know."

She pulled another face, like his males knowing about them was the worst thing that could happen to her. *The fuck!* Louise scrubbed a hand over her face. "Last night should not have happened. Look," she held out a hand as if to placate him, "I'm glad it did. We needed to get that out of our system, out of the way, *but,*" she paused, "we both need to move on like nothing happened. It's business as usual. I don't want this interfering with our working relationship. With the work I am doing."

"It was fucking, Doctor, plain and simple. Just fucking."

She flinched and something eased in him. It was good that they were on the same page. He could've used one more rut but hey, some things were not meant to be. "I think it's safe to say that we enjoyed ourselves. The research you are doing is vital to my people. I can assure you that nothing will get in the way of that. Let's finish up and I'll give you a lift."

"No need," she shook her head like taking a ride from him was the worst possible thing. "I'll call a cab."

"You're not calling a cab . . ."

She shook her head some more. "No really."

What the fuck difference did it make? He didn't offer lifts to any of the others. "Suit yourself." He made himself another pancake. Throwing on an extra piece of bacon for good measure. He could tell that she wasn't going to eat much more and it would be a shame to let all of this food go to waste.

Granite took a big bite, chewed and swallowed. He took another bite and then another. The food tasted of nothing but he needed his energy, so he ate anyway.

CHAPTER 20

Two days later...

Breeze held the baby to her breast and Crystal suckled greedily. The shifter wrinkled her nose. "I still can't get used to this whole breast-sucking thing. It is so strange. To think I need to do this for the next year," she shook her head.

Louise gently patted Gem's tiny back. The little one was slung over her shoulder, already halfway to falling asleep. She gave a toothless, milky yawn. Then again, it wasn't milk they were drinking but an essence. At least Breeze described it as such. From what she could ascertain, it was a nutrient-rich liquid perfect for a growing dragon baby. It was weird to her, then again, not so weird as the other dragon species. All of their young were born with teeth and began eating solids right off the bat. No breastfeeding. Earth babies were born tiny and defenseless.

They were minute and yet perfect. "I'm so happy that the girls are thriving. You are such a good mother." She reached for her coffee and took a sip. It was still early, her work day had yet to properly start. This was her first appointment. Checking in on the new family.

"You are a great doctor, I couldn't have done it without you."

"Yes, you could have."

Breeze shook her head. "No way! It wasn't just the birth, it was the days that followed. I had no idea how to change a diaper or how to bathe them or feed them," she laughed. "Especially the 'feed the baby' part. They would've been dirty and hungry if not for you. My girls are the first babies to be born on Earth soil in twelve years."

Louise tried not to show how shocked she was at the admission. "You would've done just fine."

"I'm always told of these instincts that females are supposed to have. I don't think I was given any," Breeze frowned. "You are apparently supposed to know when your baby is hungry or if she's messed her diaper. The cries sound different. I don't hear any difference. I end up running around. I have to check the diaper, put the baby to my breast, then I burp them. Sometimes I try everything and nothing works." Her eyes were wide and there were black smudges underneath them.

Louise leaned forward and touched her arm. "You are doing great. Babies cry, it's normal. As long as they are clean, fed and burped, there is nothing more you can do. You must remember that it's difficult for them too. They were all wrapped up in this warm confined space and now they're here, in this big, wide world. It can be a bit overwhelming and a little scary."

Breeze nodded. She let out a huge sigh. "I always feel so much better after you visit. Thank you!"

"You are most welcome."

Breeze cocked her head, a strange look appeared on her face. "You aren't going to bring it up are you?"

Louise gave a tiny shake of the head. "I'm not sure what you mean." She knew this was coming but had hoped and prayed that the shifter would let it go.

Breeze rolled her eyes. "You and Granite. The fact that his scent is still all over you. You reek of him two days after the fact," she gave a sly smile. "It must have been some night."

Louise felt her cheeks heat. "It was . . . good. It was fine. I'm not proud of myself."

Breeze flapped a hand and pulled a face that told her she was full of shit. "It's better that it happened. You guys can get on with it now."

"Yup. Totally," she tried to sound nonchalant and obviously failed.

"You're still attracted to him," Breeze choked out a laugh. "I don't believe it."

"Shut up, will you?" Louise spoke under her breath. "Someone could hear. He could find out about it and then I'm screwed."

"Yup, you would be." Breeze found the whole thing hilarious.

"This is no laughing matter. I hate that I still have a thing for him." It was worse than before. All she could think of was his mouth on her, his hands and of course, his cock. His gigantic 'I-can-make-you-come-in-seconds' cock. They could not be together, they could not have sex again. It could not happen. Yet, she craved it. Ached for it.

He'd found her scent to be needy and achy before . . . well, he would die when he caught a noseful of her now.

Breezed snickered some more. "Oh my god!"

"Stop already."

"So, when is his next appointment?" She winked and wagged her brows.

"This afternoon, but don't go there, don't even think it." Louise shook her head so hard some of her hair came loose. "It can't happen again. Any type of relationship with Granite is strictly forbidden. You know that."

Breeze sobered up in an instant. "No, you're right. It can't happen. I feel a bit sorry for you guys. You're probably hot for one another because you can't have each other. Silly really," she paused, "if only you could have sex a few more times, I'm sure it would fizzle out on its own."

"Mmmmhmmm, agreed, but it can't happen," Louise sighed. "I'm a bit nervous about seeing him again. How should I act? Like nothing happened or should I . . ." She thought on it for a moment. "I'll act like nothing happened. That would be for the best."

"Sounds like a plan. If I know Granite it is what he would want. He's the most straight and narrow, by-the-book male I know."

"Good to know. I'll go and see him as soon as we are done. I need him to sign off on some new equipment.

Blaze mentioned that it's coming out of Granite's budget and that he needs to approve it." She'd received the directive yesterday, but had been putting it off. Now she felt stupid for delaying.

"Yup, good idea. Just go over there and stick to business."

Louise put down her empty mug, sure to keep the baby securely against her, her neck well supported. "Little Gem is lights out." The tiny baby in her arms was breathing rhythmically.

"So is Crystal."

"Let's go and put the babies down and then it's back to bed for you."

Breeze shook her head. "I couldn't possibly—"

"Doctor's orders," Louise tried to sound stern, she even narrowed her eyes.

Louise could see the other woman hold back a yawn. "Yeah, okay, maybe you're right."

Louise helped put the babies to bed and then said her goodbyes. She really hoped that Breeze went for a lie down. It couldn't be easy looking after two tiny babies. She thought of them, so tiny, downy hair on their heads, toothless yawns and lots of squirming. One of these days they would start to smile and then all bets were off, her heart would turn to a puddle in her chest. Hard work, but also rewarding, fulfilling and just plain awesome. Every single maternal instinct was firing on full cylinders and her broody button was being pushed in a big bad way. She didn't understand how it was possible when she didn't have a significant other. Louise gave a sigh.

Walking quickly, she made a quick stop at her office to collect the file and request sheet and made her way to Granite's office.

The closer she got, the more nervous she felt. Maybe this wasn't such a good idea. Maybe she should get her ass back to her work chamber and worry about Granite when he came for his appointment later. *Rubbish!* The sooner she got this initial meeting out of the way, the sooner she could focus on her job. Her first patient was arriving just now. She hadn't slept well last night and if she was honest with herself she was obsessing about seeing him again. How would he act? Would she be able to keep her interest in him a secret? Although lust was probably a better word . . . interest didn't quite sum it up enough. Her hands actually shook. She couldn't believe how worried she had been feeling. She should have taken this to him yesterday.

Yes, getting this over with now was for the best. It was like pulling off a Band-Aid, best to be swift and yank it in one go. She only prayed that he wasn't still as hot for her as she was for him. If he offered to tear off her clothes and ravage her she didn't think she'd be able to say no.

Here goes nothing. Louise gave a hard knock before she could change her mind . . . again. She counted to five and entered.

Granite was at his desk, which was littered in paperwork. "What?" he snapped. "You don't have an appointment," he added.

"Sorry, I needed you to sign off on something."

His frown deepened. "I'm busy. You have half a minute." His dark eyes narrowed onto hers.

For a second, Louise was tempted to launch into an explanation. She wanted so badly to shift weight from one foot to the other. Tempted to look for pieces of lint on her coat. The last thing she wanted were those intense dark eyes boring holes into her.

Instead, she forced herself to stand her ground for a moment in order to catch her breath and to gather her thoughts. Although she was desperate to get the words out – so that she could leave – she forced herself to speak carefully and deliberately. "I need supplies and equipment." She continued to list the items in question. Some of the items were new. Louise took her time explaining why each one was needed, making sure she was quick and concise, sticking to the facts. Others were depleted or in need of replacement. Louise ended with a total sum of the costs. "All the information is in here." She gave the file a tap. "This is the form requiring your signature."

He gave a heavy sigh. "It could have waited until this afternoon. You're wasting my time."

Why was he being such a dick? Louise pursed her lips for a second, willing her composure to return. "It couldn't wait. I'm at risk of running out of one or two of those items, namely—"

"You should have come to me last week with that list then. You've left things until the last minute," Granite remained deadpan. He spoke to her like he would one of his subordinates or a naughty child. It wasn't that she expected better treatment after sleeping with him but this was ridiculous.

Quite frankly it pissed her the hell off. Louise clutched the file a bit tighter. "For your information, Blaze has been sitting on the paperwork for two weeks. He only got back to me with this yesterday, I thought you might be busy after taking the weekend off, so I delayed things by a couple of hours. I didn't want to delay them any further, so here I am. If you want to lecture someone about this, then get ahold of him and be my guest. Now, are you going to sign this or not?"

He pushed his chair back and stalked over to her. Granite seemed taller somehow. He towered over her. *Flip, he stilled smelled so good.* Pity about him being such an asshole. Then again, it was a good thing. Him being an asshole was just great. It would remind her of why they couldn't be together. Someone ought to tell her lady parts though. They wanted more of what he had to offer. They didn't care that he was an ass-hat of epic proportions.

He took the paper from her hand and she handed him a pen. Granite signed the bottom of the page with a flourish and handed the document back to her. "Anything else, Doctor?"

Yes, I'd like you to bend me over your desk. What the hell was she thinking? She'd never been all that sexual before. She didn't care about sex either way. When she was having it, it was nice and when she wasn't, she didn't really miss it – or she hadn't until meeting Granite. Everything about him screamed sex. At least, that's what her body heard, loud and clear. Louise cleared her throat. "That's all, thank you."

"The work that you are doing is beyond important, I can't stress that enough. I can't go into detail, it's something you will need to trust me on. Our species could end up being eradicated. There are those who wish to see us dead."

Louise frowned and shook her head. He had to be exaggerating. Surely.

"Yes," he growled. "I mean every word. It's why I'm pushing this therapy so hard. If there is anything you need, come to me. I would prefer it if you made an appointment going forward."

Hot and cold.

For just a second there it felt like he was confiding in her, opening up a little and then *bam* he took it back and then some, it was jarring.

"Of course," she forced herself to hold his gaze.

Granite gave a small nod and went back to his desk, picking up one of the documents. He gave the piece of paper his full and undivided attention and she felt dismissed. It was like she didn't exist. Like the weekend had never happened. Granite had gotten what he wanted from her and now it was over.

Good.

She was glad. She'd also gotten what she wanted. *This was great!* Louise let herself out, closing the door behind her. She was relicved. Things would continue as normal.

She would do her job to the best of her ability and he would run the Earth kingdom with an iron fist. In other words, he would continue being the biggest dick she had ever met. Her only difficulty would be to keep from calling him names to his face and maybe kicking him in the shin. *Life was good.*

Granite was going to be a few minutes early for his appointment. He'd decided to stop working because he found himself poring over the same document over and over. He'd logged numbers wrong on the spreadsheet. In short, he was having trouble concentrating. It was one of those days. It had nothing to do with the human visiting him earlier. Nothing to do with her scent. Or how beautiful her eyes looked when she was pissed . . . and she had been pissed.

It couldn't be helped, he had to reestablish boundaries. He thought she'd be happy given the way Sunday morning had played out.

He heard the doctor's laughter before he even arrived at her door. The laugh was followed by a squeal and then more laughter, more hysterical this time.

"No, Rock, no!" she tried to sound stern but broke into fits of laughter. The giggling kind. "I'm . . . warning . . . you . . ." The words were garbled, peppered with more laughing.

The fuck?

Granite felt everything tighten. His whole body bristled. He picked up the pace, practically running to her work chamber. The door was partially open.

Rock had the female over his shoulder. His face was red and he was laughing as well, the sound drowned out by her hysterical screams and giggles. The smile on her face was about a mile wide. It froze as it landed on him.

"Rock!" she yelled, trying to pull free. "No! You—" The male threw her onto the hospital bed and she bounced once.

"This is good for you." The male was out of breath. "It's exactly what you need."

"No, Rock! You—"

His blood boiled inside him and smoke curled from his nose and mouth. His scales rubbed so hard he knew they would be visible through his skin. His teeth sharpened up. His body tingled, wanting to shift. His dragon wanted to taste blood. "What the fuck is going on?" a deep snarl.

Rock turned. His face was suddenly white. It didn't go unnoticed how the male put himself between Granite and the female. *He could fuck right off.* He held up his hands, and his eyes took on a pleading look. "It's not—"

Granite wasn't interested in anything he had to say. He hit the male with a sharp right hook, making sure that he went flying to the left instead of backwards. He didn't want the human getting hurt. Granite bristled more at the idea of even a drop of her blood spilling.

Rock went flying and landed in a sprawling heap, just missing one of the machines as well as a table of instruments. The male gave a shake of the head, trying to fight off dizziness. He turned onto his back, groaning as he pulled himself up onto his elbows. He stayed down though.

Granite took a step towards him, turning so that he could tower over the male. The human healer jumped onto his back the moment it was turned. "Leave him alone, you big bully!" she shouted.

The female was liable to hurt herself. He hooked an arm behind his back and across her, holding her in place. "You . . . No . . . what . . ." she mumbled, trying to yank herself free.

Using his free hand, Granite pointed a finger at Rock. "You don't get to touch her . . . ever. Am I clear?"

The little doctor continued to squirm, yell and complain. She kicked at him and pummeled him with her fists. Granite ignored her, his eyes on Rock.

The male gave a nod. His lip was split and bleeding. "Yes, my lord."

"Fuck off!" Granite barked, pointing to the door.

Rock scrambled to his feet. "It's not what—"

"Out!" he roared, not wanting to hear what the male had to say. If Rock didn't leave right then, he was going to hurt the male a whole lot more. Bones would break and flesh would split. Blood would spill. His scales still rubbed.

The doctor continued to beat him with her fists, although, not as hard. She was panting heavily from the exertion. The human was going to hurt herself if she wasn't careful. He put her down and took a step back. "Stop!" he growled. "Be quiet!"

Louise pointed a finger at him. "You don't get to tell

me what to do." She was spitting mad. So much so that her cheeks were flushed red. Her eyes blazed. *Tough luck!*

"I told you to stay away from my males. Your contract is clear."

"What the hell is wrong with you? Oh yes . . ." She laughed but not a trace of her earlier happiness remained. "You're one hell of an asshole, I keep forgetting."

"There is nothing wrong with me," his voice was deep and guttural. His emotions running high. His teeth still felt sharp. His eyes might also be more reptilian than human. She didn't seem to notice. "Why are you fucking around with Rock?" He felt every muscle tense. Every single last one. His dick was as hard as nails. His dragon wanted him to take the human, to show her who she belonged to. He struggled to think rationally. His instincts rode him hard.

Take.

Have.

Now.

Louise's mouth fell open and she gasped, loudly. "You are completely out of line. There is nothing between Rock and me—"

"Bullshit!" a low rumble. "I know what I just saw. He was going to—"

"He's in love with Quartz, you idiot!" She took a step towards him. "Do you really think I would jump straight out of your bed into someone else's?"

"It looks that way." He knew he was being a jerk but couldn't seem to stop. He felt wound up in knots. Granite didn't understand what all of these wayward emotions were. He felt tense and angry and so turned on it was scary.

Her eyes widened. "I cannot believe what a gigantic prick you are. You're essentially calling me a slut. I was perfectly fine until you came along. Perfectly happy!" She pinched the bridge of her nose for a second. She was breathing heavily. "I don't want to have sex with anyone else, you moron." She made a growling noise she was so angry. "The only person I want is you." She gripped her lower lip between her teeth, seeming to realize what she had just said.

His balls pulled tight.

His skin seemed to shrink.

A need so desperate and fierce accosted him. "Fuck!" he growled as he picked her up off the floor, her body hit his just as his lips crushed hers.

She mewled into his mouth, melting against him. Her legs closed around his waist. Her arms circled his neck.

Granite walked a few steps to the stainless steel table. He pushed a couple of items to the side and put her on the very edge. His mouth didn't leave hers. Her eyes were squeezed shut. She mewled again as he pushed up her coat. He lifted Louise so that the garment, together with her dress or skirt, whatever the heck she was wearing, could be shoved all the way up, bunched at her hips.

He broke their kiss for a brief moment, first to pull her hair free from that god-awful bun and then to look between her thighs. White cotton underwear. The panel that covered her pussy was wet. Completely soaked. His dick throbbed. "Fuck!" he growled again, sniffing deeply, taking her scent right to the back of his throat. He could almost taste her. *So damned sweet.*

With a shaking hand, he reached between her thighs and tore the panties, ripping them to shreds. Her pussy glistened with her arousal. Granite took back her mouth and yanked down his own pants, freeing his cock. He'd never needed to be inside someone more. There was no holding back. No chance! Not this time.

He grunted as he thrust into her. So fucking tight, it almost hurt despite how slick she was. Louise gave a cry. She locked her ankles at his back and gripped his biceps. Their mouths clashed as he thrust back into her. Over and over. He fucked her hard. Too hard considering she was a human but he couldn't bring himself to stop or even to slow.

One hand closed over her ass and the other braced on the table behind her. He bent at the knee so that he could thrust up and into her. The whole table shook, instruments clanged. Some falling down onto the steel, others falling off the table completely. None of it mattered.

His balls were already in his throat so when her pussy fluttered around him it was over. He rumbled as the first spurt left him. Then all-out snarled as her pussy clamped down on him. Granite had the good sense to cover her mouth with his as she screamed. He muffled the noise. Muffled the crazy noises he was making as well. The sex was that good.

He could feel jets of come spurt from him in hard

bursts. Just when he thought he was done, another hard jet erupted from him. Pleasure rushed through every part of him, it caused his thighs to shake and his jaw to clench. It made him crunch at his middle, forcing him to break the kiss. Granite ended up cheek-to-cheek with her. He'd never come so hard or so long. By the way her pussy had squeezed the shit out of him he would say that it was the same for her. He felt like he was drowning inside her. Like he was dying and being reborn and all at the same time.

His frantic, jerking movements slowed until he was hardly moving. His hips rotating in small circles. It felt so damned good. It felt like more.

Then the ramification of what he had just done came crashing down on him. Granite tensed and stopped moving. He had to work to pull back, he had to force himself to withdraw completely from her; he immediately felt the loss. It was more than just her tight, warm heat, he felt the loss inside himself as well. Deep inside. *What the fuck was happening to him?*

"That was a mistake," he ground out, still out of breath. "A huge fucking mistake!" he added more to himself than to her. He needed to stay the fuck away from her.

Louise was panting as well. They were still cheek-to-cheek. He still cupped her ass, his other hand on her back. It was her turn to tense up. "Yeah," the word sounded choked.

"Shit!" He released her. "That should not have happened. I was thinking with my dick instead of my head." Panic welled as he scanned the room, his gaze landing on a roll of paper towels. Granite pulled up his pants. His cock was still hard. *Well, his erection could go to hell. Damn!* He was risking this female's career. Risking her future and for what, so that he could find pleasure inside her? It was wrong. It was so much worse than wrong. He felt like breaking something.

Granite grabbed the roll of paper towels and yanked off a wad, walking back with it to Louise. The female was looking down at the floor. She looked so upset. Her lip quivered thing. *No wonder!* She had every right to be angry, he was an asshole. A major dickhead. If this got out she was gone. Fired and packed and all in one day. She'd be dropped back in Walton Springs so quickly her head would spin.

"I'm so fucking sorry!" He tried to clean her up but she held out her hand instead. Her eyes were still downcast.

"It takes two to tango as the saying goes."

He handed the wad of paper towels to her. "No! I'm the one to blame." Granite paced to the other side of the room and back again. "I need to fix this."

"You can't possibly . . ."

"Sunday was only two days ago, we still scent of one another anyway." He ran a hand over his head. "I can't believe that just happened. It can't fucking happen again."

She finally lifted her gaze. Stunning green eyes locked with his. "You're saying that like I instigated the whole thing. You were the one who lost control."

It was all true. Every last word. Granite growled, feeling that same tense wound-up feeling he had earlier. "Don't fuck around with my males."

"I told you that nothing happened. I was feeling a little down and Rock was trying to cheer me up . . . as a friend."

"Fine! Arguing is not going to help." If they argued, he might just lose control and fuck her again. That could not happen. Not ever again. "Do you have a shower in this chamber?"

She nodded, pointing to a door behind them.

"Good." He pulled his pants off and threw them on the floor. Her gaze zoned in on his dick but she quickly looked away. "Can you make a fire?" he asked, looking at the hearth. Every room in his lair had a fireplace. This one was no exception. He breathed a bit easier when he saw the stacked firewood and kindling.

"What?" she frowned, looking half in a daze.

"We need to burn our clothes."

She shook her head, frowning all the more.

"Yes! We need to get the scent of fucking off of us and out of this room and it needs to happen quickly. If Blaze hears of this . . ." He swallowed thickly. "Can you light a fire?" he repeated.

She gave a nod.

"Good. I'm going to shower. I'll wash several times. I need you to do the same when I'm done. Light a fire in the meanwhile – it needs to be big and blazing. Toss that in when it's hot enough." He pointed at his discarded pants.

She gave another nod.

Granite headed for the door on the far side of the

room, the one that lead to the bathroom. He turned the faucet until the water was almost scalding. He climbed in, lathered soap all over himself, paying particular attention to his dick. His erection throbbed in his hand. He still wanted the female. He ignored his wayward cock. The fucker had caused enough shit for one day.

Granite stood under the water, waiting until it ran clean and all the soap was off. Then he started all over again. He lathered up and washed off.

Then he dried himself and rummaged through the bathroom cupboard. He found a tube of toothpaste and a toothbrush. It looked like the little doctor kept some of her stuff here. There was also a tube of lotion and some deodorant.

He gave a shrug and put a liberal amount of toothpaste onto the brush. Then he spent the next few minutes brushing her taste from his mouth. It was a crying shame since a female had never tasted quite so good. He could kiss her all day, eat her up for breakfast, lunch and supper. Shit, now his mind had gone south and he remembered the taste of her sweet pussy. His dick gave a twitch. Despite the situation, his erection had decided that it wasn't going anywhere.

The fire was blazing when he returned to the room. Louise had his pants bunched up in her hands, she threw them in and stoked the flames.

"I'll be back."

"Where are you going?" she turned to face him, her gaze never wavered from his. He could scent himself on her. His seed deep inside her. He liked it.

The fuck!

Granite cleared his throat. "I'll shift and access my room from the balcony. Once I'm dressed I'll head to your place and grab some clothes. Is there anything specific you need?"

Her eyes widened and she looked like she might argue with him. Then she huffed out a breath. "Underwear." Her face heated. "Do I need to burn this as well?" She fingered her white coat.

He gave a nod. "Everything but your shoes will have to go."

"Okay." She looked distraught. He couldn't blame her, he was such a prick for putting her in this position. She must be seriously worried about losing her job. "You need to bring me another medical jacket and . . . I don't know," she lifted her eyes in thought, "grab a dress. It doesn't matter which one."

"Underwear, coat and a dress. Got it." As an afterthought he took a chair and jammed it under the door. "This way no one will be able to get in."

"I doubt we'll have any visitors. I always leave your appointment as my last for the day. You normally need to be monitored for a time after our session." Her eyes widened. "Because you're still so badly affected by the silver. I doubt anyone will drop in."

"Let's hope you're right and that no one comes but if they do, tell them to go away and insist that you're okay."

She gave a nod, her eyes were wide and shiny. It looked

like she might cry at any second. Granite had to fight the urge to cup her chin and to tell her that everything would be okay. He had no right touching her though. Touching this female would lead to more. Every. Time.

"I'll be back."

She gave a nod.

His erection bobbed as he walked. It still refused to calm the fuck down. *Oh well* . . . There was nothing he could do about it. Maybe he deserved what he had coming. Payback in a way. He closed the balcony door behind him before looking back at the human female.

Her gaze was on the fire. Her hair was still loose about her shoulders. The blaze lit her face. *Fuck but she was beautiful.* He couldn't understand how he hadn't noticed it from the start. So stunningly beautiful that it almost took his breath away. He had to make this right.

A growl was torn from him as he shifted. Bone stretched, as did muscle and tendons. Agony sliced through him. His dick throbbed, this time with sheer pain. Shifting with a hard-on was not recommended. The growl turned into a soft howl as his change completed. It took a moment or two before the pain dulled enough for him to take flight.

CHAPTER 21

Louise watched as his cotton pants turned to ashes. She added another log, sparks flew as it fell on the hot embers. Pain flared inside her as she remembered his words. They had been so cruel and so thoughtlessly delivered.

That was a mistake.

It can't fucking happen again.

Then there was the doozy. *I was thinking with my dick instead of my head.* His words made her feel cheap and used. She made a sobbing noise and covered her mouth with her hand. She was not going to cry. Not over a guy like Granite.

She felt like his dirty secret. Something to be washed away in a hot shower. The guy was worried about the others finding out. He hated the idea. She was a dirty secret to him when he was becoming so much more to her. Louise squeezed her eyes shut. She was falling for him. Falling for a guy who cared nothing for her, one who was ashamed of her.

He was right when he said it wasn't happening again.

She respected herself too damned much to go down that road again.

Louise sniffed and took in a deep breath. She was going to be just fine. She'd focus on her job. No worries. Her shoulders already felt lighter.

There was knock at the door. *Damn it! Who the hell was that?* It was too soon to be Granite . . . surely?

"I'm busy with something . . . an experiment. Go away!" she added a little louder.

There was another knock and a muffled voice on the other side.

She moved closer to the door. "Please come back a bit later." Her heart was beating right out of her chest. She felt like she might be sick.

The person spoke again. "It's me . . . It's Granite." It was really muffled and sounded like Granite. *Could it be? It had to be.*

"Granite?" Her heart eased just a tad and she was able to draw in a breath.

"Yes!" More clear this time and it sounded like him. Gruff and short.

Thank god! It took a few attempts but she managed to pull the chair out from under the door handle. He strode in wearing a fresh pair of pants. His face was set with determination. The frown lines between his eyes were back and in full force. His eyes were so dark they looked almost black.

His nostrils flared. "Why didn't you shower and burn your clothes?" Straight to the point.

"I didn't relish the idea of standing around naked."

"Fine, but do it now," he said while securing the chair back under the door handle. He turned to face her. "We don't have all the time in the world," he spoke under his breath, like he was afraid someone might hear.

"Turn around first."

He narrowed his eyes. "I've seen you naked."

Louise gave a shrug. "I don't care. You can turn around." She folded her arms across her chest.

"We don't have time for this. I know exactly how you look under those clothes, every curve, every damned freckle. I've felt you from the inside, that's my seed dripping down your thighs right now."

His words still had the ability to make her feel all hot and a whole lot bothered. It irritated the hell out of her. The guy could go to hell and he could do it watching her undress. She didn't care. Not one little itty bitty bit. She was not giving in again so what did it matter. "Fine." She pulled her lab coat open with one hard yank; buttons went flying. They landed all around her, clattering on the tiled floor. She threw the garment in the fire. Next, she undid the top few buttons of her blouse, and pulled it over her head. His eyes honed in on her bra. If she had known she was getting naked she'd have worn one of her lacy sets.

What was she saying? He didn't deserve to see her in her best lingerie. Not that she had much in the lingerie department. She had a black set, the one she had been wearing at the weekend, and a red set. That was it.

The bra she had on now, like the rest of her underwear,

was practical and comfortable. It was soft cotton. She put her hands behind her back to feel for the clasp. His eyes remained on her chest. His pants tented.

Good!

Let him suffer. In fact, she was going to draw it out, make him wish he had turned around like she'd asked him. Give him some of his own medicine. She pushed her chest out some more. She didn't have the biggest boobs but she definitely had a pair of breasts to be proud of. Firm with a decent set of nipples that popped when she was turned on. She glanced down and *hello* . . . there they were. Hard like small pebbles against the thin fabric. In fact, she could see their dark pink coloring through the cotton as well. *Bastard!*

His pants tented some more and his chest rose and fell in quick succession. Good to know that he was just as attracted to her. Clearly thinking with his dick again. After another few drawn out seconds, she finally popped the clasp. Instead of just letting the bra fall right off, she carefully took each strap from her shoulders, sure to keep the cups over her breasts till the last possible second. His mouth actually fell open, his gaze locked on her chest. His breathing was definitely elevated. If she took his blood pressure now it would be through the roof.

Asshole deserved it. She pulled her shoulders back so that the girls would look their best, then she pulled the bra the rest of the way off and tossed it in the fire. It sounded like he might have made a quiet groaning noise. She couldn't be sure though. Then she unzipped the skirt. She could've pulled both the skirt and the ruined panties off in one go but she chose to first slowly ease the skirt down her hips instead. Slowly and painstakingly, one inch at a time. She tossed the skirt in the fire and then turned to face the flames.

Louise bent over, hooking her fingers in what was left of her cotton underwear and eased then from her body, lifting one leg and then the other. She threw the torn panties into the fire. She put one hand on the mantle, picking up the iron poker with the other. Louise spread her thighs just a tad and leaned over to stoke the fire.

This time there was a definite groan behind her followed by what sounded like a muttering of curse words. "Leave it, damn it!" his voice sounded thick and deep. "Go and wash up. The shower head is not fixed to the wall."

She turned, looking back at him from over her shoulder. Her breath caught in her throat. His erection was huge. His muscles bulged, especially his abs. That 'V' thing he had going on was incredible, as were his biceps. Then again, his hands were locked into fists at his sides so it was no wonder.

No drooling.

No staring.

She stood tall and gave a nod, making her way to the bathroom. Then she registered what he had said. "What difference does it make if the showerhead is fixed or not?"

He grit his jaw. "Really, female? You need to remove my scent from your body. Would you like me to draw you a picture, or better yet, I could come and help you?" He took a step towards her.

A shiver rushed through her at the thought of him wielding the shower head. Only, she had a feeling she'd get way dirtier before she got any cleaner. *Not a chance!* "Like hell you will." She turned and hurried from the room, closing the door behind her.

She did as he said, washing from head to toe several times. Then she used the showerhead . . . there. All she could think about was his hands on her. How big and hard he was. How he moved when he was inside her. Then there were the grunting noises he made as he went over the edge.

It made her feel achy and needy all over again. *Bastard!* Louise washed herself with soap again. It was only when she got out of the shower that she spied her toothbrush and toothpaste. It was wet. The ass-wipe had used her toothbrush. It wasn't like he'd a choice.

She sighed as she put toothpaste on the brush and cleaned her teeth with the same vigor she had her body.

She contemplated forgoing a towel but decided against it. Instead, she wrapped it firmly around herself.

Granite was leaning against the gurney. He got up as she entered the room. His erection problem was still in full force. She had to bite her lip to keep from laughing at him. He deserved it.

He fumbled with the bag, finally handing it to her. Louise took it from him, she unzipped it and rummaged inside.

No way! Using just a finger she lifted the red lace slip. "Really? Out of all of the underwear in there, this is what you chose?"

Granite shrugged.

Then she realized which dress he had chosen. She gasped. "This is the dress I wear to go out to dinner. It's the proverbial 'little black dress.'" It was tight-fitting, stopping about mid-thigh. She hadn't worn it in forever. She didn't even know why she'd brought it along on this trip. "I'm at work," she added. "I can't wear that."

"Wear the damned dress." He pulled it from the bag and thrust it in her hand. "You are a beautiful female and should dress accordingly."

"Oh . . ." *In that case.* "Okay." She got the feeling he didn't dish out compliments often. Maybe ever.

He narrowed his eyes for a moment. "You have fucking stunning breasts and should showcase them." He dug in the bag a second time and put the filmy bra in her hand as well. "Your pussy . . ." He made a growling noise at the back his throat. It did strange things to her clit. "Don't get me started on that part of your anatomy. So damned pretty . . . all pink and your fur is . . ." he growled, louder this time. "You're beautiful and sexy. You should own it." He handed her the tiny slip that would barely cover her sex. She'd never worn this set before.

Louise swallowed hard, trying to get herself to calm down. Her nipples were so tight. Her breasts felt swollen and heavy. She had that feeling in the pit of her stomach. Granite was doing that hot-cold thing again. He'd been so nasty to her right after they had sex and yet here he was being . . . nice to her. Calling her beautiful and sexy and making her feel things she shouldn't be feeling. The least of all was turned on.

"Shit!" he muttered, giving the air a sniff. "You're just as horny as I am . . . maybe more so."

"No, I'm not," her voice was squeaky. "Definitely not more so than . . . you." She looked at his dick. "You could drill through walls with that thing. You shouldn't say things like that to a person and not expect a reaction."

"Fuck!" Granite looked at the ceiling. He walked away from her, his hand going to the back of his neck and squeezing. He paced up and down a few times. The tension in the room was almost palpable.

He finally turned and faced her head on. "Get up on that that bed and open your legs."

She felt her eyes bug out. "What? No! Have you lost your mind?"

Granite cursed under his breath and muttered something. It sounded like he was agreeing with her about losing his mind. "Please can you just do it? Go and lie down. Spread your thighs wide."

She shook her head and even held her hand up like that might ward him off when the truth was, if he so much as laid a finger on her she would be putty in his hands. "No! We discussed this. No more sex. We just showered. I had to use that shower head . . . down there . . ." her voice tapered off.

His eyes rolled back and he groaned. "I pictured you

using it. It almost had me coming in my pants like a teenager so please don't remind me. We've established that we're attracted to each other and that we are compatible. Sex with you is the best I've ever had. I could live inside your body."

All righty. Flip it! She felt like fanning her face and other parts of herself. "This isn't helping. We can't do this."

"We can't rut but we can . . . do other things."

"What things?" She could imagine, but that crazy part of her wanted to hear him say them. Not that they were going to happen. They could not happen.

"I can make you come a whole hell of a lot with my mouth on your pussy." *Dear god in heaven but he was forward.* "I'd love to suck on your clit."

She felt like grabbing her girl parts and holding onto them. It felt like she was about to self-combust. Her clit throbbed like mad. She made a squeaking noise.

"I'd suck and lick my way to your pussy and make you come with my tongue, deep inside you."

"Oh!"

"Only thing is . . ."

Here it was, the 'but' . . .

He picked up a note pad off of her desk. "You need to write another one of those order forms. You'll need mouthwash and hand-sanitizer. Get a couple of packs of those wipes, the perfumed ones."

She nodded. *Why was she nodding?* It was like she was agreeing to this madness. *She wasn't . . . was she?*

"I can see that you're preparing to argue." He walked

up to her and put his hands on her shoulders. "We have this crazy attraction, Louise. It's there whether we like it or not. It is what it is. I've tried to deny it. I tried to ignore it but it's not going to go away any time soon and until it does, we need to acknowledge it, manage it."

Manage it.

What?

"Order the things we need. I'll lick your sweet pussy for the next week, two weeks . . ." He made a groaning noise. "Three months if that's what it takes. Let's ride this thing out and move on."

Move on.

What?

It hurt to hear him say that. "Oh, and I suppose you want me to suck your cock in return?" It just slipped out. She couldn't help herself. Granite was just too much. Handing her compliments, offering her sexual favors, there had to be a 'but' or an 'and' or a string of some sorts. *Handcuffs.* With Granite it would be handcuffs instead of string. A handcuff to the headboard. She tried not to scowl at him but only because the thought of being handcuffed to the headboard made her feel even more hot and heavy.

He licked his lips and she tracked the movement. *How could she not?* He had a gorgeous mouth. "No!" a rumble. "I wouldn't expect a thing in return. Don't get me wrong, I would love to see your lips wrapped around me. Fucking love it." He cupped her chin and ran a thumb over her bottom lip. "I think it would help me hold onto some sort of control if you were satisfied. I'll deal with this myself."

He palmed his cock through his pants and her mouth went dry.

"Get on the bed, Louise." She loved the way he said her name. He didn't say it often but when he did it made her take notice.

"This is a bad idea," an almost whisper.

"Do you have a better one?" *Dear god, he was right behind her.* Then his hands were on her hips, his front pressed against her. His cock pressed into her lower back. Thick, hard and ready.

Maybe just this one time.

One last time.

Granite picked her up as they reached the gurney. The bed was higher than a normal bed and a little narrower. She scooted to the middle. Her breathing was already heavy. Her towel still locked into place.

Calloused hands gripped her ankles and pulled her to the edge of the bed. She looked into his intense, dark stare. "Put your legs over my shoulders."

"Okay," she nodded. "Maybe just one," she whispered, more to herself than to him. Louise did as he said.

His eyes stayed on hers. "Two."

Oh lord up above. Two. Okay, maybe twice then. These last two times. Then she would be strong and protect herself from him. She really would.

Granite slowly leaned forward, moving closer and closer to where she needed him the most. "I've been dying to get my tongue inside you."

Louise let her head fall back, staring up at the ceiling.

The towel felt tight around her breasts. Everything felt tight with need and anticipation. When his tongue finally laved her clit, her back bowed off the bed and a loud groan was pulled from her.

Granite chuckled. "Shhhh. You're going to need to try to be quiet."

She looked down at him crouching over her. *So damned sexy.* Louise gave a nod, not sure if she would able to do as he had said.

Her mouth opened as he laved her again, but she managed to stifle the moan. Only just. There were no pillows. No blankets. Nothing to use to muffle the sounds she was bound to make.

His mouth closed over that very sensitive, swollen bundle of nerves and she almost gave a yell from the sheer pleasure that moved through her in a rush. Good thing he said two because the first one was happening any second now.

More laving and sucking. Louise clenched her teeth and covered her mouth with her hand. She held on tight. Her eyes were wide, her body felt tense. Poised for release.

"Mmmmmm . . ." Granite had his mouth over her clit and he started to hum. The noise of appreciation caused vibrations.

That was it.

Done.

She clapped her other hand over her mouth. Her back came off the bed. He had to know she was coming because he suckled her, hard at first and then softer and softer as she slowly came down. The guy was good with his mouth. No, he was better than good, he was fantastic.

Her body felt boneless. She could actually feel the endorphins course through her. His tongue still felt amazing.

A finger slipped inside.

Oh.

Granite pumped his finger a couple of times. His tongue remained soft, his strokes easy.

It didn't take long for that to change. Before long, there were two fingers inside her. Deep inside. She could hardly breathe. His tongue stroked her clit. Not too hard, not too soft. Just right. Just so. Just . . . *Yes . . . Oh god . . .*

She clapped her other hand back over her mouth, feeling the start of her orgasm. That familiar fluttering. That familiar tightening. Everything coiling. Then she was plunging. She could feel her channel squeeze his hand. It was quick and powerful and left her a quivering heap.

She forced her gaze on him, his eyes were dark and wild. His lips were wet. Granite licked them, slowly making her own mouth feel dry. He gave her the sexiest half-smile she had ever seen. He stood up and her eyes were drawn to his erection.

It was out there and in all its glory. Louise licked her own lips.

"Go and clean up." He looked pointedly at the bathroom. "I'll go after you."

He really didn't expect anything from her. Despite having given her two of the best orgasms of her life, he was willing to just walk away, hard-on and all. It meant something to her. It was selfless and endearing. Granite could be an asshole but he could also be a really nice guy.

"Wait." She took her bottom lip between her teeth and unhooked the edge of her towel, allowing it to slip off.

His eyes immediately focused on her breasts. He swallowed hard and his jaw tensed. Then he looked back up at her face. "You don't have to do this."

"I know." She slid off of the gurney and closed the short distance between them. She pulled down his pants and out popped his dick. Hard, thick and ready. Louise cupped his heavy balls. His eyes rolled back in his skull and he made a sexy groaning noise.

"You really don't have to," he repeated, his breathing was harder than it had been before. His chest rose and fell.

Instead of answering, she dropped to her knees and closed her hand around his thick girth. "I can't wait to suck on your big cock." Her cheeks heated. She wasn't used to talking dirty.

By the look in Granite's eyes, he approved.

"I can't fucking wait for you too either," he growled.

Louise wasn't about to make him wait any longer. She took his tip into her mouth and swirled her tongue over it. Granite groaned and thread a hand through her hair. Then she took him deeper, using her other hand to work his shaft. Up and down.

He made a grunting noise. "Not going to last," a deep moan. "You have one hell of a sexy mouth."

His hand stayed in her hair. He touched her with such

tenderness. She kept it slow and easy. Pumping her hand in time with her mouth and tongue.

After a couple of minutes, he was panting, making small circular motions with his hips. She sucked him as deep as he would go, taking the head of his cock to the back of her throat. At the same time she fisted him quicker, using a bit more pressure.

"Fuck!" a harsh growl.

She released him. "Shhh. You need to stay quiet," Louise had to giggle.

She took him back into her mouth. Hard and deep.

He muttered a soft curse. His fingers splayed on her scalp, they tangled a little deeper and yet he remained careful not to hurt her or force her.

"I'm going to come."

She sucked him deeper.

"Going to . . ." He pulled away, taking two or three steps back. He closed a hand over the head of his cock while the other pumped up and down on his shaft. His face was pinched. Granite was frowning deeply. His gaze was locked with hers.

It was the single most erotic thing she had ever seen. The sound of his ragged breathing filled the room.

She realized that she was breathing hard as well. She couldn't take her eyes off of him. Then he made a strained, grunting noise. His shoulders hunched over. He pursed his lips. Granite kept pumping for a few beats and then his movements slowed. His breaths came as harsh grunts. He finally stopped moving. "I could get used to that," he managed between breaths. "I'm just going to . . ." he nodded in the direction of the bathroom.

"Yeah, sure."

"I won't be long." He disappeared, closing the door behind him.

Louise got back onto her feet. Her legs felt a bit shaky. *Damn!* She could get used to this too. That was the problem. He wanted this to become a regular thing. Louise knew that she shouldn't allow this arrangement but she didn't think she would have much willpower where this man was concerned. It was a problem, a huge problem. If they were intimate on a regular basis she would end up falling even more for him. She knew it.

CHAPTER 22

Four days later...

There was a knock at her door.

Louise looked up from her computer. "Yes?"

Igneous put his head around the jamb, he grinned as soon as his eyes met hers. "I have a delivery for you."

It was the supplies she'd ordered a few days before. Both the legit stuff as well as the other things . . . the mouthwash and scented soaps. The alcohol wipes and sanitizer all designed to mask the scent of oral sex. Her mind went into overdrive for a few seconds even though nothing had happened between the two of them since.

The last time she had seen him, Granite had whispered into her ear. It was amazing how three little words could have such an effect on her.

I can't wait.

She'd been immediately aroused and terrified. She looked down at the boxes. There was more than one package. Three to be exact.

"Thanks, Igneous," she smiled at him.

"No, problem. Can I help you unpack?"

"No!" she said, a bit too sharply. "I can manage," she added. Louise smiled, praying she looked relaxed and carefree. "Thanks so much for these."

"No problem, Doc," he winked. "I'll see you soon."

"Yeah. Take care."

He gave her another wink and left. Louise found she could only breathe easy once he was gone. They were sneaking around, or, they were about to sneak around. Her heart also beat faster at the prospect.

She grabbed a pair of scissors from the drawer and opened it, using the sharp side to cut open the box. It had been taped closed. The box was filled with her medical supplies. She spent the next while putting them away.

Using the same scissors, she cut the next box open. The smallest of the three. There were a couple of bubble wrapped items inside. She pulled the wrap open and her mouth fell open.

"Oh my god . . ." she muttered to herself. "No!"

Louise pulled the next one out. There was a note inside.

Thank you for all your hard work!
G. X

Her certificates. The ones that had fallen from the wall and crashed. They'd all been reframed. Granite had organized this. She bit down on her lip. Louise couldn't believe it. She blinked a few times, feeling a little emotional about it. It was stupid. They weren't even together or anything. Thing was, he'd given her enough thought to go to all the trouble of fixing them. He knew how much her career meant to her. He must have seen the ruined frames on the shelf. That or Rock had told him about them. It didn't matter.

It was a small thing. An inconsequential thing, yet it meant the world to her.

Louise sniffed. She hung the frames, one by one, back in their rightful places on the wall. Then her gaze turned to the next box.

What the hell was in it?

She couldn't wait to find out. Louise grabbed the scissors and made quick work of the tape. She pulled the box open and almost fell on her ass.

Victoria's Secret was a damn sight richer, that was for darned sure. She pulled out set after set of lingerie. In all kinds of colors and types. From thin lacy numbers to push-up bras. From full sheer briefs to tiny thongs that looked more like dental floss than underwear. Louise had a goofy smile on her face. Her cheeks actually hurt from smiling so wide.

There were a couple of dresses at the bottom of the box. Sexy numbers. A red A-line ankle length dress that had no back. Nothing. The back dipped right down. So sexy it almost took her breath away. Then there was a short green, sleeveless dress. The color would suit her perfectly. The black dress was a wraparound, it had short sleeves. The next black number had a plunging neckline. It was daring and bold.

There was a note at the bottom of the box.

Because you are beautiful.
G. X

Simple and sweet. She clutched the note to her chest feeling like a teenager. Louise spied a second note.

Choose a set of lingerie and put it on. Do it now! Then put your coat back on. No clothes. Don't be a spoil sport.
G. X

Louise shook her head, she was still smiling like an idiot. He knew her well by now. He'd know she'd have big reservations about wearing a coat without any clothes underneath. She finally sighed, looking at her watch. It was ten minutes until Granite was due to arrive for his appointment.

Her heart beat wildly in her chest. She wanted to shower but at the same time, she didn't want to seem like she was trying too hard.

Louise sifted through the lingerie, finally choosing a sexy black set. It was a push up bra so she'd have a little cleavage and a dental floss pair of thongs. She packed everything else away, shoving the box in the corner. Then she headed for the bathroom.

Louise did as he said, slipping into the lingerie and her medical coat. She put her low heels back on. For a moment, she contemplated taking her hair out of the bun and then thought better of it. Lastly, she applied some deodorant and a fresh coat of lip gloss.

If anyone came to her clinic they would be none the wiser. She looked like she normally did. Louise bit down on her lower lip. She felt sexy and alive.

She folded her skirt and blouse and packed them away. There were still a few minutes to kill. Louise had just opened a file when there was a knock at the door.

Granite walked in. His gaze zeroed in on her. He stared at her for a couple of seconds. The intensity of his stare had her breath seizing in her lungs. Thankfully, he looked away. She could breathe again. He took her office chair and used it to prop the door closed.

Her heart raced and her hands felt clammy.

"Your supplies arrived," he said, turning back to her. It was more of a statement than a question.

She gave a nod. "Thank you for reframing my certificates."

He smiled. It lasted all of a half a second. "You're welcome."

"Thanks for the . . ." She felt her face heat up. "Other things as well."

"No need to thank me."

"But, I want to. I . . ."

Granite shook his head. "Those were just as much for me, so really, you don't need to thank me."

Her mouth went dry.

"Did you do what I asked you to do?" His gaze traveled

down the length of her body.

Louise nodded. "Yeah." She swallowed thickly.

"Good!" a rumble. He stalked towards her. "I meant it when I said I couldn't wait."

He stopped just short of her. His focus was on her white coat. "Undo some of those buttons."

Louise gave a nod. Her hands shook a bit as she undid the first one or two buttons. She sucked in a deep breath, continuing to open them up. One at a time.

Granite licked his lower lip. It was a slow swipe of his tongue. She couldn't help but track the movement. "All of them," he demanded, drawing her attention back to the job at hand. She did as he said, undoing the last few.

He closed the distance between them and took ahold of her hips. His hands were big and warm. Then he picked her up. She gripped his shoulders.

Granite put her down on the gurney. The mattress was firm. Her ass was on the very edge.

Her coat was still closed, even though all of the buttons were undone. He stepped between her thighs and carefully parted the starched cotton. His eyes were dark and so focused. It took her breath away to think that all of it was directed at her.

"So damned beautiful." He looked back into her eyes. Granite reached behind her and took the tie out of her hair. One by one he removed the pins holding all the strands in place. "That's better." He leaned forward and kissed her. Soft and slow. Really sweet.

Then he pulled back, looking deep into her eyes. "Lean

back," he instructed. Louise did as he asked, keeping herself semi-upright by balancing on her elbows. Her coat fell all the way open. She parted her thighs some more. She'd never felt more sensual or more desired.

Granite dragged his eyes across her body. By now he was sporting one hell of an erection.

"Take off those pants!" She was appalled to hear how husky her voice sounded.

Granite's mouth twitched at the corner but he did as she said, pulled down the elasticated pants and stepped out of them one leg at a time. He was so attractive. His naked body was something too. From his long muscular legs to his broad chest. Not to mention everything in-between.

Granite leaned forward over her, his cock rubbed up against her upper thigh before connecting with her panty-clad pussy. She made a gentle moaning noise. How could she not? His hard tip rubbed against her clit

"I want to be inside you so badly it hurts." Granite gave her another sweet kiss that made her toes curl and her breath come in soft pants.

"I want you too," breathless. Even huskier than before.

Granite kissed her neck, then he kissed the tops of her breasts before planting a delicate kiss on her stomach. Everywhere he touched felt amazing. Goosebumps lifted on her arms.

"I'll make you feel good," he said as he pulled the string-like thong to the side. "So damned good." Barely the tip of his tongue brushed her swollen clit. It was enough to make her cry out.

She bit down on her lower lip to stop herself from making too much noise.

"So delicious," he whispered against her clit. "I'm going to make you come on my mouth . . ." *a lick,* "my tongue . . ." *a suck,* "my hand." His finger pressed against her opening. Then he made good on his promise. Several times

CHAPTER 23

Two weeks later...

"I can't believe how much those two are growing."

"I should hope so," Breeze gave a tired smile. "Considering how often they drink, especially all hours of the night."

"How often do they wake up?" Louise took a sip of her orange juice.

"At around ten, then again at one and then at about five."

Louise relaxed. "Okay, so they're completely normal then. It might feel overwhelming, and it's understandable that you're tired. Do they keep you up a long time?"

The other woman shook her head. "Nah! Twenty minutes, maybe half an hour. Nothing excessive, thing is..." Breeze paused. "That's Crystal's schedule. Little Gem wakes up at about nine, midnight and four. I'm finished!" she yawned. "It feels like I just get my eyes closed and I'm awake for the next one."

"You have to get them onto a schedule," Louise

warned. "It's really important. I'm not sure how you're coping."

"I'm not." Breeze widened her eyes. "They do wake up together some of the time." She looked at the nursing babies in her arms. "Mainly during the day."

"Some of the time and during the day is not enough though."

"You're telling me!" Breeze shook her head. Her eyes were bloodshot.

"If one wakes up, you need to wake up the other one. I'm not an expert but I know a few basics and this is one of them."

Breeze nodded. "You're right and every night I tell myself I'm going to do it but then I don't." She wrinkled her nose. "I can't wake up a sleeping baby. Especially so soon after working so hard to get her to sleep."

"You have to get them onto the same pattern though. You can't go on like this."

Breeze nodded. "I know. Ugh! You are so right. I'm going to be strong and do it. It doesn't matter how hard it will be to wake up a child I only just put to bed, it just has to be done."

"For your own sanity," Louise added. Her friend looked exhausted.

Breeze gave a tired smile. "Enough about my really boring existence. I can't wait to get out and about again. To lead a bit of a normal life." She shook her head. "Don't get me wrong, I'm loving being a mom. I love these two so much." She looked down at the girls in her arms.

Gem had just fallen asleep. There was milk – the dragon equivalent – on her chin. Crystal was still sucking but the pauses between sucks were getting longer and longer. "How are things with you?" Breeze asked, looking a less tired.

"Good," she shrugged. "Doing my thing."

"I have to say, you look different somehow. Ever since you and Granite had your dirty weekend," Breeze paused, "even he seems different. Volcano and I were discussing it." Then she huffed out a breath. "Is there something going on between the two of you?"

"Of course not!" Louise answered a little too quickly. "That's nuts."

"Are you sure?"

"I'm absolutely sure. It was a one-time thing. It happened and now it's over, end of story."

Breeze kept her eyes locked with Louise's for what felt like the longest time. She finally looked away. "Alright, if you say so but I still think he has a thing for you."

"No, he doesn't." It was sexual. They hardly talked about anything other than the Resistance Therapy.

It wasn't like sex talk counted. They did a ton of that. It was seriously hot but it didn't count as actual conversation. It certainly wasn't deep and meaningful. "It's strictly business," she added.

Breeze cocked her head. "I think you have a bit of a thing for him as well. I've seen the way you guys look at each other. It's like a knowing look. Like the two of you share some sort of secret that the rest of us aren't privy to.

I can't quite put my finger on it." Her eyes were raised in thought.

"We had sex once and that's something, I think. It was to me." She held up a hand. "Not that I have any kind of feelings for him or anything. Not beyond friendship, even though you couldn't really call us friends," she was ranting and if she carried on she was sure to give them away. She didn't want to put Breeze in that position.

"If you say so. He's just acting differently that's all."

Breeze was right. Granite was acting differently towards her. He'd smiled at her a couple of times in public. Another delivery had arrived with more clothing. Spaghetti-strap tops, sundresses, the most beautiful sandals and a pair of stud earrings. They were the best cubic zirconias she had ever seen. So sparkly. She'd worn them for the last week straight.

She was enjoying the attention and enjoyed spending time with him. Despite not having actual sex, the orgasms were off the chart and if anything, he was trying harder as a result.

Granite had slipped into her room in the dead of the night and had actually fallen asleep with her last night. In her bed; she'd had her head resting on his chest. Thank god he'd woken up and left before activity started in the lair. Aside from the risk of getting caught, it was starting to feel too much like a relationship. The longer this went on, the more it was going to hurt when it ended . . . and it was going to end. That was the only thing that was certain.

There was only one thing to do about it. It would entail

guarding her heart before this went too far. Before it was too late.

"You look upset," Breeze said as she moved a sleeping Gem into her lap.

Louise shook her head. "Not at all! There is a lot of pressure on me to make this program work. To find a solution to your silver allergy. It gets to me sometimes." It wasn't a total lie, she did feel pressured and driven.

"I need to get going. You should go and nap anyway," she continued.

Breeze gave a nod. "I could do with a rest." Her friend reached out and clutched her arm. "Are you sure you're okay?" she frowned as she spoke.

Louise nodded. "Absolutely." A bald-faced lie.

"*Sure* sure?"

"Yeah definitely." She wasn't okay . . . far from it. Her wayward emotions added confirmation that she had made the right decision. She was going to stick to her guns. She had to.

Volcano leaned forward. "What's going on?"

Granite frowned. "What do you mean?"

"I don't know, you're too relaxed. You're too calm, too . . ." He looked thoughtful for a moment. "I don't know, too happy. Yeah, that's it. Not that you were unhappy before. You just weren't this content. This happy."

Granite knew exactly why he felt this way. Why there was an extra spring to his step. Why he looked so damned relaxed. It all had to do with one little doctor.

More precisely, it had to do with getting his pipes cleaned every other day. Okay, for the last week, it had been every day. They were taking more and more chances but it was too good between them not to. He'd popped into her office unannounced and had blocked her door and made her come. Quick and hard. He hadn't allowed her to return the favor. Granite loved watching as her breaths turned ragged and hoarse. He loved that look of awe she took on just as she reached the edge. He fucking loved the look of rapture when he made her come so hard her eyes watered.

Granite had also snuck into her room in the early hours of the morning and had licked her clit until her legs shook. Until she'd had to cover her face with her pillow to muffle her cries. He'd fallen asleep at her place the other night. It was the first time he had slept at a female's place. The first time he had really slept in another person's arms. It was only a handful of hours but it was the best sleep he'd had in a long time. The human was good for him. He liked to think that the opposite was true but she was as sexy as hell.

Especially when she had her mouth around his cock, her hand kneading his balls and her . . .

"Hey! You zoned out there for a few seconds. You had this . . . smile on your face," Volcano interrupted.

"I wasn't smiling."

"You were smiling. I know a smile when I see one."

Granite narrowed his eyes. "I was not smiling. It was indigestion."

"Indigestion!" Volcano laughed. "Like hell!" He

laughed some more. "If you say so, asshole."

"I *do* fucking say so."

"Sure thing." Volcano gave him a slap on the back. "Whatever."

Granite heaved an internal sigh of relief. Volcano might suspect something but he was clueless. He needed to be more careful. Was Louise acting any differently towards him? Were they any different together? With one another? Not that they were in public together very often. It was something they needed to consider. He was going to discuss it with her later. Granite had planned on sneaking into her room again tonight. It could wait until then.

They just needed to be a bit more careful and a lot more aware. The last thing he wanted was for someone to find out. If this got out it would spell the end of her time here. The Resistance Therapy meant too much to Louise. It meant far too damned much to the career she'd worked so hard towards. She might not be able to find work very easily if she was made to leave. Positions like hers didn't come around too often. Especially the research type, which was where her passion lay. *No!* They needed to proceed with extreme caution.

"How are my nieces?" he asked, trying hard to concentrate on what Volcano had to say. Granite was worried about the female. His level of worry was a worry in itself. Louise was the best person for this job, he didn't want to see her replaced and the program disrupted. That was it. That was why he was so damned tied up in knots. It helped him to relax some.

CHAPTER 24

That night . . .

There was the sound of footfalls down the hallway. Granite forced himself to stop pacing. He waited and waited some more. The person slowed and stopped. It had to be her. The door swung open. Granite sucked in a deep breath as Louise walked through the door. "I thought you would never come back to your chamber." The words left him in a rush. It felt like he'd been waiting for forever.

Louise grabbed her chest and gasped. "You almost gave me a heart attack!" She pulled in a couple of deep breaths.

"Where were you?" He was already scenting the air, trying to catch another male's scent. *What was wrong with him?* Granite forced himself to calm down. She wasn't that kind of female. The kind to fuck around.

"I stepped up the contact time with silver again. Igneous had a bad reaction. His heart stopped during the therapy session." She looked concerned.

He could see that she was shaken up, could even scent

fear on her. Granite didn't like to see her so out of sorts. "What happened?" a low growl.

Louise seemed to calm down but only slightly. "He arrested. It happened out of the blue. I managed to resuscitate him but it could have gone either way. I know you've said that shifters can come back from the dead, but I don't like taking such huge risks. I think that we need to back up a bit. We're pushing this whole thing just a bit too much."

Granite nodded. He trusted the female's judgement. "Yes, okay. Send me an amended program when you get a chance."

Louise looked confused for a moment. "Are you sure you're okay with that?"

"Yeah, very sure. I don't want anything serious to happen to any of the males and I respect your professional opinion." He fucking hated that she was nervous and upset about the incident.

It didn't seem to placate her. She seemed agitated somehow. Louise removed her coat and slung it over the back of a chair. "I'm glad you're here because we need to talk."

Granite strode to her and put his arms around her waist. "We can talk later." She was wearing one of the summer dresses he had bought for her. It was grey with big black polka dots. She looked so damned cute in it. Her little breasts pushed up against the fabric. Her nipples were hard. He could only guess at the underwear that would be beneath the soft fabric. Her gaze had dropped to his dick more than once in the short time since she had arrived.

His semi was now fully erect. He felt like a dick considering the nature of the conversation but it couldn't be helped. He hadn't seen her the whole day. His mouth watered for a taste of her sweet pussy.

Louise shook her head, she took a step back severing contact. "We need to talk. I don't think it can wait."

It looked like something serious. He reined in his need for her. "What is it? Did something happen? I told you we can change the program, I'm happy to go with your recommendations. I trust you." He looked into her wide green eyes and realized that he did. Even more than he had before.

"That's just it," she paused. "You shouldn't be happy. Up until a short while ago you would have taken my head off." She shook her head "Acted like a complete asshole if I'd attempted to table such a thing, let alone tried to implement it. Why the sudden change?"

He thought about what she had said. "You are a good doctor." It was the truth. "I've gotten to know you. I–"

"It's because we're intimate. You do know that your brother and Breeze suspect that there's something between us?"

"I know, Volcano spoke to me earlier. We need to be more careful. That's all. In fact, I'd planned on chatting to you about it after making you come a couple of times."

"Oh flip, he spoke to you?" She covered her face with her hands for a second or two.

"Yes, it's not a big deal. We can keep this a secret. We need to be a bit more careful that's all." Something in him clenched at the thought of their relationship ending. Not that they had a real relationship. He enjoyed her company. They were compatible. It was an excellent arrangement.

Louise shook her head. "No, it would be better just to stop this madness. We agreed it was short-term. We've had fun and now it should be over, before one of us gets burned." By the look on her face she suspected that person would be her.

"Neither of us is about to get burned. I won't let that happen. Besides, no one is going to find out." He put his hands on her shoulders and looked into her beautiful green eyes. "We are having fun, aren't we? You're enjoying yourself, aren't you?" It felt like an icy fist had taken ahold of his heart. He struggled to breathe. He would not let her walk away. Not yet.

"You know I'm having fun and of course I'm enjoying myself. We're having a great time but it's too big a risk," she shook her head. Her frown became deeper. "It's getting to a point where it's not worth the risk anymore, Granite, you need to understand that. Someone is bound to find out about us. You would get a slap on the wrist but I would end up out on my ass."

"We're being careful." That fist tightened a whole lot more. Granite struggled to breathe. He was losing the battle. The thought of not touching her again was too much. They were too damned good together. Another few weeks and this crazy attraction would peter out.

"Not careful enough. The dynamic between two people who are intimate is different. Those close to you are starting to pick up on it."

"Bullshit! I like your pussy and that's where it ends. No one is going to pick up on anything."

She seemed to shut down even further, looking at the ground, instead of at him. "I've made up my mind."

"Like hell!" he growled. His whole body felt tight. A need rose up in him.

Have.

Take.

He tried to calm himself down and failed. "Don't you like it when I touch you?" He cupped her pussy through the material of her dress. The need increased. He couldn't get enough air. Couldn't think beyond having Louise. Of convincing her that they were right. That this was all that mattered . . . right now.

"Yes," a moan. "Of course."

Thank fuck! Her honesty fueled him. Granite leaned down and gripped the fabric of her dress, he pulled the bodice from her shoulders, snapping one of the straps in the process. Her tight raspberry-tipped breasts sprang free. *Fucking perfection.* Soft curves and hard nubs. They begged him for affection.

"Granite," it was part warning and part plea. He chose to ignore the first and obey the second. On a groan, he closed his mouth over one of the nubs, it tightened up in his mouth.

She moaned. "No, we . . ."

"We're good together." He brushed a kiss across her lips. "Doesn't this feel good?" He slid his hand beneath the hem of her dress and palmed her slit. She wore a pair of briefs. They were silk and smooth to the touch.

"Yes . . ." another moan. Her eyes were glazed over. "But . . ."

He couldn't do buts, couldn't take not touching all of her soft skin. Hearing her moan. It wasn't about to happen, so best she accept it. "But you want to end it. Fuck that." He couldn't think clearly. Not with her pussy in his hand, the material wet beneath his touch. He needed to feel her soft skin so he ripped the underwear open, shredding the silk like it was nothing. The thought of not touching her again was maddening. It was unacceptable. He slipped a finger into her wet heat and pumped. His dick physically ached.

"We can't . . ." Her eyes closed and her head fell back. Her mouth opened. Her tight breasts rose and fell as her breathing became hard.

"I need this," he groaned. "I need you. You need me right back."

She bit down on her lip. He leaned in and suckled on her tight buds. He finger-fucked her a bit deeper, a whole lot quicker.

"No!" Hearing her say it twisted his gut into knots. It caused his chest to tighten to the point of pain. His mind was foggy with sheer need. His balls pulled tight.

"Do you want me to stop?" Her scent drove him to distraction so sweet and pungent. *So his.*

"No! Yes! No . . . Oh god, you should stop," she spoke through clenched teeth. Her breath ragged. What a picture she painted. "But I don't want you to," she managed to say through hard pants. "I want you." Her fingers dug into him. Hearing her admit the truth pushed him right over the edge.

"Good," he growled, pulling down his pants. It happened before he could think on it. One minute, she was on the end of his finger and in the next she was on the end of his dick. Her eyes widened. It felt right. It felt fucking perfect.

Her legs were around his hips and her dress was bunched up high on her waist. He was fucked if he could stop. He thrust in and out of her heat. Granite made a loud grunting noise with each thrust. Fuck if he could help it. Her back was against the wall and his hands gripped her thighs to hold her in position. Nothing had ever felt this good. This right. Pure pleasure rushed through him.

"Oh god!" she moaned. "Oh . . . my . . . god . . . Granite," she yelled his name as her pussy began to flutter.

Then she was spasming around him. Milking the hell out of him. Her hands grabbed his back. Her nails dug in. The orgasm that tore through him was enough to bring him to his knees but it didn't stop the thrusting or the pleasure.

He roared as he found completion.

It was only when Louise screamed his name that he realized he was biting her. Hard enough to draw blood. He'd come inside her and he'd marked her. What the fuck had he done? He put his forehead to hers. Their intermingled breaths were the only noise in the room. He'd fucked up in a big bad way, yet he couldn't bring himself to regret it.

CHAPTER 25

Louise leaned her forehead against his shoulder. Her body still shook. Remnants of the most powerful orgasm of her life still lingered. In the tips of her breasts as they brushed against him. Deep inside her where his cock was still buried inside her.

He had bitten her. The spot stung a little. She was sure he had broken the skin.

Louise knew she should move away. Far away . . . but she couldn't right now. Her legs felt like jello. Her eyes were at half-mast. She felt slightly drunk. It must have been from the endorphins.

She had zero will-power when it came to this man. She had been able to sense where things were headed but had been unable to stop it. In fact, she'd welcomed it. Welcomed him into her body. Even now, she wanted more. So much more. More than he could ever give.

"We'll fix this," he murmured as he rubbed a hand down her back.

"How?" a whisper.

"I'm sorry! So damned sorry. I let that get out of

control."

Maybe he would understand now. Maybe he would agree to stop this madness.

"It's just that you're . . ." he pulled back and cupped her cheeks while looking deep in her eyes, "in heat. Your scent affects me on a normal day but right now it's damn near killing me."

Heat.

What?

What the hell was he talking about?

She pulled away, trying to scramble off of his lap but he held onto her. "My heat, as in my ovulation. Is that what you're saying?" She was freaking out right now but couldn't seem to stop herself.

Granite nodded once. "Calm down, female."

"Don't you dare tell me to calm down. What the hell were you thinking? That should never have happened in the first place let alone while I am fertile. Have you completely lost your freaking mind?"

"You can't become pregnant. I would never have rutted you if that was the case."

"You just ejaculated inside of me." She could feel the wetness slipping down her thighs.

Granite shook his head which infuriated her. She reached down between their bodies and held up some of the evidence. "What the hell is this then? A figment of my imagination. I don't think so. We're not together. I can't have your child."

"You are not going to have my child. I wouldn't allow

that."

His words hurt her. Each one like a hypodermic needle to the soul. The truth was that she was ready for marriage and children and she felt far too much for Granite already. "You might not have a choice in the matter. You just ejaculated inside of me and I'm fertile. I'm still not on the pill."

"I'm not fertile."

"Oh really now?" She had helped numerous single mothers give birth and plenty of them had stories to tell. Things like, 'I'll pull out at the right moment,' 'it won't happen from just one time' and then there was the whole 'I can't have children' thing. That was her personal favorite. "Let me guess, you were gouged by a bull or had them fried by a Fire dragon?"

Granite frowned. "No! I *can* father children."

"What the hell are you saying then?" she yelled.

"I will only become fertile for a short period every year or so *after* I am mated. After," he repeated. "My mate will need to go into heat first, this will trigger my heat."

"So you've never," she looked down at his junk, "had working equipment?" She looked back up at him.

He narrowed his eyes. "My dick works just fine but I can't father a child at this stage of my life, no."

"You're sure?"

"I've bedded females who were in heat before, none of them have conceived," he shrugged. "It is the same with all of the Earth dragons. We've all had females. I have only been with humans."

Louise didn't like hearing him talk about other women. This had gone too far. She could count her lucky stars that they couldn't have a baby together, even though the wistful romantic part of her wanted just that . . . but not like this.

Louise trusted him. There would be no child. She could calm down. Relax. All she could feel was disappointment though. It told her everything she needed to know.

In that moment, she knew what she had to do. She had only partially committed before. "What will happen if Blaze finds out about this? He will find out."

Granite shifted her in his lap so that she was sitting across his thighs. "I won't let that happen."

She widened her eyes. "How can it not?"

"I'm going to call Volcano. I will confide in him. He won't tell a single soul."

"And then? Everyone will know soon."

"No, they won't." Granite looked deadly serious. "I'm going to go on a trip."

"What kind of a trip? Won't it be weird if you suddenly disappear on a trip?" It sounded nuts. "Even if you're not here, I'll be here. If one person catches my scent."

"I do travel from time to time so it won't be seen as strange. We have mines deeper in the mountains." He widened his eyes and licked his lips, like he hadn't meant to tell her that.

"What kind of mines?"

"It doesn't matter. I'll head out for a couple of days and you're going to fall ill. Think of something bad. You're holing up for a couple of days."

"What will happen if they find out?"

His jaw clenched. His eyes darkened. "It's not going to happen. I will do what it—"

"What will happen?"

"You'll be fired and sent away." He was breathing heavily, like the thought of her going was terrible. "I'd be whipped." He shrugged like it was no big deal.

"What?" she half-yelled the word. "Are you serious? Physically whipped?"

Granite nodded. "The Air king received twenty lashes for mating a female who wasn't technically available to him. It doesn't happen often."

"Whipped? I can't believe that."

"Yup! The whip has a silver-barbed tip. It's normally twenty lashes." He gripped her closer. "It's not going to get out. Blaze will never find out. I can handle being whipped but I don't want you to go."

Louise had planned on turning herself in. Blaze would fire her and send her home. She couldn't do it now though. Not if it meant Granite getting hurt. She nodded. "Okay. We can try to hide it."

"Four days will be enough to lose the scent. I bit you so it will take a bit longer," he frowned. "Three days for me but I need to go for a week. My trips to . . . My trips are always for a week so I don't want to raise any eyebrows and come back sooner."

"Why so long?"

"It's only a week. I'll be back before you know it," he

smiled and kissed her softly on the lips. It was at moments like this that she felt like she was in a real relationship with him.

"Only a week." Her eyes stung so she blinked a few times. She couldn't cry. Wouldn't cry. "I'll miss you," it just slipped out but she couldn't help it.

"Mmmmhmmm!" a deep vibration. His eyes were so dark and intensely beautiful. "I'll miss licking your sweet pussy."

Louise worked hard to stop herself from feeling hurt but failed. She nodded anyway, forcing herself to smile like she meant it.

Granite rose to his feet; he took her with him, lifting her easily. "Don't touch yourself until I get back."

A rush of need worked its way through her. It was amazing how in tune her body was to him. Louise swallowed hard. "Okay."

"I mean it." He wrapped his arms around her. "Don't you dare touch yourself. I'll know." Then he turned serious. "And don't worry. I'm going to take care of everything. We'll be more careful in the future."

She gave a small murmur of agreement.

"Now remember, you are sick. Very sick. Volcano will keep you safe. I'll see you in a week." He leaned in and kissed her. She could feel him begin to pull back but she wrapped her arms around him and licked the seam of his mouth. Granite deepened the kiss with a low growl.

When he broke away, he was breathing hard. "Save it for my return. Stay low and listen to my brother. You trust me, don't you?"

She nodded.

"I fucked up but I'm going to fix this." He ran his finger down the side of her cheek.

She nodded again, feeling like her heart might just break in two.

"Okay then," he gave her a quick smile. It was gone in an instant. "I can't wait to see you again." He kissed her one more time and headed for the balcony. In seconds, a great dragon stood in his place. The beast pulled back and then launched itself into the night sky. A single tear slipped down her cheek. Louise wiped it away.

CHAPTER 26

Four days later...

Breeze closed the nursery door behind her. She had milky vomit on one of her shoulders and a wet spot on her left boob. The good news was that she didn't look as tired as she had been a week ago. It had been a couple of days of hell, but the babies were on a schedule now.

Her friend rushed towards her and wrapped her arms around her in a hard hug. "You don't have to do this," she mumbled against her shoulder.

"I do." Louise's eyes teared up so she blinked in quick succession. It had become her modus operandi lately.

Lots of blinking.

Lots of thinking about other things.

Fanning her face if need be.

No crying. No crying whatsoever! Forget that. "I have to," she added as Breeze pulled away.

"Why? I don't understand," she shook her head.

This was the first time she was seeing Breeze since being confined to her bedroom. Her friend knew what had gone down. The only condition Volcano had to helping them was that he could tell Breeze.

Then the other woman widened her eyes. "This isn't just rutting to you. You have feelings for him, don't you?"

"Shhhh," Louise looked back over her shoulder. "He can't ever know."

"I knew it," Breeze smiled broadly.

"This isn't a good thing, so you can stop your smiling."

"Why isn't it a good thing? I'm pretty sure he feels the same way about you."

Hope wrapped itself around her for a brief moment. The good, warm fuzzy feelings didn't stay as reality set in. "No," she shook her head. "He doesn't have those kinds of feelings. He's made it clear." She put a hand to the scarf around her neck. The tiny wound was almost sealed.

"You still scent of him, you know."

"What?"

"Don't worry. It's barely noticeable. You will be with Volcano so everyone will think it is him."

Louise touched the knot on her scarf. "Why is that? Do they smell the same because they are brothers?"

Breeze nodded. "Yeah. Their scents are similar" Then her eyes filled with tears. "I can't believe you're leaving."

"I have to go."

"No you don't. You could speak to Granite and then show the guy all he's missing." She sniffed. Thankfully she didn't cry.

Louise forced herself to breathe. "I can't. The next hunt is in a couple of weeks. He'll hunt down a woman and then I'll have to watch him—" She shook her head. "Watch them. I can't."

"He never brings a female back."

"What if he does?" Her heart beat overtime. "If not this time then next time. Or the next. We can't be together. Even if we want to, we can't. Besides, it's not what he wants and this isn't me being pessimistic or negative. It's just the way it is." When she'd told him she'd miss him, he'd told her he'd miss her pussy. Her love was wasted on an asshole like Granite. Only, she didn't see him as an asshole anymore. She wished she did. It would make this easier.

Breeze paused for a few moments. "You are right, about not being permitted to be together. I'm not sure about the rest, I've seen the way he looks at you."

"That's lust."

Breeze nodded, looking sad. "You're probably right."

"I am right."

"Okay. I'm going to miss you." Her eyes flooded with tears all over again.

Louise couldn't help it when the same happened to her.

"You have become a very good friend to me." Breeze hugged her again. "I don't know what I'm going to do without you."

"You'll be just fine. You're such a good mom. I can only hope to do as well one day," Louise sniffed. A few tears may or may not have fallen, despite her best efforts.

"You'll be great." They pulled apart. Both of them wiped away the tears. "I'm going to miss you, my friend,"

Breeze said.

"You too. Very much!" They hugged again.

"Are you ready?" It was Volcano. He smiled as she turned towards him. He had her suitcase in his hand.

Louise nodded. "Goodbye," her voice cracked.

Breeze just nodded. Her friend was trying not to cry. She recognized the symptoms. There was lots of blinking. Tons of waving of the hand in front of her face.

Volcano closed the door behind them and ushered her towards the main hall. "Stick close, I don't want anyone picking up on your scent."

Louise gave a nod, she waved her hand in front of her face and blinked a couple of times.

Volcano looked her way. "I think you are doing the right thing. For both your sakes. I want you to know that I respect that. I'm grateful."

Louise wasn't sure what to say to him, so she kept silent. He was right. Of course he was. Why did she feel like she was leaving a part of herself with these people? She felt like she was letting everybody down. Granite would hate her for leaving with her tail between her legs like a coward. Ultimately that's what she was, but she couldn't face him. He would talk her out of leaving. This was the last opportunity she would have in a long while.

The vase hit the wall with a loud crack. It shattered into a hundred pieces and crashed to the ground, its contents strewn across the floor below. Granite picked up a side-table and threw it against the same wall. There was another loud cracking noise as it tore apart from the impact.

He smashed both fists on the coffee table, which splintered into several pieces. None of it made him feel any better. His scales rubbed him raw. His teeth were sharp. Rage coursed through him.

With a loud roar he lifted the sofa above his head, wanting to hoist it across the room. Sweat dripped from his brow.

"The couch didn't do anything wrong." Volcano leaned against the far wall, out of harm's way.

Granite hated how relaxed the male seemed. He envied Volcano. He dropped the sofa . . . some internal structure of it cracked. Not that he gave much of a fuck.

"I'm going after her," he growled. Something inside him eased. *Yes!* He'd been too angry before to think clearly. He was going to bring her back.

Volcano shook his head. "No, you are not."

"Don't you dare think to tell me what I can and can't do. Louise is a good doctor and we need her to beat this silver affliction."

"There are other doctors. Blaze had two others lined up, he is—"

"No!" Granite snarled. "I don't want anyone else."

Volcano narrowed his eyes. "Are you still talking about her as a doctor, or as a female?"

"As a doctor," Granite responded, his heart beating.

"Are you sure? Because you seem highly emotional. I agree that she will not be so easily replaced, but—"

"Exactly," he snarled. "I will bring her back." His voice

sounded guttural, he was on the brink of shifting and if not careful, he would shift right now.

Volcano put his hand up. "Louise does not wish to be here. She left of her own accord and made it clear that it was her wish to do so. She was worried that your . . . relationship would become public knowledge over time. It was—"

"That's bullshit!"

Volcano frowned. "I agree with her. You fucked up badly, but we managed to cover it up. Next time—"

"There would not have been a next time. We were going to be more careful."

"Listen to yourself. There is no such thing for a dragon shifter."

"We were nearly done anyway," he gave a shrug. *Fuck her! Why was he even bothering?*

"Well then, it shouldn't be that big of a deal."

"It's not. Not personally." Even as he spoke the words, his insides twisted inside him. "But our people needed that female. She let us down – all of us. I'm fucked off! She isn't the person I thought she was." He wiped the sweat from his brow. "You say that Blaze has someone else lined up to take her place?"

Volcano gave a nod. "The male wants you to contact him to discuss the details. He seemed taken aback that you were at the mines on an unscheduled visit. This whole thing could still blow up in your face."

Granite shook his head. He couldn't give two shits if it did come out. Let the male whip him. Louise was gone, so it wasn't like he was protecting her anymore. He wasn't sure why he had gone to so much trouble in the first place.

It was better that she'd left. The female had been a distraction he couldn't afford right now. There was too much at stake. He'd been blinded by lust. "I spent a couple of days at the mines, so I will be able to report back to him. What reason did the doctor give for leaving?" Why had he even asked? What difference did it make?

"She said that she was homesick. That she needed to be amongst her own kind."

Something in him knotted tight. He found it hard to breathe for a few beats. Granite had to set his jaw to keep from growling. "Let's move on. The sooner the next doctor can start the better."

"You know that the reason she gave wasn't the real reason, don't you?"

"It doesn't matter. We need to move on." He wiped his hands on his pants.

Volcano put a hand on his shoulder. "I'm sorry this happened, brother. I can see that you are upset."

"I'm pissed off that she dropped us like that," his voice was gruff.

"It's more than that."

He shrugged the male's hand off of him. He didn't need misguided sympathy. "No, it's not. This is the last we will speak of this. You were right, there is a hunt in a few weeks. I think I am ready to take a queen."

Volcano gave a nod but looked concerned. Worry lines marred his forehead. He was being an idiot. Granite planned on putting the whole incident behind him.

CHAPTER 27

Five weeks later...

"Come on," Hillary knocked shoulders with her. "Have another glass of wine." She held the bottleneck over Louise's glass.

Louise shook her head and covered the opening with her hand. "I'm exhausted. If you guys don't mind, I think I'm going to turn in. You can carry on without me."

"You sipped on that tiny bit of wine the whole evening and now you're kicking us out!" Debbie grabbed her chest dramatically. "You're killing us here."

"Yeah, we understand that you're hurt, that you think the world is ending, but it's not." Hillary gripped her hand. "It's our jobs as your besties to prove it to you."

Louise rolled her eyes. "I'm not kicking you out!" She gave Debbie a dirty look. "And, I do not think that the world is ending, trust you to be so dramatic," she looked pointedly at Hillary. "I fell for a guy who didn't want me in that way. End of story. I left before I could get too invested – just in the nick of time – and here I am. Am I a bit depressed? Yes! Do I still think of him . . . ?" *Flip!* She could feel her eyes tear up. Cue blinking and swallowing. "Yes, I do but I'll get over him one of these days, it's just going to take time." Cue sniffing.

If she was really honest, she'd hoped he would have chased after her. For those first couple of days she'd held her breath and had waited. She'd jumped at every noise. Had turned to look at the skies. She hadn't pursued a new job, she hadn't even contacted her friends. She'd waited. Lived in limbo. In hope. It was so stupid of her. Granite wasn't coming. His not turning up on her doorstep or breaking down her door had been proof that he didn't feel the same way about her. To think that she'd been ready to give it all up. To fight so that they could be together. She was an idiot, plain and simple. Granite was not coming to swoop her up into his arms and declare his undying love for her. It wasn't going to happen.

She was on her own.

Her lip quivered.

She was so afraid. What the hell was she going to do? *What if . . . ? No!*

"Oh, honey," Hillary leaned in, preparing to give her a hug.

"No!" too harshly delivered. "I'm sorry! If you hug me, I'll cry and he's not worth my tears."

"No, he is not!" Hillary said, injecting venom into her voice.

"The bastard!" Debbie added. "He doesn't know what he's missing. You're too good for a guy like that."

"He's not a bad guy," Louise shook her head, still working hard at holding back those tears. "He's just not my guy. That's all."

"Then he's an idiot! You are an absolute catch." Debbie leaned forward in her seat. "If I wasn't straight and already married, I'd snap you up myself."

A laugh was pulled from Louise.

"Yeah, what she said," Hillary piped up, she was laughing as well. Then she turned serious. "You have a good job, a family and friends who love you."

"My parents live on the other side of the country." Louise missed them. She needed to book a ticket and go to see them, the Easter holidays were coming up.

"*And* friends who love you and are here for you," Hillary emphasized the word. "You'll get over him. I promise you that much."

Louise nodded. She forced herself to smile. She knew her friend was probably wrong.

Most likely. Not thinking about it!

"I hope so," a whisper, followed by a sniff. What a pathetic thing to say. "I will get over him," more resolute, "it's going to take time though." And lots of praying.

"That's more like it," Hillary squeezed her hand.

"I love you guys." Louise looked from one woman to the other. "Thank you for being here for me."

"We'll always be here." Debbie's eyes were filled with concern. "Through thick and thin. You'll meet the right guy for you someday soon. You'll get everything you've ever wanted."

Louise nodded.

They talked for a couple of minutes longer and then Louise let them out. She put her back to the door, relieved that they had finally gone but nervous at the same time.

She pulled in a deep breath and walked towards her purse. She picked it up and then put it back down.

Louise cleared the glassed and the chip bowl. The cleaned and placed the items on the drip rack. She looked at her bag and shook her head. Grabbing a dishcloth, she dried the items and packed them away. Then she wiped the kitchen counters before wiping the coffee table. Lastly, she plumped the couch pillows.

Maybe she should sleep on it. Tomorrow was a new day with new possibilities. A fresh wave of nausea hit. Louise sat down for a second and breathed in deeply. Flip, she hadn't eaten a proper dinner. She'd had a few sips of wine. Guilt accosted her. It wasn't like she could refuse alcohol. Her friends would smell a big, fat sewer rat if she turned down Chardonnay. Another wave of nausea had her clutching her stomach. She had to face facts, the nausea was getting worse by the day and she hadn't started her period. Two weeks late. Two whole darned weeks. At first, she'd been too busy to notice, too wrapped up in her own hurt and despair to realize . . . but then her boobs had become sensitive. Not just that, they were a bit bigger. No, that was her imagination. It had to be.

Please.

Oh god!

On cue, she started blinking and swallowing, working

hard to hold back those blasted tears. It didn't help, the lump in her throat seemed to grow. *Flip!* She waved her hand in front of her eyes. Manual drying, it worked every time. Within seconds, she was feeling more composed.

Louise walked over to her purse and pulled out the pregnancy test. It had been stuffed at the bottom of the thing for two whole days. She was a chicken. Well, no more wing-flapping and clucking for her. It was time to find out for sure.

She pulled out the box and took out the instructions. Of course, she knew exactly how the thing worked and realized that this was a further delay tactic but she humored herself. She ignored the part about using urine in the morning in early pregnancy because she was . . . might be pregnant with a dragon shifter's baby. In which case, she was further along. It would mean that she was nearing the end of her first trimester already.

Panic welled up and she forced herself to breath. She needed to be clinical about this. Try to distance herself so that she could think clearly.

Right, she needed to urinate on the stick for a couple of seconds and then she'd know within a minute or two. It was easy. She made her way to the bathroom and followed the instructions to the letter. She put the stick on the basin and walked away, before pacing back.

One thing was for sure, Granite had never lied to her. She was certain he hadn't lied about being infertile. Although, that's not actually what he'd told her. He'd said that he'd only become fertile once mated, and then only when his mate was on heat. It was all too mind-boggling. From the sound of things, he'd had sex with plenty of women and had never made any of them pregnant before. Not that he knew of. Then again, if the Earth dragons were impregnating human women, it would have become headline news. Dragon shifters were very different to humans. It would be apparent very quickly that the child wasn't entirely human.

She clutched her chest. What if she was pregnant? She would have to tell Granite. Maybe he would feel obligated to be with her. She would hate that. On the other hand, she would be forced to live with the shifters and maybe she'd have to watch him take another woman as a mate. That would be sheer hell.

Louise had always wanted a family, she'd been desperate for children. Broody as hell as each of her friends fell pregnant and had their own bundles of joy. She wanted a child so badly it hurt, yet, not like this, not with a man who didn't love her. She wanted love and a family. She wanted all of it, not just one part.

Life didn't work that way though. It really didn't. Her situation was not unique. At least she was in a position to take care of herself . . . to take care of them if it came to that.

A baby.

She forced herself to keep breathing. She pushed down the nerves and anxiety. Louise picked up the stick but didn't dare look. She squeezed her eyes closed for a few seconds. Another thought entered her mind. What if she wasn't producing the human pregnancy hormone?

The stick would change color if HCG was detected in the urine indicating a positive result. If she was pregnant but not producing HCG, there would be a false negative. She'd cross that bridge if it came to it. She was worrying about things that she couldn't control.

Louise pulled in a deep breath which she'd held in her lungs. It was time. She looked at the stick and choked out a sob.

There were two lines.

Two.

They were both thick and dark. She was pregnant. Deep down she'd known it. She sat down on the toilet seat.

Pregnant.

She was going to have a baby. Granite's baby. It wasn't meant to be like this. It was all wrong. A mess.

Louise blinked hard. She swallowed a couple of times. Then she flapped her hand like a mad woman in front of her face. None of it helped. Not one little bit. She eventually made a moaning noise and covered her face with both her hands. Tears poured down her cheeks. It wasn't meant to be like this.

CHAPTER 28

Granite enjoyed the wind beneath his wings and the pitch-black silence of the night. The lair was just ahead. He flapped his great wings, feeling more tired than he'd been in a long time. He welcomed the fatigue. Maybe he would actually get some sleep tonight. A dragon could hope.

He had to be up early tomorrow. There was much to get done before his appointment with the new doctor in the afternoon. After that, his day would go to hell. Silver . . . he hated the blasted metal, couldn't wait until he was over it. Until they were all cured of the curse.

He just prayed he actually would sleep tonight. He wasn't going to hold his breath. It had eluded him of late. It was why he was so cranky. Lack of sleep had given him a short fuse. His males tiptoed around him. Not that he'd ever been a great sleeper before, but things were worse ever since—

He cut the thought in its tracks and focused on flying the last few feet. Granite slowly descended to the balcony. Many of his males were back already. The next team of scouts would have already headed out.

His body cracked as it folded back in on itself. There was a pulling sensation that lasted a handful of seconds.

"Thanks for coming out with us," Sand gave him a tap on the back. "I see you put your name down for two shifts next week as well."

Granite nodded. "Yeah, it's good for me to stay in touch with the goings on."

"Yeah, but you're still putting in just as many office hours as well as going through the Resistance Therapy. At this rate, you'll burn yourself out."

"Thanks, mom."

Sand raised his brows. "I mean it. Don't overdo it."

"I won't."

"How are you doing?"

"Great!" he forced a smile. Why did his brothers keep asking him that? It was becoming annoying.

"Are you joining the hunt in two weeks' time?" Sand asked, looking distinctly excited.

"Definitely!" Granite answered immediately. "I'm ready to take a female and start a family. The whole nine yards."

"Good," his brother rumbled low. "I'll stick with you so that when you cast your hard-won female aside I'll be there to take her for myself."

"Find your own damn female. I plan on playing for keeps this time."

"If you say so," Sand laughed. It fucked him off, so instead of continuing the ridiculous conversation, Granite walked towards the double doors that led into the great hall, leaving Sand and his irritating chuckle behind him.

Just as he was about to exit the main hall, Rock pushed the door open. "My lord." The male lowered his head in both respect and greeting.

"How was the scout trip?"

"Good!" Granite didn't feel like elaborating. The sooner he got showered, fed and in his bed the better.

"Sorry I missed it, I was man-down after my session today. Those three weeks off definitely took us back some."

Granite grunted instead of responding. It was true. It had taken three weeks to replace the allergist who left. *Not saying her name or thinking about her in any way.* It had put them behind in the therapy.

Rock frowned. "I'm still disappointed that she just up and left out of the blue like that."

Fuck this conversation! Granite took a step towards the door, not wanting to hear any more.

"I'm sure she had a good reason," Rock continued. "Louise would not have just left unless—"

"Shut the fuck up!" Granite growled as he turned back to face the male. "I thought I made it clear that there was to be no more talk of that female. I don't want to hear her name ever again."

Rock looked taken aback. The male was one of his best warriors but he could be as thick as two planks sometimes. He tried to unclench his fists and failed. Tried to stop more adrenaline from flooding his system and failed there too.

"I understand, my lord." Rock looked at the ground for a few moments before locking eyes with him. "You are hurting, it is understandable. You miss the female so—"

Something inside him snapped. Granite lashed out. He punched Rock. It was short, hard and right in the nose. There was a cracking sound and the male flew back several feet, he was unconscious before he hit the ground.

Granite instantly regretted his actions. *What the fuck had the male been thinking?*

Rock's nose was flat and it gushed blood. Both his eyes were swelling shut. *Shit, he'd totally over-reacted.* The male had spouted nonsense but that didn't mean he deserved to have his lights punched out.

At the same time, he had disobeyed a direct order. "Help him," Granite barked at some bystanders. "Take him to a healer," he added.

Several males went to help Rock. By then a small crowd had gathered. "What happened?" he heard someone murmur.

"Rock mentioned something about our previous human doctor. The one who left," another person answered, speaking under his breath.

"Oh! So?"

"We are not permitted to speak of her or interact with her when we are in Walton Springs. The female is a traitor."

Granite felt himself bristle over the insult. He quickly pushed the emotion aside. It was true. The female was a traitor.

"Well then, it is understandable," the other person said as Granite strode from the room. He hoped that this was the last he would hear of it. The last he would hear of her. Louise was dead to him.

Three days later...

Her hand shook, so she clutched the envelope a little tighter.

"Please wait here," she addressed the cab driver through his open window.

He gave a nod. "No problem, miss. I'll wait for as long as you need."

"Thank you." She turned towards The Cockpit. "Here goes nothing," she whispered to herself as she walked towards the packed bar. She was glad she had taken a cab instead of trying to drive herself. She was a nervous wreck.

Louise opened the door and loud music accosted her. It was rowdier than it had been before. Maybe it was because she was there for entirely different reasons. It was very smoky as well. The smell of cigarettes made her feel queasy.

Best she get this over with quickly. The sounds of women giggling irritated her. Louise scanned the room, there were groups of huge, muscular men everywhere. She tried to find someone she knew, or at the very least, someone who would know her. A familiar face would help right now.

Their chests were covered so she wasn't sure which dragons were which. There were guys from all four tribes present.

She checked the bar area. Her heart leapt. There was Rock. *Thank god!* Not only a familiar face but a friendly one. He was sure to help her.

She made a beeline for him, ignoring the women who clustered around him like buzzing flies.

"Rock."

He looked her way. Aside from the cigarette smoke, perfume filled her nostrils now too. This place smelled like a brothel . . . not that she knew what a brothel smelled like. She was pretty sure that this was it though.

"Rock!" She managed to elbow her way past one of the women who glared at her.

The dragon shifter finally looked her way. There were still a couple of women between them. He was head and shoulders above the ladies so she could see him, at least. She expected recognition to light his features but it didn't happen.

"Rock, it's me, Louise," she had to raise her voice over the loud noise. Over the chatter of the women. She was wearing jeans and a sweater so maybe he didn't recognize her.

He finally reacted, but not in the way she thought he would.

"Oh fuck!" he cursed. "It's you. You'd better leave doctor, do it now." He took a few steps back. He looked scared of her.

"Rock, wait. What's wrong?"

His eyes were wide and his face was pale. He turned his body away from her, keeping his eyes glued on her. It looked like he was getting ready to run. "I'm not Rock." He put a hand up. "Don't come any closer."

The guy was acting like she had the plague. Then she realized what he had just said. "Of course, you're Rock. You don't have to lie to me. I'm sorry I left like that."

"Save it female," he growled.

One of the women grabbed him around the waist, she turned and glared at Louise. He looked exactly like Rock, from his dark hair to his blue eyes, why was he lying to her?

"Stay far away from my brother, from all of us. We are not permitted to talk with you, or to speak of you, or we will have to face serious consequences."

"What are you talking about? What do you mean? You have to be Rock, I mean, look at you."

"Rock is my twin, leave now before there is trouble. He broke Rock's face, pulverized his nose." It didn't take a rocket scientist to know who he was talking about. "My brother took several hours to regain consciousness. His nose had to be re-broken and reset." He looked around him, genuine fear etched into every muscle. "Please, female, I cannot be seen talking with you. Go!"

"Holy shit!" one of the shifters from a nearby group growled. "That's her. Holy fuck! Let's move out," he shouted to those around him. The odd guy reacted . . . the other Earth dragons reacted as well, recognizing her. "We need to go." The noise picked up after that and not in a good way. Guys pointed. They looked afraid of her.

"Wait!" she shouted after them. Her whole body felt numb. "I'll go."

Her mind raced a mile a minute. She couldn't get out of there fast enough. Once the door was closed behind her, she gulped down air. Now she smelled like cloying perfume and cigarette smoke. The queasiness eased slightly with the fresh outside air. She swallowed thickly trying to get the rolling of her stomach under control.

Her cab, it was still there. *Thank god!* Walking as quickly as she could, Louise went over and got in. Granite had pulverized Rock's nose. The shifters were shit-scared to be seen anywhere near her. Granite must really hate her. This was going to be more difficult than she had thought.

"Please take me back home," she blurted.

The guy gave a nod and pulled off. It was only then that she realized she still held the envelope. It was crumpled up in her hand. It didn't matter. She had to tell Granite, he needed to know somehow. She would have to find another way to get the message to him. It needed to be his decision whether he wanted to be in the baby's life or not.

CHAPTER 29

Four days later . . . (6 weeks pregnant)

"Step away from the gate and do it now." The man was muscled. Bigger than a human, but not as big as a dragon shifter. His eyes were narrowed on her, his mouth drawn in a sneer. He wore black gear, including a bulletproof vest. The outfit reminded her of something a SWAT officer would wear just before crashing into a building.

"Please, just take the letter, give it to your commander. Then have him take it to one of the kings."

The guy pointed to a painted yellow line on the floor. It was two feet behind where she was standing. "Get behind that line and do it now."

"Please, just take the letter." She threw the envelope between the bars. It landed just inside the gate. The big guy kept his eyes on her, he growled. He was definitely non-human; she was at the right place.

"Step back behind the line. I'm not going to ask you again."

"What's going on?" Another guy approached them. He was bigger than the first. He wore black pants and t-shirt. His head was clean-shaven. His dark eyes landed on her. They were impassive.

"This female is up to no good. She won't move back, insists on handing us a letter," he spoke like it was the craziest thing he had ever heard. "Wants it delivered to one of the kings." He laughed and shook his head.

Louise wore perfume. She didn't want them to smell her unborn child. She'd decided not to tell them that she was pregnant with a dragon shifter baby. Her heart-rate kicked up a few notches at the thought. She tried to calm herself down. Tensions ran high between the different dragon tribes. She wasn't sure how things stood between the dragons and the different species. If they found out about her pregnancy, they might use her and her unborn child against the dragon shifters. The vampires seemed to be helping the dragon shifters find mates but she still couldn't take any chances. She had to tread carefully.

"Please," she could hear the desperation in her voice. "Take the letter and give it to one of your kings. I'm not a threat to you or your people."

The mean guy looked at her pointedly. "That's what they all say. Just because you are an attractive female does not mean that we trust you."

"It's a letter for goodness sake. Are you afraid of a letter?"

One of the mean guy's lips pulled back in a silent snarl. He had long canines. They were sharp. Clearly, they were vampires. Big, strong, blood-sucking vampires. She forced herself to keep breathing and to stay calm.

The bigger guy bent down.

"No, Titan!" the mean one snarled out the words. "This could be a trap." He scanned behind her. "A way to divert our attention and bomb the gate."

Louise frowned. "Bomb the gate. No—"

"Quiet!" the mean one said.

"I think it's okay." The bigger one picked up the envelope. "It's addressed to Granite." He frowned. "There is no Granite at the castle." He took a step towards her.

Louise could see that he planned on giving back the letter. "Give it to one of the kings. Granite isn't a vampire."

"Then why did you bring it here?" the big guy asked.

"I didn't know what else to do," she could hear the desperation in her voice. "Please, make sure that Blaze gets that, he'll know what to do with it. It's very important."

Something flashed in the big guy's eyes. He recognized Blaze's name, she was sure of it.

"This female doesn't know what she is talking about," the mean one laughed. "There is no one here by that name either. Do you really think we would fall for this bullshit?"

She ignored him, kept her eyes on the other one. "Please," she needed to convince him and decided to go out on a limb. "Blaze is a dragon shifter. Make sure he gets that." She looked at the letter in his hand. "He knows who

Granite is."

The mean one narrowed his eyes. "Who the fuck are you?" he demanded. "Dragon shifters . . ." he shook his head. "You need mental help, female."

She kept her eyes locked on the other one. For what felt like a long time, they just stood there. Then he gave a nod. "I will do as you say. You need to be careful how you talk and who you talk to."

"Titan, what the fuck!" the mean one spluttered.

The big guy ignored the other one. "It could land you in big trouble."

"I'm desperate, or I wouldn't have come here. Please help me."

Titan nodded. "I will give the letter to my kings and will ensure that Blaze receives it, but from there, I can't guarantee anything."

She sighed. "Thank you." Louise turned and headed for her car. She walked quickly. Her back prickled more and more with each step. She half-expected to be grabbed and carried away.

She could hear the two men arguing behind her.

"Why did you agree?"

"I don't have to explain myself to you," soft-spoken.

"Bullshit! I—"

"The last time I checked I outranked you. I made the decision and it's final."

"Fuck that I—" There was a loud thud. "Ow, you didn't have to hit me."

"Shut it or I will knock you out with the next blow."

What was it with these non-humans and violence? Then again, they seemed to operate on a more primal level. Louise finally made it to her car. She jumped in and fumbled with her keys. She sighed as she finally got the thing in the ignition. All she wanted to do was floor it and get the hell out of there, but she forced herself to take it easy.

For whatever reason, she trusted that the big vampire would do as she had asked but she had no way to know if Blaze would get the letter in the end, or if he would even give it to Granite. She'd tried emailing both Blaze and Granite but they all bounced back with a delivery failure. Louise didn't know what else to do.

The Cockpit had been a dead-end. The vampires were her last hope. She put a hand on her belly. The top button of her jeans was undone. Some of her clothes were starting to get too tight. Granite might not want her but he would want this child. The thought scared her.

CHAPTER 30

One week later... (7 weeks pregnant)

The energy that buzzed around him was off the charts. The scent of sweat mingled with testosterone filled his nostrils. Hundreds of males filled the valley in front of the Fire lair. It was mere minutes away from the start of the next Hunt.

Granite wasn't feeling it. He lurked somewhere at the back of the crowd. The thought of chasing after a group of humans didn't hold any appeal to him. He bit back a yawn.

What the fuck was wrong with him?

Once he got going he'd be okay. Once he caught sight of one of the females it would be game on. The thought of becoming a father appealed to him. He envied Volcano. His baby nieces were utterly adorable and he wanted what the male had. Granite put a hand in front of his mouth to hide a yawn. It was big, wide and unstoppable.

The fuck!

He needed to get back on track. The only way to do

that was to win a female. To get her underneath him as a matter of urgency. There was no tightening inside him. No 'zing' of need that moved through him.

The buzzer sounded and the males surrounding him took off with yells of excitement. There was also a fair bit of pushing and punching. A couple of warriors fell, others staggered. The sound of shouts, snarls, growls and meaty thuds filled the air. The scent of hormones was nauseating.

Granite set out at a walk. He would wait for the crowd to move off. He was a king, it wouldn't take much to get ahead at a later stage. His body felt heavy. Lack of sleep was taking its toll on him. In short, it was completely fucking him up. He took a few more steps and then stopped. There was always the next hunt. Or the one after that. He'd gone without a female for many years, a few more months wouldn't matter. Once he was sleeping better, he'd have more energy, more drive to pursue a mate. Even his chest hurt as of late. A dull ache. If it persisted, he'd go and see one of the healers.

"Are you alright, my lord?" a familiar voice sounded behind him.

Granite turned. It was Rock. Shame filled him. "I am fine."

"Why are you rubbing your chest?" His eyes widened. "If you don't mind my asking?"

Granite looked down and sure as fuck, he was rubbing his sternum. He stopped and dropped his hand to his side. "No reason. I'm tired, I'm going to give this Hunt a skip." A weight immediately lifted. In that moment, he realized that he hadn't been looking forward to this. In fact, he'd been dreading it. He'd be up for the next one, of this he was certain.

Rock nodded. The male smiled. "I am skipping the Hunt as well. I finally convinced Quartz to mate with me."

"That's great news!" Granite couldn't help but smile too. "How did you get that right?"

He stood there in silence for a few beats. "I have you to thank."

Granite frowned. "How so?"

"I am told that Quartz was frantic with worry after you knocked me out." He looked down at his feet for a moment before looking back up. The animated look from earlier was back. "She was very worried and sat at my side until I gained consciousness."

"About hitting you . . ." Granite rubbed the back of his neck. "I shouldn't have done that, I—"

Rock shook his head. "No, you don't understand, I'm glad you punched me. Quartz realized how much she loves me. She realized that she can't live without me and has since agreed to mate me."

"I'm glad things worked out for you." Granite took a step back. "I'm going to . . ."

"She has feelings for you, my lord. The doctor . . ."

"What?"

Rock held up a hand. "Please don't hit me."

"Then keep your thoughts to yourself." Granite started walking in the other direction.

"Hear me out, please, my lord."

Granite stopped moving. *Fucking hell!* He pushed out a heavy breath. "Fine." He owed the male that much.

"Quartz has loved me all along. She was too afraid to commit. It was fear holding her back. She thought that I would regret my decision to be with her but she was wrong. There was so much blood and my nose was flat against my face," the male gave a chuckle. "It took her thinking that she had almost lost me to realize that she couldn't live without me.

Granite folded his arms. "What does this have to do with me?"

"Don't let fear ruin your chances at happiness."

"Again," he tried to keep the menace from his voice and failed, "what does this have to do with me?"

"I suspect that Louise . . ." Rock flinched as he said her name.

Granite felt all his muscles pull tight. Finally, adrenaline hit his blood stream. He clenched his jaw but didn't say anything.

When Granite didn't react, Rock went on. "I suspect she had a good reason for leaving. I suspect that something must have happened between the two of you."

"This is none of your fucking business." A tendril of smoke spiraled from his left nostril.

"All I know, my lord, is the way she looked at you. At first, they were stolen looks filled with lust. Later, after . . . the Stag Run, those looks became more . . . much more," Rock paused. "You are angry that she left but you are wrong in your assumptions as to why."

Granite felt his scales rub, he clenched his fists. More smoke drifted, this time from both nostrils.

Rock swallowed hard, Granite could scent his fear. "If you have any feelings for the female—"

"I don't!" he snarled, a little too quickly, a little too loudly.

Rock nodded, his head bobbed up and down. "Okay, fine. Like you said, it's none of my business. If one day you wake up and discover that you do feel . . . something, anything . . . for that female, go to her. I urge you to set your anger aside and go and get answers . . . real answers."

Granite shook his head. "I'm sure she has moved on." He thought of that puny human. The male would be sniffing around if he knew that Louise was back. More smoke; this time it billowed. If he had been a Fire dragon, there would be flames.

Rock shook his head. "What? Move on in the same way that you have moved on? I suppose . . ." Rock looked at where the others had long since disappeared.

"I'm tired. My not joining the Hunt has nothing to do with . . . her."

"Please go and see her, my lord. You are not tired, you are sad. There is a big difference," Rock paused.

Sad. It was the stupidest thing he had ever heard. Granite folded his arms.

Rock stepped to the side. "That is the last I will say on it. My mating ceremony is in three days' time. I hope that you will attend."

The thought of watching Rock and Quartz take the

plunge did not enthuse him. These types of ceremonies never did. Mating was not about putting up a show. It was about two people pledging themselves to one another. It was about biting, tasting your partner's blood and binding yourself to them. His mouth watered at the thought of how Louise had tasted on his tongue, how right biting her had felt. *All a lie. It was his dick talking.* Rock was bringing things up best left buried.

Sad?

Like fuck!

"I will try and make it," Granite said, just before he shifted. He was going straight to bed. His chest hurt. This whole conversation had exhausted him.

CHAPTER 31

One month later . . . (2 and a half months pregnant)

"Surprise!" Louise said, as she opened the door.

Hillary's eyes bugged out. She gave a squeal and closed a hand over her mouth. "What the fuck is that?" Ever since having children Hillary didn't swear. Not ever!

Louise tried hard to smile. "Um, well . . ."

"This had better be a joke." Her friend's eyes were still glued to Louise's stomach. Her distended, very definitely pregnant belly. "A bad joke at that."

"It's no joke." Louise lifted her top. "I'm due in six weeks."

"Oh, good god!" Hillary's eyes were filled with panic. She stumbled inside and headed for the nearest couch. Her friend sat down hard. "How long have you known?" she spoke to Louise's belly. "You had better not have kept this from me." She narrowed her eyes, finally looking up and into Louise's. "You had to have known. I can't believe you're so far along. Is he the father? That Granite guy?"

Hearing his name out loud hurt. He hadn't come. She

had no way to know if that was by choice or not. She didn't think so. Granite might not want her but he would want the child. She was sure of it.

The little one kicked and she put her hand to her belly. "I had no idea until about a month ago."

"How the hell could you not know? You're a doctor, aren't you?"

"I don't know how I missed the signs . . ." *Shit!* She knew this was coming. Dragon shifter pregnancies only lasted four months instead of nine. She needed to pretend that she had been pregnant for six and a half months without knowing.

"And furthermore," Hillary looked mad, "why didn't you tell me sooner? No wonder you've made so many excuses over the last couple of weeks. Debbie is going to kill you."

"I needed to work through a few things first." All true. "This has come as a big shock. I told you first so that you can help me break the news to Deb." Again, the whole truth.

"Is the baby his?"

"He," Louise said. "I'm having a boy." The only reason she knew the sex of her child was because of the limited brief about human and dragon matings she had received when coming onboard as part of the medical staff. There had yet to be a female infant born to a human.

She gave her belly another tender rub. If she wasn't so afraid she would be ecstatic. There was a little person growing inside of her. She was going to be a mom.

"A boy. Oh, my god!" Tears filled Hillary's eyes. "You're having a baby boy. Oh, my word!" Her friend stood up and hugged her.

Louise's own eyes filled with tears. She nodded, hugging her back. "I'm having a baby boy," her voice quivered.

They hugged for a minute. Then they finally released one another. "Granite *is* the father," Louise said.

"But that would mean that you guys would have had sex sooner than that night at The Cockpit."

"Yeah we did." It felt awful lying to her friend. "I'm sorry I lied. We had sex soon after I got there. One time. He wanted more and I knew I might end up falling for him so I refused. It was impossible. He was impossible. It ended up happening again, you know the rest."

"You gave in that night."

She nodded. "Yup."

"You were already pregnant."

Louise nodded. "Yes, I would have been."

"Does he know?"

Louise shrugged. "I don't think so."

"What do you mean by that?"

"He was redeployed on some sort of mission. I left some messages for him but have been unable to get ahold of him."

Hillary shook her head. "Bastard is probably trying to avoid responsibility. Don't you have his cell number? Some way of getting in touch with him."

Louise shook her head. "No, it's complicated. He

works on covert operations and is difficult to track. I know he would want to be a part of the baby's life. At least, I'm sure he would." She had also been sure he would come after her and that hadn't happened, so maybe she didn't know him as well as she thought. "I don't know what to do." *Flip!* She felt herself tear up.

Hillary grabbed her hand and squeezed. "I'm here for you and I know Debbie will feel the same. We've both been there and done that."

They had their own families, their own lives. There was only so much her friends could do to help out. Louise gave a nod. "I know."

"Where are the ultrasound pictures? When are you due? Is everything looking normal?" Hillary launched into twenty questions. Her eyes were lit with excitement.

Louise forced herself to breathe. "Oh flip! I left the pics on my desk at work," she lied. "I'm due in about six weeks."

"What date did the gynecologist give you?"

Louise had to think quick. She rattled off a date around the time she was due.

"Was it easy to see that you are having a boy? I know with Miles it was hard to miss that part of his anatomy. It stuck out like a sore little thumb," Hillary giggled.

"Yup," she nodded. "You couldn't miss it," she lied through her teeth. Louise couldn't go to a gynecologist or any other medical person. They would be able to tell that this wasn't a normal pregnancy. She was on her own. The thought terrified her. What would happen when she went into labor? Could she manage on her own? What if there were complications? There would be no one to comfort her and talk her through the pain. No one to hold her hand. Louise had never felt more alone in her whole entire life.

2 weeks later . . . (3 months pregnant)

The cab pulled up to the curb and into the No Parking zone. Another cab pulled in behind them.

"Please wait here. I'll be out in a minute."

The driver smiled at her, his eyes crinkled at the corners. "A lady in your condition should not be frequenting this type of establishment."

"I need to deliver a letter." She held up the white envelope. "I'm trying to find the father of my baby."

"Oh . . ." He raised his brows. "I see."

Louise doubted that very much. "It's not like that. The dad and I . . . we . . . Well . . ." She let the sentence die. It didn't matter what this guy thought. "Please stay put. I don't want to have to call someone else. I need to get home and put my feet up." Her lower back hurt and her ankles were a bit swollen.

"No problem, Miss." He looked pointedly at her bare ring finger. "I'll be here when you get out."

"Thank you," she sighed and carefully eased herself out of the car. Her belly was pretty big. Okay, it was a lot big. She couldn't believe she still had a month to go. She gave the air a sniff. Aside from the scent of garbage and exhaust fumes, she thought she picked up Granite's scent, which was nuts. He wasn't due to go on another Stag Run for months. She probably just smelled other dragon shifters. Besides, he'd probably already found himself a mate at the last hunt. Her heart gave a clench. It wasn't the first time today that she'd been sure she'd picked up his scent. It was probably because she couldn't get him off her mind. Not after deciding to come here this evening.

"Oh and . . ." the cab driver continued as she stood up. Louise turned back towards him. "Good luck!" he smiled at her.

"Thanks." She was going to need it. Her hand shook. She was going to try to find someone who she recognized again. More importantly, someone who recognized her; that person was going to take the letter to Granite. Louise was done waiting and hoping. It was time for serious action.

One way or another, she would make them believe that she was pregnant with Granite's baby. Surely they would be able to scent it on her? She prayed they would. She needed to convince one Earth dragon – just one – and then Granite would get the letter and he would come for her. Okay, not for her, for the baby. Or, he wouldn't. At least then she'd know for certain that he wasn't interested. At least then she'd reach a point where she was able to say that she had done everything in her power to try and contact him. Her baby deserved a father.

Louise put a hand to her stomach as she half-walked, half-waddled towards the door to the bustling bar.

"Louise."

Her blood ran cold and she froze mid step. She would recognize that voice anywhere. She slowly turned. It was Granite. He wore a grey sweater and a pair of black jeans. "Oh god!" she choked out. She couldn't believe that he was there.

He was frowning deeply. There were two ridges between his eyes. "What are you doing here?" he asked.

Then it occurred to her why he was here. She pulled her shoulders back and sucked in a deep breath. "I'm sorry to have to rain on your parade. Cramp your style." Anger blossomed. She felt like slapping his cheeks until they were bright red. She felt like kicking him in both shins. Louise was stressing about letting him knowing about the baby, about how she was going to get through this alone and he was out looking for a booty call.

"What parade?"

"Don't play dumb with me. I take it you're here for the Stag Run." She rolled her eyes. "Forget it! Here." She tried to hand him the note but he ignored her outstretched hand. "Take it!" she yelled, throwing the envelope on the ground at his feet.

Granite bent over but she didn't wait to watch him pick it up. Louise took off in the direction of the cab. *The asshole! The bastard!* She could do this alone. She didn't need him or anyone else. She had her son. Her baby was the only thing she needed. She forced herself to calm down. This type of stress wasn't good for the little one.

Granite caught up and wrapped an arm around her. He

pressed himself against her back. She stopped, mid-step. For just the briefest moment she was tempted to lean back into him, into his warmth and strength. She stiffened up instead. "Let go of me."

"So, you were finally going to tell me about the baby," his voice was a deep rasp against the back of her neck.

"Let go of me now," she ground out.

Thankfully, he did as she asked.

Louise turned to face him. "For your information, I tried to tell you. I came to this place weeks ago . . ." She looked over his shoulder, at the entrance of The Cockpit, "As soon as I found out, but no one would give me the time of day. They were shit-scared of getting their asses kicked after you beat up poor Rock."

He shook his head. "That can't be right."

"It is."

"They would've scented my child growing inside of you." He reached out and put a hand on her belly but she slapped it away.

"That place is smoky and filled with so many other scents. It stinks in there. Besides, none of them would let me anywhere near them. They were scared of me . . . or rather, they were terrified of you."

He narrowed his eyes. "Your senses are enhanced."

She gave a nod. "Yeah, I had noticed." It was small things like how loud people's voices had become. She could hear what someone was saying from across the room. Smells were so much more pronounced.

"I went to see the vampires as well."

"Why the fuck would you do that?" he growled. "They are savages, you could have been hurt." He seemed to genuinely care.

"It was after I couldn't get through to anyone here. I was desperate to get a message to you so I took them a letter. One of the guys promised it would be delivered to Blaze. His name is Titan. I trusted that he was telling the truth."

Louise could see a look of disbelief cross his face. "No, that can't be. I'm sure Blaze would have told me if he received a letter."

She shrugged. "All I know is that I did my best.

His gaze softened. The frown had all but disappeared.

Louise let out a soft sigh. "Well, now you know. You can go back in there and do whatever it was you planned on doing before I showed up."

"You think I'm here for the Stag Run?"

She nodded. "Why else?"

"I'm here for you, Louise."

It hurt to hear him say it. Especially since it wasn't true. "That's the biggest load of rubbish, you're just saying that because you've just found out that I'm pregnant with your son." She held in a breath for a few moments before letting it out. "I won't keep you from him. Please don't feel obliged to pretend that you have feelings for me all of a sudden. I know you don't and I—"

"Stop!" It was a low growl that caused goosebumps to rise on her arms, legs . . . heck, everywhere. "I'm not here for the Stag Run. I've been following you all day."

"What? Why?"

"Because I'm a pussy." He was breathing deeply. "I came to Walton Springs to talk to you but when I saw your pregnant belly I couldn't bring myself to approach you. For a little while there I thought you might be pregnant with another male's child. A human. It happened to the Water king. The scent of a human baby is not as easy to detect. It's only apparent if you are looking for it."

"You thought I had been with someone else before coming to work for you? I told you I hadn't had sex in a long time and I meant it."

"People lie."

"I didn't," she shook her head and her braid whipped left and right.

"I wasn't sure. I was too afraid to find out. I had to work up the nerve to get close enough to check. Then I was upset that you hadn't told me. I don't know how the fuck this happened." He scrubbed a hand over his face.

So it *had* been his scent earlier. It wasn't just her imagination. Granite didn't look happy about the prospect of becoming a father. "I tried to send emails to both you and Blaze."

Granite shook his head. "Our firewall would have blocked you. We don't communicate with unauthorized URLs."

"I tried," she whispered.

"I know. When I saw you come here I knew that you were trying to communicate with me. I've never been happier in my whole life. Fuck!" He reached out and touched the side of her face.

"Why did you come?" She stepped away from his touch, despite feeling much better with the knowledge that he wasn't here to hook-up. She wasn't sure why he was here. Maybe he had come to try to get her to take her old job back.

"We need to talk but not here. It's time that we lay a few things out on the table." He took her hand.

For a moment she wanted to pull it free. but decided to go along with it for now. "You don't have to do this. I told you I would let you be a part of his life and I meant it."

"I came to talk to you, Louise. This has nothing to do with the baby," he paused, "I think that this conversation became a lot more important because of our son though. I finally realized a couple of things," Granite smiled. *God, but he was beautiful when he smiled.* "A friend helped me see things more clearly. I've been an idiot. Let's get out of here."

Louise nodded.

It was the longest fucking cab drive of his existence. It was like time slowed. There was so much he needed to hear. So much he needed to say. There were a couple of important things. One or two in particular. Things Louise had no idea about. For the first time in his life he was nervous. His heart beat a bit faster and his hands felt clammy.

He couldn't help but sneak glances her way. Her skin glowed. Her cheeks were flushed. Her eyes were brighter than he remembered. Her belly was deeply curved. Swollen with life. She scented of them both and of new beginnings.

Never sweeter or more tempting. She was more beautiful right now than ever before and that was saying something. She'd taken her hand back as soon as they had sat down. Both hands were now clasped tightly in her lap. She stared at the road ahead. Granite wished he knew what she was thinking.

He prayed that Rock had been right. Louise had been jealous when she thought he was there for the Stag Run. *Fuck that.* He couldn't think of being with another female. They held no interest to him. All females paled in comparison since meeting Louise. Granite almost laughed out loud thinking about how he'd tried to deny his attraction to her from the start. He had fooled himself and only continued to do so.

Sad.

Rock had been right, although sad didn't cut it. Completely ripped apart. So out of sorts it was scary. That's how he had felt when she'd left him. Like a part of him had gone with her. Like he was empty. Only, he hadn't acknowledged what he was feeling. He had allowed anger to manifest instead. It was easier to be angry than heart-fucking-broken. He was exhausted because he spent every hour of every day trying not to think of Louise. He worked at keeping his anger levels high so that he wouldn't have to feel anything else. When Rock had told him he was sad, that he missed Louise, he had realized in that moment that it was true. Sure, he'd tried to ignore it. Tried to keep up the pretense, but it didn't work. Once he started thinking about her, he couldn't stop. Once the emotions started up, they wouldn't let up.

Sad? He was completely fucked up without her.

Now, at least he knew why.

The cab finally pulled up outside her apartment building, jolting him from his thoughts. He glanced at Louise. How was he going to break the news to her? How would she take it?

He peeled off a few dollars. "Keep the change."

The guy nodded. "Good luck with everything." He turned to Louise. "I'm glad you found him. I hope you can make it work."

"Thanks," Louise gave a tight smile. He helped her out of the cab. She stuffed her hands into her coat pockets, so he put a hand to the small of her back as they walked in silence.

The keys jingled as she fumbled with them. This type of entrance was not safe, especially at this time of night. Louise dropped the keys and they fell onto the cement floor with a clang.

"I'm such a klutz." A pink blush crept up her neck, spilling onto her cheeks.

Granite bent down and picked them up. "Let me." He opened the door.

She walked in and straight to a door that led to the stairs, which she began to push open.

"What about the elevator?" he asked, following a step

or two behind her.

"It's under repair . . . again." As she said it, he noticed the hand-written note that had been stuck to the door.

Louise said it like this sort of thing happened all the time. "I'm on the third floor, it's not so bad. I feel sorry for the people on the eighth floor." She was breathing heavily as she walked up the stairs. "It will be fixed within a day or two." *Unacceptable!*

She paused on the second landing, her hand on her lower back.

"Are you okay? Can I carry you?" Fuck, every instinct told him to go over and pick her up. To protect her . . . but he forced himself not to do it. They slowly climbed the last flight of stairs.

"I'm fine." Louise pushed a door open. The number '3' was painted on the surface of the wood. Just as the stairs had been, the hallway was clean. The tiles were a cheap porcelain. The lighting came from long UV bulbs.

They walked down the hall, passing several doors. Then she pointed at one. "This one is mine."

Granite nodded. He took the second key on the chain and used it to open the door. He stood back, allowing her to enter first. She flipped the light switch and he watched as she unbuttoned and removed her coat. She wore a white, cotton top. It pulled tight across her stomach and breasts. *So plump and rounded.* Granite lifted his eyes; he needed to get his mind out of the gutter. There were important things to discuss. It would be uncomfortable doing so with a stiff dick. He had a feeling it would piss her off as well, and he couldn't blame her. Having said that, he'd almost forgotten how attracted he was to the little doctor . . . nothing had changed in that department. If anything, his attraction had grown.

"You're welcome to help yourself to something to drink," she widened her eyes. "I only have orange juice or water. It's that or herbal tea." She gestured towards a door. "The kitchen is through there."

Granite nodded.

"I need to use the restroom, I'll be right back." She pulled a face and made a barely audible groaning noise. "I think he's punching my bladder."

"Can I get you anything?"

She nodded. "A glass of juice would be great." Granite got to work pouring two glasses of juice and then walked back into the living room area. He put the drinks down and paced back and forth a few times. Then he forced himself to sit.

Granite jumped up as she walked back into the room. She was barefoot and held a pair of socks. "Are you feeling okay?"

"I'm fine."

Louise sat down across from where he had been sitting. She sat with her legs splayed and put one foot onto the thigh of the other leg. He noticed that her feet were a bit swollen.

"Let me help you with that." He went down on his knees in front of her.

"I can manage."

"Let me help you, please." He held out his hand, his eyes on the socks still clasped in her fingers.

"I've managed just fine on my own up until now."

"I'm glad, but you aren't alone anymore."

She narrowed her eyes. "I told you that you don't have to go into 'happy family' mode just because I'm pregnant. I can cope on my own."

"I'm sure you can but you don't have to anymore. I'm here now." He looked pointedly at the socks.

"Please don't take him from me." Her lip quivered so she bit down on it. "Don't take my baby."

"Where did that come from?" Granite growled. She must think him to be some monster. "I'm not going to take him from his mother. I would never do such a thing."

"Okay," she seemed to calm down. "It's the one thing I was most afraid of. I can deal with anything else. I can." She sounded like she was trying to convince herself.

"What other things did you think you might have to deal with?"

"It doesn't matter," she shook her head.

Granite took the socks from her and helped her put them on. He noticed how her jaw clenched and her back straightened. He also noticed how she curled her hands around the curve of her belly. Already a fiercely protective mother; his heart warmed.

Granite stood up and sat in the chair next to her. She looked distinctly uncomfortable. Tough luck, he meant what he said, he was here now. He wasn't going any-damn-where. Not any time soon. Louise wiggled to the edge of the seat, widened her legs to make room for her belly and grabbed the glass of juice. She studied the glass before taking a small sip and then went back to studying the contents again.

"I had no idea that you were pregnant."

She finally looked his way, but didn't say anything.

"The reason I came was to find out why you left. Don't give me some bullshit about not enjoying your job. It had nothing to do with your work. I tried to convince myself that was the case. That maybe you had received a better offer elsewhere, that you left us for more money or better benefits."

She shook her head. "That's not it."

"Also, I don't believe that you left because you were afraid of us getting caught."

Louise chewed on her lower lip for a second. "I was afraid of that but it's not the real reason behind my leaving."

"Why then?" he asked when she didn't offer anything more.

Louise shrugged. "It's not important."

"It is important. It's all important."

Louise chewed on her lower lip but she didn't say a thing. Not a single word. If this was going to work, they had to communicate. She was still running scared. It was his own fault.

"I'll tell you why I came. I wanted to find out the real reason why you left, because I realized how much I cared that you were gone. Up until recently I had been fooling myself into thinking that I didn't care, that we were better off since you had left. That I was better off, but I'm not." He paused to gather his thoughts. "Making you come had become my single most favorite pass-time. I was convinced that I'd get over you sooner rather than later. That next time would be my last time. I was wrong."

Louise licked her lips. She was blinking hard.

Granite leaned forward. "I'll never get enough of you, Louise. There is no such thing as one more kiss or one more touch. I've never had such little control before meeting you."

"Our relationship was out of hand," Louise's voice was soft. "It was only a matter of time before someone found out. I couldn't keep . . . on like we were." She sniffed and blinked. "It wasn't working for me. I won't go back to that."

"No, we can't," Granite shook his head. "I refuse as well. I want you in my bed . . . every night. No more sneaking around."

"And what would you tell everyone?" Louise looked horrified. "Would it be acceptable to bring your . . . What would I be? Your girlfriend? Your lover? Your piece of ass back with you? Will Blaze agree to such an arrangement?"

"I don't give a fuck about what Blaze has to say about it. I want you in my bed. Go and pack a bag . . . Do it now."

"Still trying to boss me around, I see," she sighed. "I had my reasons for leaving and they haven't changed."

"Everything has changed," he insisted.

"This pregnancy doesn't change anything." With difficulty, Louise managed to get to her feet. "I told you that you can be a part of his life. You don't have to take me on just because I'm the mother of your child."

"Take you on . . . What are you talking about? It wouldn't be 'taking you on.'"

"What about when you decide to take a mate? How will it work then? Will I be your piece of ass on the side or—"

"You are my mate, dammit!" he roared. "Fucking hell! You need to listen to what I am saying. I want you in my bed. I came here today to tell you that I love you. I crave you. I need you. I've been fucking miserable since you left. I couldn't understand why. I even went to see a healer. I haven't been able to sleep. I'm useless without you. Those are the reasons for wanting you in my bed, for wanting you period."

Her mouth hung open. Her eyes were wide and her skin pale. "Are you just saying that because of the baby?"

"No! Fuck!" He ran a hand over his scalp. "I came to tell you this before I found out you were pregnant. I was hoping you would admit that you love me too. I know you fucking love me."

"That's a bold statement." Her freckles were pronounced against her milky white skin. He noticed how her shoulders lifted a bit, how the corners of her mouth turned up just a bit.

"We're mated, Louise. We're already mated. I can't even look at another female. I don't want anyone else. I know you love me. I love you so damned much." He cupped her cheeks. A few tears had fallen and her silky lashes clung to the moisture. "Don't cry, please."

"I'm happy." She didn't look fucking happy. He used his thumbs to wipe them away. Louise smiled. "I do love you, that's why I left. I couldn't stand to be near you and not have you," she paused, smiling through her tears. "Are you sure we're, mated? We can't be."

"There is no other way you would be pregnant. Our bodies have been so in tune with one another from the start. When I bit you . . . it had to be then. I couldn't have impregnated you otherwise. We must have mated in that moment. Our bodies knew before we did."

"Speak for yourself," she whispered.

"I'm sorry I didn't see it sooner, that I put you through all of this. I love you and you love me. You're having my babies and you're moving in with me today. It's simple."

"I have a job."

He shook his head. "I don't give a fuck. Your place is with me. My place is at your side. We belong together. You know it and I know it. We were both idiots to try to deny it. Let's not waste any more time."

"I thought it was purely physical for you. I thought that I was the only one falling in love. That's why I had to leave, to try to protect myself."

"You're right, it was mostly physical."

Her mouth gaped and he could see her mind working at about a mile a second. "No, sweetness," he murmured. "You don't understand. *Was* is the operative word here. I just realized that I don't know anything about you. Well, that's about to change, I want to know more about you. We can spend quality time together . . . not just fucking. Although we will make plenty of time for that. I have so many questions. Do you have brothers and sisters? What is your favorite color? There are so many things I am desperate to know about you . . . about my mate."

"Hold up." She was frowning deeply. "I just realized something."

"What?"

"You said babies. Not baby. It was a mistake right? A slip of the tongue?"

Granite shook his head.

"Why are you shaking your head?"

He had to smile at her. She was adorable when she panicked. She was adorable no matter what she did. "Earth dragons always father twins."

"Always?" Her eyes lifted in thought. She mouthed 'Oh my god!' "You and Volcano—that's why you look so alike. Breeze's babies. Then there's Rock and his look-alike," she gasped. "There are more examples. Loads of them." She clapped a hand over her mouth. "Why didn't I realize? Wait . . . your sister isn't a twin."

"We lost our twin sister at birth."

"I'm so sorry," she mumbled. "Oh god!" Her hands went to her belly. "Twins. Seriously?"

Granite put his arms around her. "We'll get through it. I'm here." It felt like his heart was too big for his chest.

Her arms went around him as well and she squeezed

him tight. "Please tell me this means you agree to go back with me. You agree that the four of us can be a family?" His voice was thick with emotion.

"Yes," there was a quiver in her voice.

"Thank fuck!" he growled.

"Twins. We're having two," Louise was crying.

His own eyes felt damp so he buried his face deep into her neck.

CHAPTER 32

Five days later...

"Put that down." He pointed at the vase in her hands. "Sit down right this minute." Granite scowled at her.

"I'm pregnant, I'm not an invalid." She put the flowers on the center of the coffee table. Orange tulips, her favorite. Granite had bought them for her after finding that out about her. All he did was ask her questions. They'd talked for hours and hours over the last few days.

He took a step towards her. "You've worked hard all morning decorating our new chamber. You shouldn't overdo it."

Louise gave him a dirty look. "You and Rock moved the furniture. I told you where to put everything. That's not hard work."

"You've fluffed pillows and made the bed." He pointed to their extra-length, extra-width king-size. "You hung up the curtains in the nursery." She could see his whole demeanor soften as his mind turned to the babies.

"Fluffing pillows isn't heavy labor." Her back did hurt a bit and she was feeling a little tired. Not that she would admit that to him. Growing two babies in a matter of months was taking its toll on her. Granite was overprotective though. If he could wrap her in cotton wool and keep her on bedrest he would.

"I went to see Blaze yesterday," Granite blurted, looking at the opposite wall and then back at her.

"Oh, I wondered where you had gone to." It was the first time he had disappeared for so long – the whole day to be precise.

"Yeah, well, it had to be done. We broke a couple of lores," he gave her a tight smile.

Louise gasped. "What happened? Don't tell me he plans on having you whipped. That's so juvenile. It's not like we planned—"

"We snuck around. I rutted you on dragon soil. What we did was forbidden," he smiled.

Louise couldn't believe he was smiling at a time like this. "What are you saying?" she could hear the panic in her voice. "When does he plan on doing it? I'm totally against this."

"Shhhh, my love." Granite cupped her chin. "I'm not sorry. I would do it all again in a heartbeat." He brushed a tender kiss across her lips and released her.

Louise gripped her belly. The babies were squirming inside her. There wasn't much room left for kicking, although once in a while one of them got it right. "When then?" she asked with a tremble in her voice.

"I accepted my punishment yesterday. No use putting it off."

She felt herself frown. "That can't be. He couldn't have used a silver-barbed whip."

"It's working," his smile widened. "The Resistance Therapy is working. It only took a few hours to recover. The silver didn't affect me too badly."

"You told me it normally takes days. You didn't have a scar. At least, I didn't notice one." She walked around and touched the smooth, unblemished skin of his back. "It must have hurt though." She looked him in the eyes and touched the side of his arm.

"I told you it was worth it. Besides, I only got ten lashes – although I would have taken a hundred to be with you."

"I'm glad all of the pain and effort has been worth it. The new doctor seems to be really good." She couldn't remember the woman's name and had only met her once. "Not that I'm complaining, but why only ten lashes. I thought you said the punishment was twenty."

Granite nodded. "Yeah, it is normally twenty. And the new doctor is good, although, not as good as you." He kissed her forehead before going on. "Blaze felt guilty." Granite clenched his jaw for a few seconds. "He did get the letter from the vampires but decided not to give it to me. It was sitting in his desk drawer all along."

"Why didn't he give it to you?" her voice was shrill. "I don't understand. I went through so much effort."

"He told me he's not an idiot. He suspected that something was going on between us. His males told him that we spent Stag Run together; and then there was my unplanned trip to the mines."

The mines.

The reason humans would take a keen interest in the dragons if they ever found out what the dragon shifters were sitting on. Louise shoved the thought aside. So, the therapy was working. *Really working.* She sucked in a deep breath. "I told you it was bound to come out."

"Yeah, you did and as usual you were right. Blaze planned on speaking with me about it but then you resigned and left," Granite paused. "He said that despite you being a good doctor, it was a relief when you went. He knew where things were headed." Granite narrowed his eyes. "Then a month or two later, he received a letter addressed to me, from you. He decided not to give it to me, not to say a damned thing about it. He didn't read it, just put it in his drawer. He was highly apologetic."

"The asshole! He had no right to interfere."

"He thought he was doing the right thing at the time. The road to hell is paved with good intentions," Granite chuckled. "Probably why he only gave me ten lashes."

Louise had to smile. "I'm still pissed off but I'm glad it saved you more pain and suffering." She put her hands around his waist. Her belly knocked against his abs.

"It was so worth it." He rubbed her back. "Now, you go and lie down, I'm going to take a quick shower and then I'll make us lunch."

"How about you go shower, I'll make us lunch and . . ." It would take five minutes to fix them some sandwiches or a steak. Her mouth watered at the thought of meat. "Then we could go to bed together. We need to christen our new place." They needed to have sex . . . period.

His whole demeanor changed. Granite tensed up. He looked to the far wall for a few beats before looking back at her. "You need rest," deep and husky. "Go and lie down. I'll organize lunch." He turned and disappeared into the bathroom before she could argue the matter.

What was wrong with him?

He hadn't touched her once since coming back. Not once. Sure, he held her close every night. He couldn't tell her enough how much he loved her. He gave her back and foot massages. He held her hand and kept his arm around her but nothing sexual. In fact, it was so bad that he turned away when she was naked or made excuses to leave the room.

It was starting to worry her. They had a healthy sex life before. Yet, now that they were free to go at it like rabbits he didn't seem interested. She was worried that he might not be attracted to her. She'd heard of men losing interest in their wives during pregnancy.

Well, it was time to find out what the hell was going on. Louise pulled the maternity dress over her head. Her panties and bra quickly followed suit. Her belly was well-rounded but neat. Okay, it was just plain old well-rounded. Her boobs were huge. *Good god!* Nothing neat about those either.

She wasn't sure how she looked *there*. On account that she couldn't see down there anymore. It would be a bit of a mess but she didn't care. She was pregnant with his babies.

She could hear the shower running and entered the bathroom. Although the glass shower door was already a bit steamed up she could still see in easily. Granite hadn't been in the bathroom for very long.

She stopped in her tracks. He had one arm braced on the wall and the other wrapped around his cock which he pumped furiously. A zing of need coursed through her. He was magnificent. Her clit gave a throb, letting her know it was still there and that it still worked. Her girl parts turned wet in an instant. Her body didn't seem to care that she was pissed off. Her boobs suddenly felt swollen. Her nipples puckered up.

What the hell!

His head whipped up and his dark eyes locked with hers. Okay, so maybe she'd said that out loud.

"I just offered you sex and you turned me down," she put her hands on her hips.

"Fuck!" Granite's voice was thick with lust. "I . . . um . . . I . . ." He took his hand off of his cock, which jutted between his thighs.

The man was something to behold. Water cascaded down his chest. His short hair was wet. There were drops on the end of his lashes. Wet from head to toe. He was nowhere near as wet as she was right now. She'd heard that pregnant women generally tended to be hornier than normal. It was true for her. Big time!

"It's not what it looks like." He turned off the water

and stepped out of the shower.

"I'm pretty sure it's exactly what it looks like. Is my belly too big?" She rubbed the heavy curve. "Look, I know I've put on a few pounds. My ass jiggles and my boobs bounce."

Granite groaned. His dick twitched. It honest to god twitched. He gripped his cock, squeezing the tip. "You're killing me here."

"I don't understand," she frowned.

"I want you really fucking badly." He looked her up and down and groaned again. His eyes were heated. "All I can think about is sinking into your heat. It's what I picture every time I get myself off." He walked towards her, stopping just short. Water still dripped down every muscled inch of him.

"I thought you were turned off by . . ." She stopped talking when he shook his head.

"The opposite is true." His face had this pinched look. "I want you, Louise. I want inside you so badly, I—"

"Let's go have sex then. Hard, hot sex," her own voice was husky now. Her own skin felt too tight. She was sure she felt something trickle down her leg, she was that turned on, that wet.

Granite went down onto his knees, he kissed her belly. "I'm afraid of hurting you, of hurting them."

"That's silly!" She stopped when she saw the worry on his face, etched into his frown lines, it was also reflected in his eyes. It would be wrong of her to make light of his fear.

He nuzzled her belly. "I love you so much. I don't know what I would do if something . . ."

"I'm fine," she smiled at him. "I'm great! The babies are fine. You heard the healer." They'd gone to see one of the local doctors a few days ago. "I specifically asked if it was okay for us to have sex and she said that it would be good for me." She gave a sigh when she saw she wasn't really getting through to him. "I'm a doctor. You can't hurt me or them. Your cock is really huge but it's not that big. You can take it easy. I know you can be gentle with me. You don't have to be though, I won't break but we can take it slow if you are worried."

"I don't think I can be gentle." He parted her thighs, his nostrils flaring with every deep breath. "Look how wet you are." He slid a finger over her clit. "So damned swollen."

Louise cried out. "That feels so good. I need you, Granite."

He gave a nod. His gaze was feral. "I want you so damned badly. Are you sure . . . ?"

"Yes . . ." It came out sounding like more of a moan. "You won't hurt us. Endorphins are released every time I come. It is good for the babies. I need this so badly." He rubbed against her clit again and another deep moan was torn from her. "I want you inside me."

Granite licked his lips. "Let's go to our bed," he murmured. He was up in an instant, she was in his arms before she could blink.

He walked quickly, putting her down at the foot of the

bed. Louise crawled onto her hands and knees. Her clit throbbed. Her channel felt slick and so empty. She'd never been so turned on before. She doubted she ever would be again. It had been too long since she'd had sex with her man. Granite was hers and she was his. Not just some dirty little secret but his for real and for always.

"You are so damned beautiful." The bed dipped as he crawled up behind her. He palmed her ass. "I love the extra pounds." Next his hands slid over her belly. "Every part of your pregnant form excites me." He clasped her breasts. "So goddamn lush." He gently tweaked her nipples and she gave a moan. Her boobs were so sensitive. He gave another squeeze. She could feel his cock against her ass. Big and hard. He was still damp from the shower but she didn't mind.

Next, he closed his hand over her slit and she moaned again. "Your pussy is swollen and dripping for me."

"Please." She couldn't wait. She pushed back against his hand.

She heard him swallow hard. "I will try and be gentle. I might need to bite you though."

Louise looked over her shoulder. "I loved it when you bit me before." She rubbed herself against his hand. She moaned and whimpered. His fingers felt good but it wasn't what she needed. Nowhere close.

"Here, my love," he reached over and grabbed a pillow which he used to support her belly. "You promise to tell me if anything hurts?"

"Yes," a moan.

"I mean it," his voice was thick with need. His cock did that twitch thing against her. Every time she rubbed against his hand she also rubbed along his dick. He moaned, the sound heavy with lust. "Stop that or I'll come before I'm even inside you."

"Take me already."

He pulled back, putting one hand on her hip. He used the other to line himself up with her opening. Then he was pushing inside her. His breathing immediately became labored. "Even tighter," he growled. "Swollen."

Louise immediately made soft noises in the back of her throat. It was so good, she couldn't help it. He felt amazing. So thick, hitting every nerve-ending inside her.

Granite grunted as he pulled out, pushing in further with each stroke. "So good!" he rasped, squeezing her hips a little tighter.

His hips finally collided with her ass as he seated himself fully inside her. Her boobs gave a wobble. Granite shook. His body vibrated. "All good?" His voice was choked.

She glanced back. His face was red. Veins stood out on his forehead. There were deep frown lines between his eyes.

Louise took her bottom lip between her teeth. She was breathing heavily as well. She gave a nod.

His abs were ripped. His biceps bulged. Those muscles on the sides of his neck were roped. Her pussy gave a flutter and squeezed him. Granite made a grunting noise. His jaw clenched.

God but he was beautiful. She still couldn't believe that he was hers. The desire in his eyes amazed her. It meant that he felt the same, even now, in her heavily pregnant state. Louise gave another nod. There was no way she could get a word out right now.

Thankfully he understood what she wanted . . . what she needed. He looked down at where their bodies were joined. He made a growling noise as he pulled out and plunged back into her. Not too hard but enough to have her crying out.

Pure ecstasy graced his features. He tipped his head back and closed his eyes, his throat worked and he made a rumble of pleasure. Then his eyes were back on her. "My mate. My everything." He pulled back out and pushed back in, keeping it slow and easy.

After a time, he realized she was fine. That they were fine. That the little cries she was making were from pure bliss . . . because he stepped it up a notch. Until his balls slapped against her. His fingers dug into her. Her breasts jerked back and forth with each thrust. Next time she needed to remember a pillow to support them as well. Her body tightened. His grunts became more pronounced.

"Fuck!" He leaned forward, caging her with his body. "Can't hold . . ." He strummed her clit.

If her back had been able to arch, it would have done so then. She cried out as her channel clenched tight. As everything in her pulled tight.

Granite roared. He jerked against her. Then he pinned her down. Enough to keep her immobile but not enough to hurt her. He bit her on that soft spot at the base of her throat. A second much harder orgasm ripped through her. Louise screamed, she buried her face into the comforter. Granite jerked again, he grunted as he released his hold on her.

Then he froze, mid-thrust. "Are you okay? Did I hurt you?"

"I'm good," her voice was shaky. She had a goofy smile on her face. "That was amazing."

"I didn't hurt you." It was more of a statement than a question. "I didn't hurt you," he repeated sounding shocked.

She shook her head, as much as she could in her current position. "I'm stronger. Sex is natural, even for a pregnant woman. We'll just have to get creative with how we go about doing it."

Granite kissed her neck. "I love you." He pulled back so that she could stretch out.

"I love you too."

"Stay right there, I'll bring a towel."

She nodded and stifled a yawn.

"No sleeping just yet, you still need to eat," he wagged a finger at her. Granite got up off the bed. She noticed how hard he still was.

"Then . . ."

He looked back over his shoulder.

She smiled. "We can have round number two," Louise said, as she bobbed her eyebrows at him.

Granite shook his head. "Nope!"

"What do you mean, no?"

"We'll eat a couple of steaks." He was definitely getting to know her. "And then I'll have dessert between your thighs."

Her clit did that throb thing again.

Granite chuckled. "I might even skip straight to dessert." She watched his sexy ass clench as he walked.

Louise lay back against the pillows and smiled. "Sounds like a good plan." She had a feeling he would have plenty of those.

CHAPTER 33

Three months later...

All four babies lay on the blanket in the middle of the living room. Louise picked up her herbal tea and watched Breeze do the same. The other woman blew on the steaming brew. "So," Breeze smiled. "When do you plan to go back to work?"

Louise shook her head. "I'm in no rush. A couple of months, a year and then probably only part-time. They employed Monique, she's doing a great job. I don't want to miss out." She looked down at the two little ones staring up at their colorful mobiles. They both had dark hair like their daddy and green eyes like her. A bit of both of them.

It was hard work. Most days she felt like a milk factory, her boobs leaked whenever they felt like it, which was all the time. It also felt like all she did was change diapers. That and their clothing. If they didn't spit up on themselves, they made humungous poops that leaked out from all sides. It was an ongoing, seemingly never-ending workload... and she loved every minute of it.

Smelling their baby scent. Feeling their soft skin. Those toothless grins were enough to make her broody all over again. Well, not really . . . not yet anyhow. Granite helped out a lot and it was nice having a friend like Breeze, who was going through the same. They spent loads of time together. She emailed back and forth with Hillary and Debbie who were thrilled that she and Granite were together.

"Mmmm . . ." Breeze made a humming noise that brought her back from her thoughts. "I think that staying home for a good while is wise. They grow up far too quickly. Just look at Gem and Crystal."

Louise turned to look at the baby girls. Crystal was gurgling and chatting away to herself. They were both chewing on toys. Gem was drooling. They were huge compared to her own boys. It was amazing what a couple of months' difference could make. "Is she cutting another tooth?" Louise twisted her stud earring as she spoke. She'd since discovered that they were real diamonds and not cubics like she'd thought.

Breeze nodded. "Yup! She'll soon have two."

Gem dropped her toy, tried to find it and ended up rolling onto her tummy.

"Oh wow! That's great," Louise smiled as she watched the little girl pull herself up onto her elbows.

"She's been doing that for a couple of days already. Mummy's big girl," Breeze spoke in baby talk, directing her words to the little one on the floor. "It won't be long and you'll be crawling. Then it's watch out world."

Gem cooed and smiled. Lines from the markings on her chest peeked up above her vest. Golden. Just like every other royal dragon. Earth dragons might have black etching, Water dragons green and Air dragons blue but they all had gold in common.

Louise felt a pang. Her boys' also had markings but they weren't golden or silver. There were no specific etchings either. Her boy's markings were just an outline. They had no filling. It was baffling. Granite tried to hide it when the babies were born but she had seen the worry for a moment before he schooled his emotions. Another thing she had noticed was that he hadn't look shocked. It was like he had been expecting them to have the colorless markings.

Granite had since confessed that Blaze had told him about it sooner. Both the Fire king and Fire princes' sons had the same colorless outline. It seemed that this was normal for royal young born to human women. Although, so far, no other royal young had been born. The Water king's mate had conceived a human child but with some dragon DNA. The little girl wasn't marked at all.

The Air king and his bride were trying to conceive but hadn't had any luck. His mate, Tammy, had emailed her asking for help. They'd apparently been trying for a couple of months now. Louise had given her some basic advice, like only having sex every second day leading up to and during ovulation and had advised that Tammy go on a good multi-vitamin. The general rule of thumb was that a couple try for a year before seeking fertility treatments. Louise would definitely go and meet with them if they didn't conceive naturally in the next couple of months. She wasn't a fertility specialist but she could help out.

Gem's grin grew wider as her gaze landed on the toy she had dropped earlier. The little girl gave a squeal. Then she turned her head slightly and frowned.

The baby girl was looking at one of Louise's sons, Declan, named after her grandfather. Granite hadn't been too thrilled at first because it wasn't a name suitable for an Earth dragon but hey, Declan was half human, they had brought human women into their world, so as far as she was concerned, some of the regular traditions would need to change. Declan's identical twin was called Quake after Granite's grandfather. It was a strong name that suited him perfectly. Declan was her softer, more sensitive son. He cried more easily and liked to self-soothe with a pacifier.

It looked like Gem spotted Declan's pacifier because she reached out and grabbed it. She then proceeded to try and get it into her own mouth.

"Gem!" Breeze said using a stern tone. "No!" The little girl ignored her mom.

Declan clenched his tiny fists and gave a yell. He scrunched his eyes shut and wailed. His tiny face turned red and smoke wafted from his nostrils. Both she and Breeze were rooted to the spot. When Declan wailed a second time, a couple of orange flames shot from his mouth. Only about a foot but they were there.

"By Claw!" Breeze yelled, grabbing her chest. "Did you see that?" Her eyes were wide.

Louise nodded. She was too stunned to talk.

Declan was pulling in a deep breath. He was preparing to give another loud yell.

"You'd better get him before he burns the chamber down."

A thousand questions raced through Louise's head as she picked up her baby and cradled him to her chest. She made soothing noises. Declan instantly calmed. "What does it mean? He shouldn't be able to breathe fire," she shook her head, looking down at her son. He was still so tiny.

"I . . . I don't know." Breeze was also staring down at him, a look of awe on her face. "Only Fire dragons can breathe fire."

"Not anymore," Louise whispered. Her little boy smiled at her, all gums and drool.

AUTHOR'S NOTE

I had a blast writing this story. I hope you enjoyed reading it.

A big and heartfelt thank you to you . . . my readers. For reading my work and for all your messages and emails. Also, to those of you that take the time to review my books. It means the world to me. You are what keeps me writing on days that I might not feel like it so much.

If you want to be kept updated on new releases please sign up to my Latest Release Newsletter to ensure that you don't miss out www.mad.ly/signups/96708/join. I promise not to spam you or divulge your email address to a third party. I send my mailing list an exclusive sneak peek prior to release. I would love to hear from you so please feel free to drop me a line charlene.hartnady@gmail.com.

Find me on Facebook—
www.facebook.com/authorhartnady

I live on an acre in the country with my gorgeous husband and three sons and an array of pets.

You can usually find me on the computer completely lost in worlds of my making. I believe that it is the small things that truly matter like that feeling you get when you start a new book or a particularly beautiful sunset.

BOOKS BY THIS AUTHOR

The Chosen Series:
Book 1 ~ Chosen by the Vampire Kings
Book 2 ~ Stolen by the Alpha Wolf
Book 3 ~ Unlikely Mates
Book 4 ~ Awakened by the Vampire Prince
Book 5 ~ Mated to the Vampire Kings (Short Novel)
Book 6 ~ Wolf Whisperer (Novella)

The Program Series (Vampire Novels):
Book 1 ~ A Mate for York
Book 2 ~ A Mate for Gideon
Book 3 ~ A Mate for Lazarus
Book 4 ~ A Mate for Griffin
Book 5 ~ A Mate for Lance
Book 6 ~ A Mate for Kai

Demon Chaser Series (No cliffhangers):
Book 1 ~ Omega
Book 2 ~ Alpha
Book 3 ~ Hybrid
Book 4 ~ Skin
Demon Chaser Boxed Set Book 1–3

Excerpt

Chosen BY THE VAMPIRE KINGS

The Chosen Series ~ Book 1

Chapter 1

IT HAD BEEN MANY years since he had been in such close proximity of his birth enemy. Zane looked as arrogant and as full of shit as ever. Barking orders at his royal guard like they were his servants instead of trusted subjects. In some cases, those receiving the harsh treatment were probably his best buddies. Then again, the bastard probably didn't have any friends. Shaking his head, Brant turned and surveyed the crowd. He felt sorry for the female that would soon be chosen to become queen to the likes of that ruthless king.

It wasn't his concern though. His own queen was out there. Brant shuddered, praying that the events of one hundred years ago would not repeat themselves. A bloody war between their fathers had been the result of the last choosing. It couldn't happen again, the vampire species would not survive another war at this point.

As his mind returned to thoughts of his own female, he knew that he would not be able to remain sensible where she was concerned. His focus was on protecting his coven, and he would dispatch the other male without hesitation if he so much as looked at what was his. No matter the odds, and the knowledge of Zane's ruthlessness, Brant would allow nothing to harm her. She was too valuable, too precious of a gift to him.

Turning, he surveyed the crowd again. Feeling the electric pulse of her closeness. According to the lores, he would be able to sense her and to tell of their compatibility almost instantly even in a crowd full of females. From the noise projecting from outside, he could tell there were many females present. He hoped his chosen would be willing from the start. The last thing he wanted was to force her, to have to go caveman on her and throw her over his shoulder. The thought did not appeal to him, but the choosing was not something that could be ignored. She would feel it as well, whether she wanted to or not.

"Ready?" his head guard Xavier asked as he moved in next to him. His brother's eyes never faltered as they stared straight into his. Brant knew the reason for the intenseness. Xavier harbored similar feelings of distaste and distrust for their neighboring king. In order to maintain their strenuous hold on the truce between them, it had always been necessary to keep interactions between the two covens to a minimum. This event was no exception.

"Yeah, as ready as I'll ever be," Brant replied while taking a moment to scan the room.

"Your eyes are glowing my lord, maybe you should stop looking in that direction."

Brant looked into Xavier's clear grey eyes. *Always the cool one in a situation.* "My eyes have nothing to do with that bastard at the moment, and everything to do with my female. I can sense her, and the urge to mate is strong. I just hope that she'll be agreeable to a speedy union."

"I told you to take a female, ease your need. Humans are . . . easily broken. We don't want any accidents." Xavier spoke softly, ensuring that no one else would be privy to their conversation.

"I have a plan."

"Please, tell me you at least drank recently," Xavier's eyes narrowed. When Brant didn't reply, his brother's eyes narrowed even more. He made a sound of disbelief and continued, "Brother, should you harm our future—"

"Enough," Brant growled.

Xavier lowered his eyes.

"I said I have a plan. My future queen will come to no harm."

Xavier nodded. "Yes, my lord. It is time."

Brant took a deep breath. He had been raised for this moment. His decision and the events of the next few minutes would determine the future of his coven.

No pressure.

Tanya had seen tabloid pictures of the vampire kings and they really weren't all that attractive, unless you were into the ultra-big, ultra-built and ridiculously bad non-human types.

She so wasn't.

The whole choosing ceremony was so outdated to the point of being down right sexist. Yet, every hundred years, all of the eligible women would assemble to be chosen. A queen for each of the kings. The worst part was that vampires and humans never mixed so there was very little known about them. Their traditions, their ways, their expectations, she shuddered.

For at least the twentieth time, she wished that her best

friend Becky was there with her. The whole thing was a real circus. Tanya hadn't realized how many women there were in Sweetwater between the ages of twenty one and thirty. Aside from age, there had been a long list of requirements. Everything from weight and height to a clean medical exam.

Tanya sighed as a group of giggling women squeezed past her trying to find a spot closer to the podium. Becky was divorced, a complete no-no. It had automatically disqualified her from being allowed to attend the choosing ceremony. Attend, hah, not hardly, the right term would be forced. If all aspects of the criteria were met, it was mandatory to be here. For whatever reason, the human justice system went along with this whole farce once a century. Only those wanting a fast track to jail failed to show up. What scared her the most though was the thought of how many of these women were actually hoping to be chosen today.

Vampire queen.

Tanya cringed at the thought. For once she was thankful for being a little curvy. Most men were into wafer thin model types, so she would be safe.

The whole courtyard vibrated with an excited hum.

The two kings were royalty but they were also vampires. They drank blood for heaven's sake. Had these women lost their freaking minds?

It was early afternoon yet you wouldn't guess it by how some of them were dressed. Little back numbers, low cut tops, sequins and jewelry were the order of the day. The amount of skin on display was obscene. Tanya did a double take as one of the ladies walked by, she was wearing a sheer dress without underwear. Her lady bits on display for all and sundry. With all that exposed skin, she hoped that the woman had used sunblock. The highest possible factor.

Tanya looked down at her jeans and t-shirt. Maybe she should've tried a little harder but then again, she wasn't planning on getting noticed. She had a life to get back to. It wasn't much but she had her little book store. Some might consider it to be boring, but she liked it just fine.

She'd owned The Book Corner for two years now. Reading had always been a major passion, that and coffee. It had been her ultimate dream to own a little coffee shop on the side. That way potential customers could browse through purchases while enjoying a cappuccino and maybe a little pastry. So far she was way behind on those goals. She was supposed to have had half the money she needed already saved in order to do the required renovations. As it stood though, she may not even have a store soon, let alone an additional coffee shop. She couldn't afford to hire someone to fill in for her today. Just the thought of the closed sign on the door, of losing potential customers, had her looking at her watch. Hopefully this would be over soon. The last thing she needed in her life was a man . . . let alone a vampire who would not only uproot her from her goals but from her friends and family as well. She only had one BFF and her aunt, but she loved them both a ton.

It had been a while since she'd dated and her last relationship had ended . . . badly. Sex was overrated anyway. She could just imagine how much worse it would be with a blood sucking vamp. Wishing she was back at the store, she glanced at her watch a second time.

It wasn't like one of the kings would ever think of choosing a plain Jane like her anyways. What a waste of her precious time.

There was silence followed by gasps as two of the biggest, meanest looking men she'd ever seen walked onto the platform. Tanya had expected fanfare. A trumpet call. An announcement at the very least. What she hadn't expected was to be shocked stupid. Pictures she'd seen of the men didn't do them justice.

Tall, *check.*

Built, *check.*

Mean, *check.*

Ridiculously hunkalious, *double check.*

Several women swooned. One woman, closer to the front, fainted. Medics pushed their way through the thick crowd and placed the young women on stretchers.

The king on the left was slightly shorter, from tabloid pictures she'd seen, he had to be Zane. Although short was the wrong description, the big vampire must be at least around six and a half feet. He was meaner looking, with close cropped hair. From this distance she could tell that he had dark, hard eyes. A nervous chill radiated through her body.

King Brant was taller and even though he had a massive chest and bulging arms, he wasn't quite as broad as the scary one. Neither was classically good-looking. Though both radiated raw energy and sex appeal like nothing she'd ever seen before.

"Pick me!" One of the women closer to the platform shouted waving her arms.

The kings ignored her.

A group to the side hoisted a '*Look over here'* sign. *What was it with these freaking women?* For some reason it bothered her that they were so desperate to become one of the next vampire queens that they would do anything to get noticed? And the question of the hour was, *why?*

Turning back to the platform, she noticed that the taller one, Brant, had medium length dark hair, his eyes were dark and his mouth generous. Tanya was certain he would be even more attractive if he smiled.

Both men were tense. They just stood there, hands fisted at their sides. The crowd grew restless. Some women tried to push to the front while others tried to catch the attention of one or both of the men on the elevated platform.

Eventually, Zane stepped forward, his hard eyes were fixed on her. *What the hell?* Adrenaline surged through her blood, but her mind immediately rejected the idea that he was actually looking at her. It had to be some sort of mistake. His eyes seemed to stay on her for a few more seconds. Just as she began to feel the need to look around her for the true object of his fascination, his gaze moved to the back of the crowd. She breathed out in a gush.

"You," his gruff, smoky voice was a low vibration. He pointed somewhere behind Tanya.

An equally big, equally mean looking man came onto the platform from the side. King Zane didn't take his eyes off the female he had set his sights on the entire time he spoke to what had to be his head guard. All of the surrounding men were dressed in full leather. Though, this one wore a silver family crest on his chest.

Tanya shivered, thankful she hadn't been chosen by the likes of him.

Zane continued to shout orders. The head guard, flanked by two vampires, stepped off the platform and stalked through the crowd. Tanya shifted to the side as they approached. They were big bastards. The women surged forward. One dared to touch. The king's head guard paused, without turning to face the culprit, he growled. His top lip curled revealing sharp fangs. The air caught in her lungs. Her pulse quickened.

They were so close, Tanya could smell a musky male scent, could almost feel heat radiate off their huge bodies as they passed.

"You," a deep growl sounded through the crowd.

"No," a feminine wail responded. "Let go of me!"

Tanya was too afraid to turn. So close to the action, she was fearful of being noticed.

Another wail, louder this time.

"Put me down!" the woman shrieked. It seemed Tanya was not the only one there that didn't want to be chosen.

Tanya moved with the crowd as the guards passed, the woman was slung over the shoulder of the head guard. She kicked and screamed. The big vampire didn't seem to notice though. Tanya caught the look of sheer terror on the young woman's face.

This wasn't right.

How could this be allowed to happen? Tanya looked around her at the multitude of willing ladies. Women that were practically throwing themselves at the vampire kings. *Why did the SOB have to go and pick one of the few that wasn't interested?*

Tanya took a few steps in the direction of the platform. *Not happening.* She stopped. She didn't want to get involved. Couldn't afford to. She didn't even know the girl. It wasn't like she could change the situation even if she tried. This ritual had been going on for hundreds, possibly thousands, of years.

A large group of women at the front screamed to Zane that he pick them instead. One of the young ladies even lifted her top.

The king didn't take his eyes off his chosen woman the entire time that his guard maneuvered through the crowd. They narrowed though as they got closer. The girl screamed louder.

"Please don't do this. Please, I beg you." The screams had turned to sobs at this point.

Tanya couldn't bear to hear them. Each word struck a nerve.

Zane nodded in the direction of the waiting SUVs.

"Oh God, please no," she was sobbing in earnest.

The nerve quickly rubbed raw until Tanya couldn't take it anymore. "Stop!" She marched in the direction of the vampire king. "Stop that at once. Let her go."

Neither king took any notice. Maybe some of the others in the crowd were feeling the same way as she did because the women parted to let her through. "What you are doing is nothing short of barbaric."

The crowd hushed.

"She doesn't want to go with you. Let her go right now." Tanya projected, sounding more confident than she felt.

Zane glanced her way before turning in the direction of the waiting vehicles.

"This is a sexist, disgusting tradition that needs to be put to an end. Why can't you choose someone that's actually interested in going with you? Why does it have to be her?"

He turned back, his dark eyes zoning in on her. Her breathing hitched. Her heart rate increased, a whole damn lot. *I just had to get involved. Couldn't leave it alone.*

"This woman has been chosen as my mate. What is done cannot be undone." He turned and made for the waiting vehicles. Like that was a reasonable explanation. *So not.*

"Bastard! Leave her alone!" She must have completely lost her mind because she walked after him and straight into the massive chest of one of the guards. There was only one thing to do in a situation like this, she beat against the chest in her way while screaming obscenities at the retreating back of the bastard king.

"Easy," a low rumble that had her insides vibrating.

Tanya looked up into a set of dark, penetrating eyes. She froze. It was Brant. The second vampire king.

"What would you like me to do with her?" asked a voice to the right of the king.

His eyes stayed on hers. His nostrils flared and his body tightened. It was then that she realized that her hands were flattened on his chest. She snatched them away.

"Lord Brant?" the voice enquired.

"She's coming with me." He took her hand and strode towards the remaining vehicles. She wanted to pull away, to dig her heels in the ground, but her traitorous feet kept on moving in time with his. It was only when they reached the waiting SUV and Brant opened the door and gestured for her to enter, that she finally snapped out of it. Part of her didn't want to believe this was happening. As ridiculous as it seemed, King Brant had chosen her.

No. Surely not.

"Wait."

His eyes snapped to hers. Dark, fathomless, deadly.

Chosen by the Vampire Kings (Ménage)—available now

Printed in Great Britain
by Amazon